Kate Cann is the author of many books for young adults, including LEAVING POPPY, POSSESSED and FIRE. She lives in Hampshire with her husband.

www.katecann.com

KATE CANN

WITCH CRAG

SCHOLASTIC

First published in the UK in 2012 by Scholastic Children's Books
An imprint of Scholastic Ltd
Euston House, 24 Eversholt Street
London, NW1 1DB, UK
Registered office: Westfield Road, Southam, Warwickshire, CV47 0RA
SCHOLASTIC and associated logos are trademarks and/
or registered trademarks of Scholastic Inc.

Text © Kate Cann, 2012

The right of Kate Cann to be identified as the author
of this work has been asserted by her.

ISBN 978 1407 10702 8

A CIP catalogue record for this book
is available from the British Library.

Printed and bound by CPI Group (UK) Ltd, Croydon, CR0 4YY
Papers used by Scholastic Children's Books
are made from wood grown in sustainable forests.

1 3 5 7 9 10 8 6 4 2

This is a work of fiction. Names, characters, places, incidents
and dialogues are products of the author's imagination or are used
fictitiously. Any resemblance to actual people, living or dead,
events or locales is entirely coincidental.

www.scholastic.co.uk/zone

To Jeff. Who else?

CHAPTER ONE

Kita crawled the last stretch of the bramble tunnel on her stomach to protect her face and hands from thorns. Then she wriggled out on to the flint ledge, and gazed down at the grasslands that sloped away below.

Nada's funeral procession had just emerged from the great outer gates of the hill fort. Two men carried the flimsy stretcher with the old woman's body on it; two boys, who had opened the heavy wooden gates and who now ran back in an arc to close them again, followed behind.

Females never followed a funeral. Or watched one, or talked about it, even if the body taken out was someone you loved.

Tears skidded down Kita's grimy face. She was glad to be on her own, with no one to censor her emotion as wasteful. No one knew about her flint ledge, thin and perilously high on the rocky outcrop which was part of the hill-fort barricades. Crouched on it, she was perfectly screened by brambles. She came here to hide, and think, and gaze out at the grasslands and the forests beyond where she was never allowed to go. And today, she was here to grieve for Nada. She smeared the tears from her eyes and stared at the tiny funeral procession as it trooped under the great rock overhang. If she craned over the edge, she could still see it, Nada so small and still between the two marching men, and the boys circling the stretcher, proud of their responsibility, alert for danger.

Nada had cared for her as a child in the pens, where all infants went as soon as they were weaned, because the headman decreed it was more efficient that way. Kita had gone there too early, barely walking, because her mother had died of a chill. Nada had nurtured her. And when she was about six, old enough to be of use and leave the pens, Nada had looked out for her. Covered for her, taught her, whispered her stories, and sometimes risked hugging her. Friendships, special bonds, were frowned on in the hill fort, but Kita and Nada had formed a bond.

The funeral procession had disappeared from sight. Kita couldn't see the men tipping the stretcher sideways and Nada's body sliding off and bumping on to the ground, but she knew this was happening.

The sheepmen of the hill fort always dealt with death this way. Death was inevitable; to survive, you spent no time on the death of others. A dead sheep was worth something, you could eat it – but a dead human was worthless. There was no ceremony, no words, just a body thrown like meat to keep the forest dogs and the black cloud of crows satisfied, and away from the fort.

The men reappeared, jogging with the empty stretcher; the boys raced ahead of them to open the great gates. No one wanted to be outside when the crows and the dogs came.

Kita made herself stay still, made herself wait, and listen. This was the third funeral she'd watched; she knew what was coming. She stared at the close-set trees that ringed the grasslands. There was a stirring and thickening at the base of a nearby clump of firs; then a surging black shape broke free, and streamed into the open.

A pack of dogs, racing to Nada. She could hear them now, a rushing, crackling noise as they sped through the undergrowth.

Up above, another dark shape shifting; a flock of giant crows, gathering. They always came just after the dogs; they'd wait for the body to be torn open so they could feast too when the dogs were glutted.

Kita felt her stomach squirm; she retched twice. Then, hating herself, she clapped her hands over her ears so she wouldn't hear the snatching and cracking and gorging.

"Goodbye, Nada," she whispered, eyes on the sky. "Thank you. Thank you for saving me."

Something was happening with the crows, something weird. They separated, cawing in panic, and then instead of flying lower, they suddenly wheeled upwards, higher and higher. Kita heard sharp yelping, long, terrified whining, and looked down at the grasslands. The dogs, a black, sinewy mass of them, were streaming back towards the forest. She stared, amazed, as the dark trees absorbed them. Why had they left their grisly feast? She craned forward, but the angle was all wrong, she couldn't see Nada's body. And now all she could hear was silence.

About two hundred sheep people lived on the hill fort, and most of them were already queuing for the end-of-day meal when Kita skittered into the food hut. She grabbed one of the little scoured wooden troughs from the pile, then spotted Quainy ahead of her, yellow hair shining. She pushed and wriggled and pleaded her way through until she was standing directly behind her.

"Quainy!" she called, softly.

Quainy turned round, big blue eyes wide, smiling. Her beauty always made Kita blink. The women had rubbed ash into Quainy's hair as a child, to dull it. And at the quarterly shearings, they'd shaved her as close as they could. Beauty was a distraction; it didn't help you survive. But for the last half-year, Quainy's hair had been left to grow. Quainy was trade. She was nearly sixteen; she'd be going soon as wife to one of the horsemen, to strengthen the link between the two tribes. Kita couldn't bear to think of it.

"Where have you *been?*" Quainy whispered. "I had to cover for you. I said one of the pregnant sheep was sick and you were nursing it."

"Thanks. I was up high." Up high was the nearest Kita got to telling Quainy about her flint ledge. "Watching Nada get taken out."

Quainy shuddered. "Ghoul," she muttered. "How could you bear it?"

"Because I owed it to her. I owed it to her to see her taken. But Quainy, listen. She—"

"Less chattering!" barked the head cook. "Save your breath to eat and work!"

Quainy held out her little trough, and the scowling cook dolloped a scant ladleful of brown porridge into it.

The end-of-day meal was always the same. Porridge made from grain gathered on the lower slopes behind the hill fort at the end of summer, cooked in stock from sheep bones, with scraps of mutton added.

"Tell me tonight," murmured Quainy, as Kita stepped forward with her trough.

The girls sat together silently at the girls' end of the young ones' benches, pressing their near knees together by way of communication. Their friend Raff was sitting opposite, with the boys. He didn't look across at them. He had a bright new bruise by his left eye, and even at the distance they sat, Kita could see his hand shaking as he spooned up his food.

*

Night-time was the best time. The need for warmth meant you could sleep close in the girls' hut, all bundled together under old, worn sheepskins, little ones just out of the pens cuddled and mothered by older girls. Kita crawled across two solid forms, wincing as one of them elbowed her, hard, and slithered down alongside Quainy.

"Did you see Raff's face?" Quainy mourned, softly. "Someone hit him again."

"I know," said Kita. "Those bastards, I hate them."

They'd grown up with Raff, and despite all the obstacles and sheepman-creed disapproval, they'd formed a strong friendship with him. But they'd watched in sorrow as he'd slowly changed from a bright, funny, defiant child to a boy with hunched shoulders and a hunted expression.

"If only he could *grow* a bit," Quainy said. "I'd give anything to make him bigger."

"I know," said Kita. "So he could stick it back to them."

"And get made a footsoldier. Then they'd leave him alone."

Kita sighed. She knew Raff would never be a footsoldier, and Quainy must know it too, but they never admitted it to each other. Footsoldiers, with their short, battling lives, were the elite of the hill fort; the young ones formed its fighting core. And they treated the other young men – the ones who stayed safe, who shared the women's work – like dirt. Raff's life was set to get even worse.

"So," murmured Quainy, gently, "Nada's funeral. Tell."

"It was weird. I watched them take her out and tip her off – I saw them jog back with the empty stretcher, but I couldn't lean out far enough to see her body."

"Oh, Kita. Your high place. You'll tumble down one day."

"Too bad. It's worth it. Anyway, the dogs came, then the crows. . ."

"Wuuurgh. How could you stomach it?"

"I told myself I had to. I had to be there, it was the least I could do when I hadn't even said goodbye to her. . ."

"That wasn't your fault," soothed Quainy.

"But . . . but then this weird thing happened . . . the crows flew away, and the dogs ran off. They seemed full of panic, cawing, yelping – they didn't even touch her, I'm sure of it. It was all too fast."

Quainy shifted away from Kita a little. "Did you hear anything else?" she whispered. Kita stiffened. She knew what Quainy meant – any other predator. There were rumours of monstrous unnamed creatures prowling outside, and birds even bigger and more savage than the crows.

"No, nothing," she muttered, fiercely. "If it'd been . . . I'd've heard it, if she was taken – I'd've heard it."

"It's OK, Kita," said Quainy, and she pulled the sheep fleece round them more snugly. "Go to sleep now."

"It all happened so fast, her dying," muttered Kita. "Why didn't they tell me she'd got sick? I can't bear it that I didn't see her, didn't kiss her goodbye. . . D'you think she asked for me?"

But Quainy, exhausted, was asleep.

CHAPTER TWO

The girls only slept for a few hours. They were woken by the harsh sound of iron clanging against iron. This summons meant one of two things – attack from a gang of marauders, or heavy rain. Usually it was rain.

All but the youngest girls struggled to their feet and out of the hut into the downpour, running to get in line. Everyone knew their places, even in the dark; water was as necessary to survival as the sheep were, and water drill was practised too often for anyone to forget.

As the headman shouted orders, eight vast oiled sheets made of stitched-together sheepskins were unrolled. Each one was stretched between four sturdy wooden stakes and tied securely. Then thirty-two footsoldiers seized a stake each, and stood braced under the teeming sky.

Everyone watched as the sheets bulged and filled with the precious rain, waiting for the headman's next order.

It came. *"Fill!"* The footsoldiers holding the front stakes dipped their load, so that water poured off the sheets and into waiting skin buckets, each replaced so fast that barely a drop was spilt. The buckets were fed into a chain and passed from hand to hand until they reached the footsoldiers at the well, who emptied them into its stone depths and fed them back into the chain to the sheets again.

The well was not a true well but a great container, and it was the main reason the first headman had made his hill fort here. Made in the time before the Great Havoc, when nearly everything had been destroyed, it was of stone without seams, square and massive and deep in the ground. Far beyond the sheepmen's skills to build.

Kita and Quainy were at the top of the line that handled full buckets. They'd been moved up from the empty line that summer. It was exhausting, seizing the wet handle of a heavy bucket with two hands, turning to pass it on, spinning back in time to get the next one. If you were slow, if there was a build-up behind you, the flow of emptied buckets would be stalled, and water wasted. But to hurry too much meant you might slip over, slide on the mud. . .

The winter before last, Raff had slipped and sent himself and a full bucket sprawling. The boy next to him, a newly promoted footsoldier, had jumped forward on to his back and retrieved the bucket. Then he'd closed the chain with the footsoldier next to him, each of them stretching their arms out long. Raff had struggled to his feet, slimy and dripping, but the two jeering boys hadn't let him back in the line. When the headman praised the young footsoldiers afterwards, it had been the absolute seal on Raff's humiliation.

Kita screwed up her face, peering through the dark and the rain. The boy who'd grabbed that fallen bucket was there, close to her, holding one of the wooden stakes. He was called Arc, and the headman had great hopes for him; he'd recently made him leader of the young footsoldiers. Arc trained his fighting band relentlessly, and longed to be tested in a fight.

Kita realized with a start that Arc was staring straight back at her, raising his eyebrows like a question. She glared down again. Raff was three beyond Quainy; as she passed her full bucket on, she willed all their hands strength.

The rain began to lessen; the storm was gathering its skirts and heading northwards. The sheets had been filled and emptied five times; a great haul. Exhausted, everyone waited for the order to cease.

As the sheets were emptied for the sixth time, the headman shouted, "*End!*" And then the words everyone longed for.

"*Fire! Soup!*"

While the storm lasted, four older men excused from the rigour of the water chain had been busy piling brushwood and thick sticks into carriers made from yet more sheep pelts. At the headman's command, they hobbled with their loads to the fire pit, pulled off its cover, and tipped in the brushwood. One of the cooks ran from the kitchen with a flaring rag that she dropped into the pit; carefully, the men fed in the sticks as the fire took hold.

Kita and Quainy hurried past the sheep pens towards the fire pit. The pens were solid and roomy; better made than the girls' sleeping huts. The dry sheep looked out at the drenched girls, and shifted comfortably on their hay.

Flames were just beginning to dance above the rim of the pit; smoke swirled, scattering sparks. Kita smiled at the sight of it. Two cooks staggered out from the kitchen with a great cauldron of soup they'd heated on the stove that was always kept alight. Two more followed with the little wooden troughs and a huge ladle. The dripping workers in their rough woollen tunics gathered round the fire, privileged footsoldiers at the front, everyone else clustered behind.

It was a strange gathering. A fire at night, under the stars; the glow of success, of much water saved and stored; hot soup, warmth and companionship. But apart from some joshing among the footsoldiers, there was no festivity. No singing, no chatting, no laughing. Everyone sat alone, to dry, and drank the soup, to warm up, and the only object was – to survive. Cold and wet meant chills, meant illness and possible death. The fire was there for survival, nothing more.

But Kita couldn't keep the smile from her face as she watched the flames flare.

And then, too soon, much too soon, the headman said, "Put the fire out. Dawn is close. Set to work."

CHAPTER THREE

"I feel dreadful," muttered Quainy, as they scrambled to their feet. "We've hardly had *any* sleep."

"I know," Kita murmured back. "It's ages till dawn."

If the rain summons came early enough in the night, the headman would let them go back to the huts to sleep again afterwards. And then the soup didn't count as the start-of-day meal, and they got fed once more when they woke. But that was rare. Usually, they had to stay on their feet, and work right through until the midday meal.

Kita was on sheep work for that day. Quainy was spinning skeins of wool. The older women who drew up the rotas and read out the next day's tasks at the end-of-day meal rarely let them be together.

Kita risked reaching out her hand and squeezing Quainy's. "Tonight," she whispered, and Quainy nodded. Lying side by side, whispering in the blackness – it was all they had to look forward to.

As Kita collected her bucket and rake, she saw Raff heading off in the direction of the latrine holes. It seemed to be his permanent job, shovelling out the latrines. Which was cruel, which was sad, but it meant she might see him later, when she emptied her bucket full of droppings on to the huge, stinking dung heap outside the rear stockades. Nothing was wasted. Once rotted, the manure nurtured the coarse grain that grew on the slopes at the back of the fort.

Kita let herself into the first sheep pen, where the mature ewes lived. Ma Baa trotted over, raised its blunt head and sneered at her, stamping its hard little feet.

"Sod off, you old bitch," Kita muttered.

She'd named Ma Baa, and she hated it. Queen of the sheep, it had birthed countless lambs and seemed to be aware how valuable this made it – far more valuable than the girls who tended it. It would nip the carers, or back into them and tread on their feet.

Kita shook her rake at it, but it pranced closer. Then it turned around and urinated copiously, splashing her bare feet.

"You *wait*," spat Kita, "you evil wool bag, you can't have many more lambs inside you, and once you're spent, we'll stew you up. . ."

But Ma Baa was oblivious to the threat. It swaggered over to the troughs, which were being filled with grain by two little girls, one on either side of the grain sack. Kita sighed, set her bucket down, and started raking up the dung and spent hay.

*

Kita was in luck. As she staggered along the narrow, steep-sided passage between the inner and outer barricades, heading for the dung-heap gate, Raff was just coming back. They put down their buckets, hers full, his empty, leant back against the barricade planks, and grinned at each other.

"Well met, mad one," said Raff. "How's life?"

"What life?" said Kita.

"Complaining is futile," Raff intoned. "Hope is futile."

"Survive, survive, survive," Kita chanted, giggling. They'd made it up in childhood – the game of the Sheepmen's Song – and played it still.

"Care for the sheep. Nourish the sheep. The sheep are our saviours."

"Baaa . . . baaa . . . baaaaaa. . ."

"Watch out for marauders. Those who would gut us."

"Survive, survive, *survive!*"

The dung passage was one of the very few private spaces where they couldn't be seen or overheard. Where they could indulge in the shocking game of mocking life on the hill fort, where the fortunate few had survived.

"You've been hit," said Kita, and she reached out her hand and stroked his forehead just above the bruise. "Again."

"Arc's mob. One tripped me up, the other put the boot in. I made out I was dead so I got off lightly."

"I hate them. *God*, I hate them."

"Hate is a waste of useful *energy*," Raff intoned, trying to resurrect the song game, but Kita had tears in her eyes, and wouldn't join in.

"Hey," he said softly. "I heard they took Nada out yesterday. I'm really sorry."

Kita gulped. His voice was so beautiful, so unlike the other sheepmen, she wanted to fling herself into his arms and howl. . . She wanted to tell him about the weirdness of the crows and the dogs running from Nada's body.

But Raff was tactfully changing the subject. "Any news on Quainy's trade?" he asked.

Kita stiffened. She hated to think of Quainy going. "No," she said. "She's safe while her hair's still short. If I could think of a way to make her bald. . ."

"Then they'd slit you as a witch. And think of *her*, Kita – she'll have a better life with the horsemen for sure. They're fierce but they're democratic – they vote on things! And she'll have more colour, and pleasure, and *fun*. . ."

Stories of the horsemen's lavish feasts had been brought back to the hill fort. Jumping to a drumbeat, strange berry juice that made you crazy and full of laughter . . . but Kita didn't want to think about it. "Can't you tell the headman?" she asked. "About the way the footsoldiers treat you?"

"Oh, he sees. And knows Arc won't let it go too far."

16

Kita reached out and hugged him. She knew it would go too far, maybe already had gone too far – Raff's rare bright spirit crushed.

"Come on, mad one," he said, gently disengaging himself. "We'd better go before we're missed."

Kita sighed, and said goodbye, picked up her bucket and headed for the narrow gate in the outer barricades that led to the dung heap. There was always a guard on it, but they'd kept their voices low so he wouldn't hear them talking.

No one knew how long it had been since everything stopped, since the time of Great Havoc, of earthquakes, floods and wars. Five generations was the usual tally. Memory went back three generations, when the truce with the ferocious horsemen tribe was made, and life became safer. Vague myths circulated about how people had come to the hill, driving the sheep that were their main means of survival ahead of them, bringing basic tools and weapons, then building the fort, but storytelling was discouraged. What mattered was the here and now. Do the work, grinding work. Keep the sheep safe. Collect water. Guard the barricades. Survive.

The headman was not a cruel man, nor especially callous, but everything he ordered was about survival. A badly wounded footsoldier wasn't kept alive. A weak baby wasn't fed. The very old weren't cared for.

And no one challenged the headman, ever, because

they knew he kept them from the terror that threatened to devour them. Terror of the past, that strange time of fevered plenty when people had given over their souls to things and let screens and machines do their living for them, ushering in the Great Havoc. Terror of the cannibals who lived across the wastelands in one of the foul, decaying cities of the past. Terror of roaming, scavenging marauders. Terror of nature, how it crept forward, engulfing the past, reclaiming the land, its trees hiding wild dogs and sheltering giant crows.

And most of all, terror of Witch Crag.

CHAPTER FOUR

Witch Crag was always in view, from every part of the hill fort. Lowering, jagged, like a broken fingernail scraping the sky, its lower slopes thickly forested with dark pines that never changed whatever the season, its top harsh bare rock. Sometimes, at night, green and purple lights flickered on the summit. It was forbidden to look at them, because they were made by the witches who lived there, and could be part of how they lured girls to them.

The last girl to go to Witch Crag was many years ago, when the headman was a young man. Her name was Vild. Mystery surrounded her going, whether she was taken or had been bewitched and escaped. It was forbidden to talk about her.

But once, when Kita was a child, Nada had talked about Vild. It was spring, and Kita had found an abandoned fledgling bird cheeping desolately by the kitchens. She'd scooped it up and made a straw nest for it behind some old wooden staves; she fed it with crushed worms, and as it grew stronger it started to flutter from stave to stave. It started to call to Kita when she appeared with its food; then, one day, it flew to her and landed on her shoulder. Laughing in pleasure, she'd turned to find Nada standing there, white faced.

"I saved it, Nada! It knows me!" she'd cried in triumph. Then, "Why are you looking like that?"

Nada had glanced hurriedly behind her, then got hold of Kita's arm. "You must drive it off," she said. "You're a kind girl to save it but you mustn't keep it tame."

"I know. I know it's foolish, time wasting. Animals are here to feed us, not for our pleasure or to be our friends. *But*—"

"It's more than that," said Nada, urgently. "They'll think you're a witch."

"*What? Why?*"

"Because you befriend beasts. Vild . . . Vild could do that. She had a little wild dog, a puppy. The headman found her with it – he . . . crushed the life out of it. In front of her. She grew hysterical. She was screaming, cursing. They tied her up and left her in one of the storage huts while they decided what was to be done. But in the morning . . . she'd gone."

"To the witches."

"They were sure of it."

Kita shuddered. "And you think I might be one."

"No. *No.* It's what others think, dearling. If she hadn't gone . . . they'd've slit her for sure."

*

26

Everyone knew the witches were evil. They had a fearful history. Abducting girls, or luring them with witchery; murdering any men who dared venture on to the crag slopes – there were sightings of their corpses hanging like grotesque puppets from the pine tree branches.

Not long after Vild disappeared, three witches had been discovered lurking in the woods near the hill fort. They'd been dragged out on to the plains and slit as they stood, the headman himself executing one of them.

Their bodies had been left for the dogs and crows, but that night their bloodstained garments had floated eerily down into the hill fort, causing panic and dismay among the sheep people, who were sure they were now under a curse.

Rumours of witches inside the hill fort grew with the panic and swarmed around two women skilled in healing, despite all the good they did. Then, one dawn, the women were discovered crushing and boiling herbs. The headman ordered them to be tied up while he decided their fate. Which was to be taken outside the hill fort walls the following dawn, and slit.

Soon afterwards, a marauding tribe intent on stealing sheep had besieged the hill fort. As their pact demanded, the horsemen had answered the bonfire summons and joined with the sheepmen; together they'd driven the marauders off. The fierce fighting had lasted until nightfall; the loss of life had been terrible.

But less terrible, somehow, than what they saw from the hill fort walls when the sun came up the next day.

Three great stakes had been driven into the ground on the edge of the battlefield, stakes with crossbars. On one side of each crossbar dangled a crazy bouquet of teasels, thistles and yellow flowering broom, all tangled up with ivy and vines. Beautiful in their way.

On the other side of the crossbars three dead footsoldiers swung, hanging by a foot. Naked but for more vines and ivy coiled over them.

A message from the witches.

The headman had let out a roar of rage and disgust. He ordered the gates open and limped at speed on to the grasslands, several of his best men following, all of them ignoring their battle wounds. The wild dogs and crows still gorging on the dead had scattered at their furious advance. The soldiers had tried to reach the vine ropes that tethered the boys, but they were too high. So they'd hacked at the stakes, felled them like trees with their tragic fruit, then left them for the crows and the dogs.

"I don't think you're a witch," Nada had whispered, "but it's not me who matters."

CHAPTER FIVE

In the girls' sleeping hut, Kita snuggled up to Quainy under the heavy sheepskins. "Oh, at *last*," she mumbled. "A bit of space at last. No one ordering you about. Quainy, pinch me if I doze off, if we don't *talk* this whole day will have been crap. . ."

"Shhhh," said Quainy, stroking her hair sadly, "shhhhh."

"I saw Raff today. In the dung tunnel. Fitting, isn't it, that the only place you can get a bit of privacy is in the dung tunnel. He's being so brave, Quainy, but this place is killing him, no one sees what he has. . ."

"No one wants what he has."

"Apart from us! His creativity, his words, his *curiosity* — d'you remember how he used to try to get the oldies to tell him anything they knew about before the Great Havoc, and they'd cuff him aside?"

"Yes."

"And when we were just kids, and he did that amazing picture, on the rocks, drawing with a burnt stick. . ."

"The headman hit him and locked him up in a storage shed."

"And he told us he made a huge sculpture, out of the grain," Kita giggled, "and knocked it down when he heard them coming to let him out. . . He *won*, he won in the end, they never knew."

Quainy was silent, although usually she was happy to talk about Raff. "What's up?" asked Kita.

"I heard today," Quainy murmured. "I'm to go on a visit. The horsemen are having a feast next big moon. Six of our footsoldiers are going, to renew the bond of our tribes. And . . . and I'm going, too."

Panic seized Kita. "But you'll come *back*?"

"They say so. But not for long. There are three men who I might marry. Once we've all met, we decide who I wed. . . Then I go back for the marriage feast."

"But your *hair* isn't grown!" Kita wailed . . . and was silent. She knew that didn't matter. Long hair, short hair, Quainy was beautiful. She'd be excellent trade with the horsemen, who seemed to value beauty. "Are you scared?" she whispered.

"Of course. I've felt sick all the time, since I heard. And I can't bear it that I won't see you again, or Raff. . ."

"But you'll have a better life there. Everyone says so. Especially as a *wife*. Maybe you'll fall for one of the bridegrooms, they say the young horsemen are gorgeous, and he'll fall for you too and love you. . . Oh, I wish I wasn't so skinny and odd-looking, Quainy, so they wanted me too!"

"I love how you look," Quainy said, "but I'd change it if it meant we could be together."

The night of the big moon came round fast. In its morning, six footsoldiers set off to walk the seven miles to the horsemen's fort, with Quainy and a sheep destined for the spit walking with them.

Kita had no chance to say goodbye to Quainy. She escaped from her work hauling water up from the well only in time to see the great gates swing shut behind her. She waited until the central yard was empty, then raced over to the rocky outcrop, clambered up it, and wriggled through the brambles to her ledge to watch her friend go. The footsoldiers surrounded Quainy and the sheep, two of them carrying a huge bale of woven wool, on poles – more trade. She was dressed in a fine, new woollen tunic, and her hair was washed. It fanned round her face in corn-yellow waves.

Kita watched until they were out of sight, a stone of grief inside her. The wind was up, and she had to lie flat to feel safe in it. The high rock and wooden barriers kept the wind out of the hill fort – it roared overhead as though you were in the bottom of a bucket. But up here, Kita liked to feel it on her body. She let it buffet her for a while, then she scrambled down and stood leaning against the wooden stockade to catch her breath. Forking her fingers through her dark spiky hair, she was suddenly aware of someone behind her. Then a hand shot out and grabbed her arm.

Shocked, she spun round. To face Arc, grinning at her. He squeezed her arm hard, then let it go. "You climb like a tree rat," he said.

Her heart pounded in shock and fear. Had he seen where she'd come from? Was her flint ledge discovered?

"What the hell were you trying to do?" he demanded.

"They've taken Quainy," she muttered. "I was trying to see her go. But I couldn't."

"Course you couldn't. Unless you could fly, h'n? Like a witch?"

She hung her head, didn't answer. She thought she'd got away with it.

"You're not the only one sad to see Quainy go," he sneered. "Bray was meant to be in that guard today, but he's fallen for her looks so bad the headman noticed. Said he had to stop behind in case he caused trouble. *Idiot.* Missing out on a feast with the horsemen. Over a *girl.*"

Everything in Kita wanted to get away from Arc. He exuded a kind of menace, a violence. But she wanted information more. "You went the winter before last, didn't you?" she asked.

"Yes," he said. "For a feast – the biggest feast of the year. We stayed three nights. I'd just been made footsoldier – they were the best nights of my life. The horsemen know how to live. Their staple food is the boar they hunt in the forests behind them, not stupid sheep. Their hall is decked with plunder from tribes they've battled with. And they honour their warriors."

"You're honoured here," Kita ventured.

"Not the same," he scoffed. "Yes, we get fed the best, warmed first, wear leather . . . but just to make us fight better. There, they get proper respect. The warriors – they sat on a high table, above everyone else, and when the drums stopped, everyone shouted their names, *saluted* them. . ."

"For that feast – didn't some of our girls go?"

Kita hated the way Arc leered at her when she said that. "Three of them," he said. "You know *why*, don't you?"

"I thought . . . I thought they went like Quainy's going. To be considered as wives. But none of them went back again. Did no one want to keep them?"

Arc threw back his head and laughed. "And you're hoping no one will want Quainy, and she'll stay here too? Forget it. Those three girls had a good time for a few nights. There was no plan for more. Remember the baby that was born, nine months later?"

Kita went pale. With shock – and at her own stupidity. Of course. Of *course*.

"We boys were put to work, too," he said. "Two babies came from us. Don't look so sick. My father was a horseman, I'm sure of it. That's why I'm drawn to them. That's why I'm – like I am."

"I never . . . I just never thought of it before."

"Oh, Kita. *Dumb*. Why d'you think the headman's glad if someone brings in a wild sheep, found wandering? Fresh blood is good for breeding. Strengthens the strain. Better sheep, better men."

CHAPTER SIX

Depression settled on Kita like a dark fog. Her grief for Nada opened up again, and threatened to engulf her. All she could think of was Nada, and Quainy going for good to the horsemen. Of never seeing her again. Sleeping alone in the huts, with no one to talk to. None of the other girls wanted a bond, a friendship – they kept to the sheepman creed. She had Raff, of course, but meetings with him were rare now they were no longer children. And she could only see bad things ahead for him.

Two days went by, and Kita worked mournfully in the kitchen, stripping meat from sheep bones and chopping the tough root vegetables they cultivated near the dung heap. One of the older women said how good it was that Kita had matured at last, settled to steady work, and stopped being so jumpy and fanciful. Then, with the air of someone bestowing a great honour, she told her she'd recommend her for work in the infants' pens. Kita thanked her, but her heart turned over. She remembered the pens as loss, as terror, a desolate space where she'd begged for Nada's fearfully rationed comfort. She dreaded revisiting them.

Later, when the next day's tasks were announced during the end-of-day meal, she learned she had to report there. The next morning, reluctantly, she made her way over. The pens consisted of a long hut, for sleeping and protection from the weather, and a series of interconnecting cages built from sturdy bamboo.

Nada had been a little girl when the cages were built. She'd told Kita that after the Great Havoc, some of the creatures who survived evolved fast. The crows who circled the hill fort in their murderous flocks grew bigger and bolder, perching on the great wooden walls and swooping in for lambs and carrion. Then one dreadful day a newborn baby, swaddled in wool and asleep on the ground, was carried off by a huge crow. Distraught, the women resolved to be more vigilant, but a few days later six or seven of the great birds soared in together, harrying a woman and the three little ones in her charge. The decision to build the cages was made that day. Small children would be kept safe like the lambs; bamboo bars would free their mothers for other work. And free them from the maternal bond, which was no help to survival, after all.

The heavy-set matron in charge of the pens opened the cage gate to Kita and Erin, the other girl on duty there that day, with one eye on the sky. "Quickly," she barked. "See those buggers flapping over there? Oh, they don't miss a trick." She ushered the girls in and slammed the gate to. "They'd be in here if I let 'em."

"That's horrible," grimaced Kita.

"Oh, they're *waiting*. To get their claws into something small enough to make away with. I came out here the other day, two of them perched on the roof bars, peering in."

"The littlies must've been terrified."

"Screaming fit to split, but the crows took no notice. Ugly evil buggers. Now. Erin, here's a broom, you sweep up. Kita, I want you on drilling. And none of your wordiness – just stick to what's needed. Then both of you – food duty. Follow me."

Kita's heart sank further. "Drilling" was the only teaching the children got; an endlessly repeated series of dull commands ("Pick up the stick! Give the stick to the one on your left! March to the end of the pens!") that had to be obeyed immediately. It was designed to make them biddable workers. Food duty was worse though. However rank the mutton broth or porridge, the children were made to eat it, so they'd grow too big for the crows to carry off.

As she walked through the pens, dark memories settled on her. There was no play here and only one dreary little song the children knew; she shivered when she heard them intoning it, remembering how much it had scared her as a child.

Don't look at the witches,
In trees or in ditches,
They'll grimly enchant you,
They'll gobble you up.

But somehow she got through the day. Few of the children reminded her of her younger self; most of them were well on the way to becoming stoical little sheep people, dull-eyed and obedient. She ached to pick up one crying toddler but was told "Leave her be – she's got to learn."

Whenever she looked up, the sky was criss-crossed with cage bars. Overhead, black as her thoughts, the huge crows circled.

The matron in charge of the pens was pleased with Kita, said she had a way with the little ones, so she was sent there for the next day, too. Girls had to take a turn with all the tasks but if they showed a real aptitude for cooking, say, or spinning, they were sent to those tasks more often and, once adult, that would be all that they did. Kita thought about ending up like the matron, living her life in the pens, and decided death would be preferable.

The moon was waning; the footsoldiers and Quainy were due back that afternoon. Kita's longing to see her friend was made more desperate by knowing how brief a time they'd have together. She told herself not to be selfish; maybe a handsome young horseman had fallen for Quainy, and she for him, and she'd be happy. Maybe he'd be high up the ranks, with power, maybe he'd call for Kita to come and be Quainy's help and companion. . .

Maybe, maybe.

She heard the great gates grind open as she was feeding the babies their last mush before bed. It had to be Quainy and the men, returning home, but there was no sound other than the gates; no fuss was made of their homecoming.

As soon as she was released, Kita ran to the food hut and scanned the queue. Raff was there, too far away to speak to, head down and shoulders hunched as if warding off a thump or mockery. But Quainy wasn't there, nor did she come through the doors that Kita watched anxiously throughout her sparse meal.

She was there, though, in the sleeping hut when Kita ran to it, her blonde hair glowing above the stained old sheepskin wrapped tightly around her.

"Quainy!" Kita cried.

"*Shhhhh!*" went the hut.

"*Shhhh* yourselves! Dumb sheep! *Quainy!*"

Quainy turned, waved. Kita scrambled down beside her and Quainy pulled the sheepskin over them both. "You weren't at dinner," Kita whispered.

"I ate with the headman," Quainy muttered. "It was terrifying, I could hardly swallow. He *interrogated* me about how the visit had gone."

"*Well?*" Kita demanded. "How did it go? Did you like any of the three possible husbands? Is the decision made?"

Quainy was silent for a moment, then she said, "I don't know. It's nothing to do with me. I don't get a choice. I don't get a say. I know I'm trade, but I thought they'd ask what I felt. But they didn't. I'm not even sure who the three men are. There were five of them who came in, all leering and laughing and prodding me. All of them are old, like our headman, old warriors who have 'earned' me. All of them are disgusting."

"Oh, *Quainy*," Kita groaned. Devastated.

"The young footsoldiers who went with me – the ones who've never been before – I know they were shocked, though they tried not to show it. And a couple of the young horsemen – they tried to cheer me up, afterwards, but they got shouted away by one of my 'bridegrooms'. After that I kind of – froze up, for the rest of the visit. And then – I couldn't stop crying on the walk back here, and one of our men – he said marriage was my duty and I just had to get on with it."

"That's gross. And unfair."

"He said we needed the horsemen's alliance to survive."

"Survive, survive," hissed Kita. "Why do we bother?"

"Don't talk like that, Kita."

"I mean it. When I think of them treating you like that, I. . . Sometimes I. . ." She trailed off, a vision of death in her mind like a beckoning witch. Then, hopelessly, she said, "No wonder the headman wouldn't let Bray go with you."

"Bray?"

"You like him, don't you. He likes you. If he'd seen you treated like that. . ."

"Maybe."

"It was Arc who told me he'd been banned. *Arc's* been before. Getting their girls pregnant. He likes their ways."

"Then I don't think he can have *seen* their ways!" Quainy burst out. "I think he just saw the surface. Kita, we were wrong about the horsemen. We thought they were better, more advanced, because they marry, and have fun and feasts and dancing. . ."

"And they're democratic – they vote on things?"

"But not in any way that has meaning! One of the girls told me – it's only the men who vote, and they're told which *way* to vote by whichever old warrior is their protector, their *master*."

"I don't understand."

Quainy sighed, shakily. "The old warriors, the strong ones, who've fought countless battles – they rule the fort. The younger men and the weaker men – they have to ally themselves to one of the strong just to survive. And the old warriors strut and shout and backstab each other, constantly vying for power, and making and breaking alliances with each other, and there's a horrible atmosphere of fear everywhere." She paused, then added, "The old warriors are the only ones allowed to have wives. And those wives are shut away, like prisoners."

Even in the gloom in the hut, Kita could see how white Quainy was. She took hold of her hand, and squeezed it.

"Kita, I think . . . I think our way is best," Quainy whispered. "Even if it's narrow, pinched. It's . . . safer. More predictable."

Something in her voice made Kita go colder still. "Did they hurt you?" she choked out.

"No. No, dearling. It was just what I *saw*. What I sat through. They feasted on our sheep, ripping into the meat, wasting it – the children scavenged under the table. No order. They were drinking that stuff they brew from berries, it made them loud, frightening . . . and I was the only girl at their high table. Sat there like . . . like trade. But there were some girls fetching and carrying, and they. . ."

"What?" whispered Kita.

"The old men mauled them. As if they were *things*. And they made them dance to drums. That's how the women live, unless they marry and get shut away. They dance, and drudge, and mate with outsiders to strengthen the bloodline."

A sad silence descended. Kita knew about mating. Rams tupped ewes to get lambs; babies were needed, too, for the tribe to survive. The sheepmen had a practical attitude to sex. During early spring, the rules were relaxed, and mating was encouraged. The sleeping huts were left open for this very purpose. If a girl and a boy were drawn to each other, they had sex. Pregnant girls worked through the summer and autumn and then gave birth in the winter, when there was less work to do. . . It was efficient. Basic.

But this . . . what Quainy had described. . .

"We always said our way was terrible," Kita muttered, at last. "Bonds discouraged. Men just around for the stud. Children taken from their mothers and put in the pens. . ."

"It's better," croaked Quainy. "Our way is harsh, theirs is *slavery*. And the boys suffer too. They got this boy . . . he was under the table, scavenging, but he was older than the other kids, just thin, nervous-looking. . ."

Like Raff, Kita thought, knowing Quainy was thinking it too, but neither of them said it aloud.

"They . . . they dragged him out, and then they made him fight. With one of the warriors."

"Oh, no."

"No weapons, but he was . . . it was hateful, Kita. He was knocked down, right away, and then he was crawling, begging, while this posturing old . . . *ape* kicked him and . . . and *stamped* on him and all the big warriors shouted *get up and fight*."

"Did . . . did he die? What happened?"

"I didn't see. I ran out. I threw up. But the girl I'd spoken to before, Lilly, she told me one of the younger horsemen intervened to stop it."

"He risked his neck."

"Yes. He was cunning, though, he made a big joke of it, Lilly said, insisted the boy wasn't worth the killing, then he picked the shattered boy up and carried him out."

Kita sighed, exhausted by all she'd heard. "Quainy, you can't go back to the horsemen," she murmured. "Not to live among that. Not to be some old man's slave."

"I haven't got a choice, have I? Get some sleep."

CHAPTER SEVEN

The days went by. The treacherous moon waned, then began to wax again. Soon it would be full and at the next big moon, Quainy would be taken to the horsemen's fort to be married.

They told Raff what had happened to Quainy there, but apart from that, they didn't talk about it. It was like stone inside them.

Then something happened.

It was at the start of the working day, and Kita was in the sheep pens. She disliked the rancid smell from the animals and the spitefulness of Ma Baa, the prime ewe, but the work was so simple no one was in overall charge to nag and watch over her, so she felt a certain freedom. And there was always the hope that she'd bump into Raff on a trip to the dung heap.

She was drearily sweeping up when she heard a drumming noise, growing louder. She stopped to listen. The noise grew louder still; it was hooves, horses, she was sure of it – then there was a thundering, heaving noise, the horses being reined in, it had to be, and a man bellowed, "*Open the gates! The horsemen ask it!*" Before she could feel afraid, she dropped her broom, raced out of the pens, ducked behind a bale of hay and peered out at the central yard to watch. The headman was striding across the yard, yelling orders; four young footsoldiers raced over, unbarred the gates and ran out in an arc, two to a gate, opening them wide.

Then six horsemen rode in, horses prancing, snorting, tossing their great, handsome heads. Kita was awestruck; she'd never been so close to horses before. They looked so wild and noble compared to sheep. The gates thudded shut behind them; the headman shouted greetings. Two cooks ran out from the kitchens with mugs of sweetened ewe's milk and water; the horsemen reached from their horses to take the drinks, and didn't dismount.

In her hiding place, Kita was seized by the terrible thought that they'd come to get Quainy and take her to her new home early. Then the leading horseman spoke. He had long grey hair tied back, and a great scar across his cheek.

"We ask your help," he said, loudly. "And come to warn you. Two of our girls have gone missing. They took a horse. We discovered their loss first thing this morning. The gates were still barred; impossible to know how they got through our barricades, but get through they did. We set off, following the tracks. Which led us to Witch Crag."

The horses shifted, stamped; the sheepmen were silent, listening, waiting.

"They were two fine girls," the horseman went on. "Soon to be brides. One of them my bride. Some of us were for going back, but I led the men round the foot of the crag, searching the lower slopes, and found single horse tracks going higher. And found not our girls, but bones. Bleached skeletons, a dozen or more of them, shining white, arranged in a great circle, a wheel, skulls inward, legs and arms all overlapping in a great, grim wheel. And nearby, a few weapons, broken and useless. Some marauding gang's crude clubs and daggers, nothing we or you sheepmen use."

"You turned back then," the headman said. As if needing to be reassured.

"Yes. The whole place was rank with necromancy. And on the way back, we found the horse wandering."

"But no riders."

"No. Witches have taken our girls. Seduced them and called them; hexed the gate bars or bewitched the horse so it could clear the barricades. There is no other explanation."

The headman glared at the ground. "It's years since anything like this has happened," he growled.

"Long years. It's starting again, sheepman. The witches have got stronger. That obscene wheel gave news of their power and intent. So. We warn you, and we ask you to search and keep watch. If the girls escape the witches, like the horse did, you may find them."

"We will search and watch," said the headman, grimly.

"Open the gates," said the horseman.

It was all anyone talked about that day. In muted, frightened voices, they discussed the witches. Witches getting stronger, luring young girls, boiling dead men to eat the flesh and make grisly patterns with the bones. Patterns that emanated evil into the land.

At night, in the hut, Quainy cuddled up to Kita and murmured, "In the kitchen, they were saying witches can fly with crows. Holding on to their wings, riding their backs. Imagine."

"Nonsense," said Kita. "If they could do that they'd've come for us long ago, over the walls."

"H'm. I don't know. What I *do* know, though, is the horsewomen will suffer worse things now those two brides have gone. They'll be controlled, constrained, kept under tighter chains than ever, in case any more are seduced by sorcery. We will be, too. I heard that no girls are to be let out to watch the sheep in the spring."

"Oh, *what*?" wailed Kita. She'd never once been outside the hill fort walls, apart from to the dung heap; she was longing for late spring, when she might be allowed to help mind the sheep driven out to the grasslands to graze. The space, the lack of barriers – she was longing for it.

"It's the headman's orders," said Quainy. "We're in danger, outside."

"I'd rather be in danger than kept in a bucket!" Kita exploded.

"Kita, *shhhh*!" Quainy murmured, looking around nervously. "Don't even *think* that. The witches are evil. They bewitch girls and steal them away so our tribes can't thrive, can't breed and multiply, everyone knows that. . ."

"Do they?" said Kita.

A party of young footsoldiers, led by Arc, was sent out from the hill fort early the next day to march the perimeter of the grasslands and look for the missing brides. No one had any real hope of finding the girls but it was vital that the sheepmen's obligation to the horsemen be fulfilled. At the same time (efficiency being central to the sheepman creed) the footsoldiers were to hack down the brush that was encroaching from the forest. The forest was dangerous – it sheltered savage dogs, maybe worse – and must not be allowed to creep closer. Especially as spring was coming and soon the sheep would be let out to pasture.

But the footsoldiers came back early, well before midday, the hacking only half done, and shouted excitedly for the headman as they approached the gates.

Kita was working in the spinning shack that day, and she was just crossing the deserted central yard with a fleece when she heard the shouting – urgent, triumphant shouting. She dumped the fleece behind a rock, swivelled her eyes to check no one was watching her, scrambled up the rock face and crawled on to her flint ledge to look out.

It was a serious matter, opening the gates. Instead, the headman ordered the parley ladder to be propped up against them, and climbed it. Kita, peering over her ledge, watched as the footsoldiers came to a halt on the steep, grassy slope.

Two of them were carrying something. The first thing she noticed was its colour – a glorious, russet red, like berries in autumn, glowing and rich.

Then its shape. Human shape.

Arc stepped forward and saluted the headman, who was now looming over the gates on the top rung of the parley ladder. "A witch!" Arc cried. "Sir, we caught a witch!"

The headman started. "Stay back!" he roared. "Are you mad? Bringing her here?"

"Sir, she has no power!" shouted Arc. "We saw her in the undergrowth, stooping, shuffling. She saw us, and tried to run. But Drell caught her a blow with his scythe end, and she went down."

"She could have destroyed him – destroyed all of you!"

"But she didn't!" Arc yelled back, defiantly. "We overcame her!" Then he turned, and gestured to the two

44

footsoldiers carrying the russet bundle, who dropped it on the ground.

A slender girl unfolded from the cloth, and scrambled to her feet. The red cloth billowed around her; a shower of bright-red flowers dropped from her hands. She had long, wild brown hair, a white pointed face, huge, terrified eyes. Kita stared; her mouth dropped open. Somehow the girl was more stirring to her even than the magnificent horses had been. The girl was beautiful.

And yet she was a witch.

"Sir, she has no power," Arc yelled, again. "If she had power, she would have used it by now. Maybe she's too young. If we bring her in, we can work on her. We can find out how they make their necromancy. We can learn about the two missing girls. The horsemen will be pleased."

There was a silence, as the headman glared down over the gates. Then he said, "It is too dangerous to bring her inside the gates. She is evil." Then he said, "Slit her. Do it now."

"But *sir*!" Arc erupted.

"*Now!*" roared the headman, but Arc still made no move, defying him.

Then Drell drew his knife. He knew how to slit a witch, all the young footsoldiers knew, though none of them had seen it done.

He planted himself in front of the swaying witch,

then he thrust his knife into her throat, leaving it there as the blood spurted.

Soundlessly, weirdly, she spun, and then for a long instant she looked straight up at Kita, hidden on her ledge. Kita flinched back into the brambles, trembling.

Drell seized the witch by her arm, steadying her. He took hold of his knife again and dragged it down, down the witch's breastbone to her stomach, and the witch folded up, gushing more bright blood on to the ground.

Chapter Eight

"*Get back to work!*" the headman bellowed. Arc rapped out a command, and the footsoldiers turned on their heels to go back to clearing the perimeters.

The witch's body was left on the ground to be cleared by dogs and crows.

Kita scrambled down from her ledge, shaking. She was awash with horror, but she made herself focus on the here and now — collecting her fleece and returning to the spinning shack before anyone realized she was missing.

She worked at the mindless spinning until the day's end in a fog of fear and confusion. She thought endlessly of the slight body on the ground, the red of the blood and the flowers and the gown, as questions hurtled through her mind. The witch had seemed powerless. Until she'd looked straight at Kita, penetrating the brambles hiding her, when she'd seemed to have a power beyond anything Kita had come across before.

At the end-of-day meal, everyone was talking about what had happened in front of the fort walls. Talk rose so far above its usual dull murmur that the head cook came out from the kitchen and insisted on silence.

Kita sat with Quainy, as usual, but said nothing to her of what she'd seen. It was too horrific, too overwhelming, to talk about yet.

They left the food hut together. It was a bright, clear evening, stars beginning to prickle the sky. "Bed?" asked Quainy, shivering.

"In a minute," said Kita. "I want some night air. Clear my head."

"I'll save your place," said Quainy, and she hurried off.

Kita looked up at the black, silent sky for a long moment, then she wandered towards the great gates. If anyone was out too late, a guard would shout at them to get to bed, but during the half-hour after eating it was all right to walk in the compound. Few chose to, of course, because everyone was so tired after their day's work.

As Kita rounded the corner, she heard voices. Someone other than her was still up. She crept nearer.

Arc, with Drell and a few other footsoldiers, were gathered by one of the massive gate posts, talking intently. Suddenly, Arc rounded on Drell, who stumbled backwards. "I'd slit twenty witches," he snarled, "if it was right to do it!"

"But you were *ordered*—"

"It takes no courage just to follow *orders!*"

The boy next to Arc put a hand on his arm, but he shrugged it off violently. Then there was more fierce talking, but lower, so Kita couldn't hear.

Kita looked at Arc hungrily. She was desperate to question him, as if that might salve the trauma she felt. He'd taken the witch, and she wanted to know all about it, all about *her*. She wasn't sure why she felt this way, but she felt it strongly. Arc had some kind of key and he must be made – somehow – to pass it on to her.

But just the thought of approaching him, of walking over and asking to talk to him, made her feel sick with fear. He'd mock her, he'd laugh; she couldn't do it, couldn't expose herself like that.

And yet he had the key, and she needed it.

The group of footsoldiers was dispersing. Drell's head was low. Arc had reasserted his authority.

Kita breathed in, and stepped out of the shadows. "Another witch!" Arc crowed. "Slit her, Drell!"

The footsoldiers laughed; Drell grinned, sheepishly.

"Arc, can I speak to you?" Kita blurted out.

She wasn't prepared for the jeering laughter that followed her question. All of them, all the footsoldiers, laughing at her and mocking Arc, who grinned and swore. She waited, heart hammering, desperate to run, making herself hold her ground. Then Arc said, "Get on, you morons, I'll be along later," and with more laughter the group walked away.

And Arc leant back against the huge gate post, arms

folded, and all she had to do was cross the space of ground between them.

Somehow, she made it. She came to a halt a short distance away from him, and said, "It's about what happened today."

"Come closer," he said. "I don't want to shout."

She edged a little closer. Arc was scary, close up. An even face, handsome, like a mask, strong teeth like a dog. She couldn't meet his eyes.

"Did you get into trouble?" she asked. "For defying the headman?"

"What's it to you, *tree rat*?"

"I'm curious."

Arc grinned. "Yes, I did. He clouted me, warned me never to talk to him like that again. Said I talk too much altogether. But he's got me marked as his successor. He's all but told me so. He knows I need balls for that job. So. . ." He grinned again.

"Why weren't you more afraid of the witch?"

"If she'd been able to hex us, she'd've done it as soon as we flushed her out. She was the one who was terrified – I could smell it on her. Drell overreacted. He laid her out – if he hadn't, I'd've made her talk."

"Did she say *anything*?"

"Not a word. She didn't even beg for her life."

Kita's throat seized, but she made herself flatter him, made herself say, "I'd've been terrified. Weren't you scared at *all*?" She knew he was looking straight at her, and she made herself look back, meet his eyes. They were grey and oddly beautiful. "Everyone knows the witches do terrible things," she went on. "If you go too near Witch Crag – you're done for. They hang you from the pines to die in agony or boil you and gobble you up—"

"Stories," scoffed Arc. "Scary tale crap from the infants' pens."

"But what about those footsoldiers, after the battle, stripped and covered in ivy and strung up by their feet. . ."

"They were *dead* when they were strung up. And killed by marauders, not witches. And the bones the horseman spoke of . . . who knows how they got killed. Maybe two gangs slugged it out and slaughtered each other." He paused, still staring at her steadily. "Maybe the witches just tinker about with corpses."

Something shifted in Kita's mind when she heard that, something she knew she didn't understand the importance of yet; she tucked it away to examine later. "Everyone was talking tonight," she went on. "Everyone was saying what a risk you took."

"I was ready to take it," he said. Then he unfolded his arms, and stopped leaning against the wooden post, which made Kita want to take a step back, away from him, but she stopped herself.

"Why?" she asked.

"Instinct. Like when a dog knows to attack. Maybe she did have power, but I knew it wasn't dangerous to me, right there and then. *Or* to the tribe. The headman bottled it. He threw away our chance to find out more."

"How d'you think they bewitched the horsemen brides?"

Arc laughed. "Maybe they didn't. Maybe the brides just didn't want to be married to old men."

"Are you *serious*?"

"Maybe. What about you, Kita? Where does your taste lie?"

She stared at him, stunned, and he said, "Spring's nearly here. I can fight and you can climb like a tree rat – we'd make a good baby. And I don't think the *real* reason you came to talk to me was because you wanted to hear about a dead witch."

Then, fast, sure of himself, he was right in front of her, his arms around her. His mouth went down on hers. She jerked her head backwards, wriggled furiously, and ducked down out of his grip.

His laughter followed her as she raced for the sleeping huts.

"Nice walk?" mumbled Quainy, sleepily, holding out the sheepskin cover for Kita to get under.

"No," wailed Kita, heart still pounding. "I saw Arc and asked about the witch, and now he thinks I want to breed with him."

"Oh, *Kita*. Of course he does if you went to talk to him."

"*What?* Oh, lord – I didn't think of that."

"Oh, Kita – you know what the footsoldiers are like. They all think they're prizes for the girls to fight over. And Arc likes you – I've seen him watching you."

"That's insane!"

"It's *true*. I'd've told you before but I knew you'd react like this. Why shouldn't he like you? You've got more life in you than most of the girls here put together."

"I'm going to be sick."

"No, you're not. You're flattered. I can see it in your face." For answer, Kita pulled the sheepskin right over her head, making Quainy laugh. "He's young and strong," Quainy teased, "and good looking. Even if he is a thug – and let's face it, footsoldiers are trained to be thugs."

"Mmmmph," groaned Kita.

"Lots of girls would jump at the chance of sleeping with him this spring. I'd say yes if I were you."

There was a long pause. Then Kita reappeared solemnly from under the sheepskin and said, "Quainy, don't say that. Don't be like the others. I don't want to just – *get pregnant*. I don't want to be a sheep, making babies. I want more than that."

"Sorry," murmured Quainy. "It's just – Arc, for all his arrogance, he's . . . he's a better choice than what I've got to go to."

"I know, dearling," said Kita, sorrowfully, snuggling closer. "Oh, lord, Quainy, there has to be a better way than the sheepmen or the horsemen. There has to be something more. Something with order, respect . . . *and* dancing."

"There isn't," muttered Quainy. "Go to sleep."

But Kita lay awake for a long time that night, staring at the low black ceiling of the sleeping hut. First, she admitted to herself that Quainy was sort of right. Part of her was flattered, stirred, that Arc seemed to like her. She hadn't been as appalled as she should have been when he'd grabbed hold of her. His kiss hadn't been . . . it hadn't been vile.

But that was irrelevant. There, she'd admitted what she felt about it, now it could be set aside.

The horror of the witch, spinning and dying, looking straight at her, took over her thoughts. Things – confusing, challenging, terrifying things – were clicking into place in her mind.

That night she dreamt she was chasing after Nada through the forest. She was scared that Nada was a ghost but she still ran after her. She went faster and faster as skinny winter branches caught at her face and tripped her. But the old nurse wouldn't let herself be caught.

Chapter Nine

Two more days passed. The moon was no longer like a nail-paring in the sky, but bulbous, ominous. And as the moon waxed, and her departure as trade bride drew nearer, Quainy's stoicism waned. She was anxious, tearful. That night, she cried herself to sleep with Kita failing to comfort her.

An hour or so before dawn, the clanging of iron against iron woke most of the girls in the hut to the sound of heavy rain drumming on its roof. Rain collection was vital in the spring; the well had to be full for the long dry summer, and that morning the clanging was even more urgent than usual.

"Come on," Quainy groaned, shaking Kita, who was still asleep. "We've got to get in line. Kita, come *on*!"

Kita sat up and rubbed her face with her hands. "I was deep in the most amazing dream," she murmured, "about Nada again, but this time I caught up with her. We were in the middle of a wood, she told me to be strong, she told me to trust what I knew even if I didn't have a name for it. . ."

"Later, Kita," snapped Quainy, pulling her to her feet. The two of them scurried out into the downpour.

The rain was so heavy that the eight great sheepskin sheets filled in record time, and the bucket handlers had to work murderously fast. Kita's muscles and sinews screamed as she seized handle after handle and passed the heavy brimming buckets on to Quainy. She didn't dare to look further down the line to see how Raff was faring, but she heard the headman shout, "Keep up, boy, keep the rhythm, the girls shame you!" and she knew he'd been shouting at Raff.

Then, as dramatically as it had started, the rain stopped, and the headman gave his welcome cry of "End! Fire! Soup!"

Raff caught Kita and Quainy up as they hurried over to the fire pit. "My arms are out of their sockets," he groaned. "How do you two do it?"

"That was harsh," agreed Quainy. "That was faster than I've ever known it."

"At least I didn't fall over," he muttered.

They reached the crowd by the fire. Its glow illuminated the footsoldiers standing at the front; cocky, self-assured, they waited for the soup that would be passed to them first. Kita could see Arc's strong profile against the firelight – he shook his dark wet hair over Bray, and laughed; she saw his teeth glint.

Usually, everyone tried to huddle as close behind the footsoldiers as they could, to get warm, but Kita took hold of her friends' arms and said, "Wait. Let's stay back here."

Something in her voice made them stop, although it was risky for Raff to be seen in the company of the girls; he risked the young footsoldiers turning on him. But the moon was behind thick grey clouds still, and no one could see them so far from the fire.

"What is it, Kita?" asked Quainy, as they sat down on the wet ground and huddled together.

Kita knew she had to talk fast, because an opportunity like this might not come again before Quainy was sent to the horsemen. She didn't know what she was going to say, beyond the first few shocking words; all she had were fragments that formed a vague and terrifying shape in her mind. She took in a deep breath, and began.

"We have to get out of here. All three of us. Quainy can't become some old man's slave; Raff can't be bullied any more; I can't bear to be here any more. It's like death and I'd rather be actually dead. We have to go. *Don't* say anything. I know you think I'm mad. I know how we can do it. My high place – it's a ledge, on the rock by the great gates."

"I thought it was," said Quainy. "Though I've never seen you climb up there."

"I hope *no* one has. There's a way down from my ledge to the outside – where the wooden barricade joins the rock. I . . . . I've done it."

"You've been *out*?" said Raff, stunned.

"No. Last summer, I climbed down as far as I could, then saw the drop, and bottled it. Actually, I didn't really mean to escape, not on my own. But we can do it. Climb halfway down, at night, then drop."

"Right," said Quainy, sarcastically. "Drop right on top of a night guard."

"We'd be between the guards at the gates and the one at the dung gate – they won't see us. Not if we go *soon* – before the moon's too big."

"They'll hear us when we scream because we've smashed ourselves on the rocks."

"Quainy, I've been down, I've seen it – we can do it. Where we have to drop, the rock face slopes inward, we wouldn't touch it. We'd land on brambles but we could throw sheepskins down first, to break our fall."

There was a long pause. "Brave Kita," Raff said, at last. "Brave plan. So we escape. Then what? We're living alone in the wilds. Fodder for dogs and crows. Or cannibals. Or worse."

Another silence, then Kita blurted out, "Not if we get to Witch Crag fast enough."

"You're mad," breathed Quainy. "Go to the *witches*? They'd destroy us, grimly enchant us – gobble us up. What are you *saying*?"

"I don't know," whispered Kita. "I don't know how to explain."

Raff nudged her in warning as three bowls of hot soup were passed to them by a frowning cook, who'd heard their animated talking and didn't approve of it. They took the soup, sipped, and waited for the cook to move out of earshot.

"Listen – I've had this . . . *doubt* . . . for a while now," muttered Kita. "Like fog in my brain, like something you can't pin down or put a name to. And then when Arc dragged in that witch, it all seemed to . . . it started to take shape. And then I talked to him and it took a stronger shape."

"And what was it?" asked Quainy. "This shape?"

"Just – I don't think the witches are as dangerous as everyone makes out. If they were – why wouldn't they do more harm to us?"

"Other than stealing girls, you mean?"

"Suppose they don't steal them. Suppose the girls want to go."

"Oh, right," said Raff. "Go to women who boil the meat off men's bones?"

"Arc said this thing, about the witches. He said – maybe they just tinker with corpses. And I thought – maybe they do it to scare people away. To keep themselves safe."

There was a pause. They drank their soup in the silence. Then Quainy said, softly, "The horsemen . . . at their gates . . . they had a row of poles. With the heads of marauders spitted on them. And boar heads, interspersed. Rotting, flyblown, disgusting. Done to put the fear into people, to show how terrifying they are. . ."

"Yes," said Kita, "*yes*. Suppose the witches are like that. Suppose all their displays, footsoldiers hanging, skeletons in rings . . . suppose it's the same thing."

"But that means they're like the horsemen," said Raff, dully. "Barbarous. Cruel."

"Not necessarily. Think. *Think*. The horsemen are warriors, hunters, fighters. They ride out to defend and attack. Those heads on poles show what they *do*. What is the one thing, the only thing we have proof of, that keeps the witches safe?"

There was a pause, then Quainy said, "The stories. Our fear of them."

"Yes. Exactly. Suppose they've *created* this fear to keep themselves safe? They've said to themselves – people hate us, they think we're evil, they'll hunt us down – all right then, we'll play it their way, we'll put on a display of necromancy so twisted and dark it will create terrifying stories that will swell and spread and they'll be afraid to come after us. The weird lights, the grotesque corpses – it could just be their protection. The making of their reputation. What man dare venture up the crag if he thinks his bones will be boiled and made into a daisy chain?"

Raff shook his head. "So there's no sorcery," he said, slowly. "The girls who go to them – they work this out like you've done?"

"I don't know. Maybe there's some kind of magic, some kind of contact. Something to tip the balance.

For me it was. . ." She paused. Then she said, "I saw the witch that Arc dragged up to the gates."

"*What?*" said Quainy. "How?"

"I was up on my ledge. I watched her get slit. It was horrible. She was beautiful, and scared, and she didn't hex anyone. And she looked straight at me, as though she was trying to tell me something. I was hidden, in among the brambles, but it was as if she knew I was there. And I've been having these dreams. . ."

Quainy and Raff, speechless, stared at Kita.

"It's an almighty gamble," croaked Raff, at last. "Based on a look and some dreams."

They'd finished their soup. Any minute now the headman would set them to work. By the fire, the young footsoldiers were getting restless, and looking around. If the three were spotted together, there'd be trouble.

"Are you sure you want to go, Kita?" asked Quainy, urgently. "Arc has singled you out. You'll have privileges if you carry his child."

"Yes," said Kita. "I'm sure."

"Then I'll come too," said Quainy. Her eyes were huge. "I trust you, Kita. I trust your instinct."

Kita took hold of her hand, squeezed it tight, no need for words.

Raff exhaled shakily. "You've made your mind up fast," he muttered.

"Because there's no time to waste," said Quainy. "And anyway, if it's death we're going to, death by dogs or cannibals or the witches, bring it on. Sooner that than what's waiting for me with the horsemen."

"OK," groaned Raff, "but you're both girls. The witches might accept you but they'd *slaughter* me—"

"Maybe not," said Kita. "You're clearly not a threat – not a warrior."

"Thanks."

"*Raff*, you're an artist! And maybe they love beauty, and they're enlightened, freethinking. . ."

"That's just your hope, Kita. Your longing."

"Well, maybe it should be your hope, too. Maybe you should trust like Quainy."

"Let me think," he muttered. "I can't *think* so fast."

The quiet was shattered by the headman's roar. "*Put out the fire! Get to work!*"

"Raff – meet me tomorrow in the dung passage," whispered Kita, as they scrambled to their feet. "Soon as you can after the midday meal. You have till then to decide."

Kita spent that day in the infants' pens. Because the day had started so early, dawn only just turning the sky a dull grey, the infants were all still asleep when the matron let her through the cage door. They lay in rows in the shed, snuffling and whimpering under their lamb fleeces. "Sort the washing till it's time for them to wake," the matron ordered. "Then you can dish out their porridge."

After a while Kita paused in the queasy task of piling soiled napkins and shifts into separate leather buckets, and stared down at the rows of little ones. *Do they realize the drudgery waiting for them?* she wondered. *Do they dream of more?* She was gripped, suddenly, by a fierce desire to rescue them, set them free – create a happier life for them.

"Hurry up!" the matron barked. "No dawdling! It's just you and me today, I can't have dawdling!"

The huge crows circled above the bars as Kita washed clothes in the morning, ate her midday meal with the babies, and spent the afternoon leading cheerless obedience drills. She wasn't let free until all the infants had eaten their last mush and been settled for the night. Then she ran to the food hut, hoping Quainy would be there. She was, but she was already seated, on the adults' benches, and eating, flanked on either side by a drab looking woman. The three of them were talking quietly together. Kita felt her heart sink. What did it mean? She and Quainy always tried to eat together, they'd hang back until the other one arrived. . .

Then, with a sick thump to her heart, it hit her, what it meant. Quainy had changed her mind. She'd rejected Kita and her mad plan; regretted her own wild, determined words of last night. She was going to be a good, stoical sheep girl and do what she was told and go to the horsemen to be married.

For all Kita knew, the two women were discussing her wedding clothes.

Rage and jealousy and disappointment and hurt boiled up in her – a toxic brew. She stood there, glaring, willing Quainy to look up, but she didn't. She was on the verge of storming over, shoving one of the sheep-faced women to the floor, slamming down beside Quainy, *accusing* her, when her neck started to prickle, and she looked round.

And there was Arc, staring at her. He was sitting at one of the footsoldiers' tables, with a dozen of his mates. Three of the prettier hill fort girls were sat there too, in among them, flamboyant with excitement. This mixing was allowed, now that spring was near – it was the start of couples pairing off.

She looked back into Arc's strangely beautiful grey eyes. He jerked his head, beckoning her over.

And she went.

CHAPTER TEN

"Eat with us, tree rat?" Arc asked.

"No room," she said. She didn't know what she was doing, she was so furious with Quainy.

"Bray'll shift. Won't you, mate?" He put his hand on the back of Bray's neck, ready to push him from his seat.

"Tell your friend to come over, too," said Bray, resisting the pressure. "Tell Quainy."

"Oh, get *over* it, Bray!" snorted Arc. "She's *going*. Not like Kita. Kita's staying." His eyes never moved from Kita's as he spoke. Locked together. "Get your food, Kita. Go on. And Bray will shift."

She turned, and headed for the serving table. A burst of laughter followed her, like the laughter she'd heard when she'd first got up the courage to speak to Arc. The young footsoldiers were gloating, watching Arc add to his conquests. She had no idea what she was going to do. As she queued for her bowl of mutton porridge she glared over at Quainy, who was still deep in conversation with the two drab women, still refusing to look up.

Something was spinning and screaming inside her

head. She swayed. She'd go over to Arc, she'd let this thing with him run. . .

But as she walked towards him she found herself sinking down on a bench next to the matron from the pens, then eating fast, with her head down.

Kita was one of the first into the sleeping hut that night. She went to her usual place by the wall, rolled herself tightly in a sheepskin, and turned to face the bare wood. Before long Quainy lay down beside her. And punched Kita sharply in the back.

"Ow!" snarled Kita. "What the *hell*—"

"Shut up!" Quainy snarled back. "Wait till the others are asleep."

It didn't take long. Sheep people were always exhausted; soon the hut was full of slow breathing. Quainy jabbed Kita again. "What's up with you?" she hissed. "Ignoring me, not sitting with me."

"Why would I sit with you when you were with those *trolls*?" Kita hissed back.

"Kita, don't be so *childish*! Those *trolls* both work full time in the kitchen now. Marth is in charge of *supplies*. The dried food, the stored food, all kept in those huge boxes at the back of the kitchen. Guess where this is going?"

"No," said Kita, sulkily, but she felt as though she'd come back to herself again. The terrible, frightening feelings that had possessed her ebbed away.

"We'll need supplies, won't we? That hard grain cake

they make with sheep fat . . . dried berries . . . whatever we can get. I did a real weepy on Marth today, saying how scared I was about going as trade. She's taken me under her wing, teaching me how to cook breakfast because I'll need to as a wife. She'll make sure I'm in the kitchens until I go. And I'll be helping her get things from the supplies boxes. *Look.*" Quainy pulled a little dead-leaf package out of her pocket, and unrolled it. It contained a precious slab of wild bees' honeycomb, used to sweeten the sheep milk. "This'll keep us healthy. It's magic stuff. I snatched it when Marth's back was turned. I'll get more stuff tomorrow. Here, hide it under your bedding, that far corner, no one'll look there, they know you bite."

Silently, Kita did as she was told. Then she said, "Quainy, I'm ashamed."

"So you should be."

"I doubted you. I felt – it was horrible. I thought you'd decided not to go."

"The opposite."

"I know. You were stealing honey and plotting to steal more . . . you're brilliant. I didn't so much as thieve a bit of old wool rope. It didn't cross my mind. You're way ahead of me."

"Yes, Kita, because the moon's halfway to being full. We must go *soon.*"

"I know, I know. Look – we'll know tomorrow if Raff is with us."

"What about going the night after that?"

"Will it give you time to get enough supplies?"

"Yes. We can't carry much, after all."

"Good," said Kita, "the night after next it is." And she suddenly felt full of the most wonderful, confident, exhilarating energy. "I can hide what you get up on my ledge, we can pick it up when we go."

"What route do we take, Kita? Only I was thinking – if we go straight towards the crag, across the grasslands and the wastelands beyond, we'll be seen. Clear as an ant on a bone."

"We won't go that way. We'll go roundabout, under cover of the forest. Disappear into the trees from the east and head south. Get to the crag from the other side."

"That'll take a lot longer. And it means going near. . ."

"The old city. I know. It's a huge risk, but only a risk, and crossing the open plains we'll be caught for sure."

"All right. Maybe we'll make it. What about dogs, though? And crows?"

"Make ourselves big and noisy to scare them off."

"And shout to the cannibals that we're here!"

"Look," said Kita eagerly, "we can't plan all that, we don't know what's out there. But we'll deal with it! We'll deal with things as they come at us."

"Let's just hope they don't come at us too hard," said Quainy.

*

Kita woke the next morning determined to make amends for the day before. She was in the infants' pens again, and that was a blow as she'd hoped to be with the sheep, unsupervised, so she could leave easily and meet with Raff in the dung tunnel.

But she'd find a way round it, she'd think of something, she knew she would.

The matron almost smiled as she let her through the cage door. "Here again, Kita!" she said. "I asked for you again today. Well, we get on, you and I, don't we?"

Kita made herself smile back. *She thinks we get on. Just because I sat down beside her at the meal table. What desolate lives we lead here.*

"And you've a way with the little ones," the matron went on. "They cry less when you're here. Keep on as you are, and you'll be here all the time, and then you could be my successor, you know."

A bigger smile was called for now, although the prospect horrified Kita. She forced herself to bare her teeth, muttered "thank you", as if overwhelmed, then hurried off to help the infants get dressed.

The solution to getting out to meet Raff hit her almost immediately. The infants used a row of little clay potties at the far end of the shed; they were tipped into a large malodorous bucket which was emptied at the end of the day. When the matron wasn't nearby, Kita scooped up sandy earth from the ground, flung it hastily into the bucket, then tipped a brimming potty on top of it.

By the time she'd done this three times, the bucket was full. After the midday meal had been eaten, she drew the matron's reluctant attention to this. "H'm – upset stomachs again," the matron sniffed. "That broth they sent over wasn't all it should be. . ."

"I'll empty it now," said Kita, piously.

"Oh, you're a good girl. Thank you."

Kita staggered lopsidedly along the narrow, steep-sided dung passage towards the outer barricade, carrying the heavy, reeking bucket. It was some time after the midday meal by now, but Raff wasn't in the passage waiting for her. The guard let her through the gate at the end; Raff wasn't by the dung heap. She emptied the bucket, then went back through the gate and lingered in the passage, wondering how long she could afford to wait, what possible excuse she could make to the matron about why she'd taken so long. . .

I'll have to go in a minute, she thought. *And if Raff doesn't come – well, that's told me his decision.*

Slowly, resignedly, she began to walk towards the entranceway. Someone appeared in it, and for a moment, the light from above blanked out who it was, it was just a shape coming towards her. . . She held her breath in hope.

It was Raff, a bucket in either hand. "*Back up!*" he breathed, and she spun round and headed for the middle of the passage once more.

"Well?" she demanded, as he came to a halt beside her.

"Well, you're mad," he said, putting down his buckets. "You're mad to even let that crazed Witch Crag idea enter your skull. And—"

"*And?*"

"And if we don't die getting there I'll almost certainly get killed on sight because I'm a boy."

"*And?!*"

"And I'm coming with you."

"Oh, *Raff!*" she cried, joyfully, dropping her bucket, flinging out her arms to get hold of him. Quick as a flash, he caught her by both wrists, mouthing, *Shhhh!*

"When do we go?" he whispered.

"Tomorrow night."

"Good. It'll be cloudy still, if this weather holds. Hide us from the moon."

"Quainy's getting food supplies. I'll take them to my ledge, and tomorrow night we can talk after the end-of-day meal, make last-minute plans – and meet at the rock base when everyone's asleep."

"Good," Raff repeated, then he fumbled in his waistband and held something out to her. "Here. You hide this."

Kita found herself taking hold of a knife. It was old, forged in the days before the Great Havoc, but still strong and sharp. She turned it over on her palm. "Only footsoldiers have these!" she breathed.

"I know." He grinned. "And some footsoldiers like to take off their weapon belts when they take a dump. I stole it. It's the only good thing that's ever come from working endlessly in the latrine pits."

"But *Raff*. . ." Kita's mind spun. Footsoldier knives were precious, brought with the sheepmen when they first travelled to the hill fort, and handed down from old to young. "If they suspect you . . . if they *search* you. . ."

"If they search me, they won't find it, 'cos you'll have it, won't you?"

"But – that might not keep you safe from a beating. If the one you stole it from works out where it went missing. . ."

"Too bad. I'll deny all knowledge and act dumb. Anyway, I think I'm safe. This particular footsoldier is pretty stupid. Now – we must go!"

"Who was it?" she asked, softly.

"Drell," he mouthed back, then he picked up his buckets and hurried on down the passage.

Chapter Eleven

Heart pounding, Kita tucked the knife into her shift sleeve, gripping it, concealing it, not knowing how she could bear to touch it.

Drell's knife – the knife that had slit the witch. She saw again the piercing look the young witch had given her as blood gushed from her throat.

Then she picked up her bucket and hurried out of the dung passage, and through the storage huts and work shacks. When she reached the central yard, it was deserted. She knew she had to hide the knife. It had a murderous past but it had sparked into life her plans to escape, and it might save their lives in the future. And her friends, her true friends, not only did they trust her crazy plan enough to risk their lives, they'd stolen stuff, wonderful stuff. . . Suddenly she was racing for the rock barricade. She hid the bucket behind a thorn bush at its base, then scrambled up her steep, secret route to the top. She tucked the knife into a hollow in the rock by the thick bramble bushes, then crawled through to her thin flint ledge.

And crouched there, looking out at the grasslands and the wasteland and forests beyond.

Looking out at freedom. They'd be out there the day after tomorrow.

She stared at Witch Crag, tiny in the distance. It seemed to her like a black, cracked finger beckoning.

"What took you so long?" demanded the matron, as Kita slipped back through the cage door to the pens.

"I'm sorry. . ." Kita began.

"Oh, sorry be damned. I know what you've been up to!"

Kita's mind skidded in horror. Had she seen her? Did she *know*?

The matron's face puckered up unpleasantly; then, shockingly, she winked. "I'm not so old that I don't remember spring," she said, archly. "Who is it then? Is it Arc? I've heard the gossip."

Eyes wide, throat dry, Kita nodded. "Don't tell!" she begged.

"Flirting with a footsoldier when you should be tending the babies!" the matron tutted. "Go on, put that bucket back where it should go, and get on with something useful!"

Kita whirled into the shed and out again. Drawn by her energy, the little ones gathered about her, and she started the drills, making them into a game, clapping and using a sing-song voice. Soon the infants were marching in time, up and down the cages, and clapping too. The matron appeared, frowning, then she shook her head, smiling, muttered, "Springtime!" – and left them to it.

Kita was smiling, too. She'd spotted a sturdy woollen bag, used for storing napkins, lying in the corner of the shed. If she could smuggle it out, it would be perfect for carrying their supplies in. . .

That night, when everyone was safely asleep, Quainy unpacked from her pockets and sleeves an impressive haul of food. Grain cake made with sheep fat, more honeycomb, dried berries, and a slab of cold mutton. Kita was delighted with it all, and Quainy was delighted with the woollen bag, and especially delighted that Raff had agreed to come. And she was pleased and terrified in equal measure when she heard about the knife.

Together, they packed all the food into the bag, then Kita slipped out into the cloudy night to climb up to her ledge with it. She was surefooted, steady, even in the dark. She looked out for possible pitfalls, places where she'd need to guide her friends, and noted them for tomorrow night.

The knife was still there in its hollow at the top of the rock face, glinting dangerously. She left the food in the brambles near it, taking the bag back with her. Quainy had another day in the kitchen; there would be more food to carry.

*

"I can't sleep," Quainy whispered, as Kita snuggled back down next to her. "I'm scared. *Excited*. It's suddenly all so real. That we're going, I mean."

"I know," murmured Kita. "But you must sleep, dearling. You need to stock up on sleep for tomorrow night. I doubt we'll get much rest then."

But Kita couldn't sleep, either. She lay awake staring at the drab wooden walls, thinking of all the things that could go wrong.

The next evening, Kita and Quainy, sitting some way away from Raff, ate what they hoped would be their last hill-fort meal. Then they left the food hut and Raff led the girls to a quiet spot by the sheep pens, where they wouldn't be seen in the damp dusk.

"Quainy got loads more food," Kita said. "I hope it'll all fit in the bag."

"I got these," Raff said, holding up two sticks, one curved like a little bow with notches at either end and a skein of wool tied in the notches. "And this." In his other hand he held up a stone with a hollow in it.

"Adorable," said Kita, sarcastically, fondly. "What are they?"

"My fire-making kit. I'll show you, it works. We'll catch rabbits, if we're lucky, and cook 'em."

"Was there any fuss about the knife?"

"Not so far. Although I did see Drell searching all

along the fort walls today, looking like he wanted to throw up. . ."

"He'll get into real trouble," murmured Quainy.

"Oh, do you *care?*" demanded Kita. "He used that knife to murder a girl."

"A witch. And he was following orders."

"So you feel *sorry* for him?" erupted Raff. "You think I shouldn't have taken it?"

"Did I say that?" squawked Quainy.

"Stop it!" hissed Kita. "Stop it, *please*. We can't afford to fall out."

"We're not," breathed Raff. "We're just jumpy. Quainy – think. When we can't be found tomorrow, he'll blame us – or the witches – for the loss of his knife. He won't cop it too hard."

"OK," whispered Quainy. "Sorry."

"Let's focus on the practical," said Kita. "When we go, take a sheepskin each. To drop on, and for warmth, later. Tie it round your neck, like a cloak."

"I've got some wool rope we can use," said Raff, rifling in his pocket – then he froze. They all did.

Suddenly, like a dog springing out from nowhere, Arc was among them. Eyes glaring; fists clenched. The air shook with violence.

Arc grabbed Raff's shoulder and shoved him backwards, but Raff stayed on his feet, facing him.

"What're you doing talking to Kita, you runt?" Arc snarled.

"She's my friend," said Raff. He was white with terror, standing his ground.

"*Friend!*" Arc spat. "You're coming on to her! You think she'll take you off to the huts, don't you?"

"We're just talking," said Kita, desperately, "it means nothing. . ."

"It means something to *him!*" exploded Arc, and he shoved Raff again, much harder this time, and this time Raff fell, he sprawled on the ground, and Kita knew the next movement would be Arc's boot in his back, on his head, and she acted swiftly, before her mind knew what she was doing.

She flung her arms round Arc's neck. "Are you *insane?*" she cried. His mouth was just above hers. "You don't really think I'd sleep with *him*, do you? When *you* said to me that we'd make a good baby. . ."

"You ran off when I said that."

"I was shocked."

"And you wouldn't eat with me."

"I was shy. *Then.* Now I'm not. You were right. It was why I came over to you, why I spoke to you, both times, I just didn't know it at the time."

Arc laughed, and put his hands on her waist. "And you know it now?" he asked.

"Yes. I do."

"Then let's do it now."

"No," she croaked. "Too near sleep time. Tomorrow. After the end-of-day meal."

He ran his hands up her body, on to her breasts. "All right, tomorrow," he said. Then he dipped his head, and kissed her.

And Kita responded. She told herself she had to, because he had to be convinced she was sincere, she told herself she hated it. But her tongue moved with his, and she held his head as they kissed.

"We've got time, tree rat," he breathed. "*Now.*"

"*No.* Tomorrow."

"All right. But you kiss like that and then you – you're cruel."

She smiled, and disentangled herself. "See you tomorrow, Arc."

"Yes. And may the time run fast." Then, amazingly, he pulled Raff to his feet, and said, "Sorry. Just stay away from her, all right?" Then he strolled off.

A kind of humming silence followed his leaving.

"Oh . . . my . . . *lord*," breathed Quainy, at last.

"He was jealous," Raff said, shaking his head in amazement. "He was jealous – of *me*."

"That was . . . *almost* . . . romantic," said Quainy, sarcastically. "*May the time run fast.*"

"He apologized," said Raff. "He apologized to *me*."

"He's got it bad, Kita," said Quainy. "Are you sure you can bear to leave him?"

"All right, stop it," exploded Kita, red faced. "I had to do that or he'd've laid into Raff. It was all I could think of."

"And my *lord* did it work," said Quainy. "He was *totally* convinced you wanted him."

"One more word," railed Kita, "I swear, Quainy, one more word, and you'll end up on the ground like Raff did!"

There was a shocked silence, then they all burst out laughing and *shhhhing* each other. "They have *so* much in common," murmured Raff. "Really — they're *so* alike!"

CHAPTER TWELVE

The hill fort was asleep. Kita (heart pounding so hard she thought all the girls in the sleeping hut would hear it and wake) nudged Quainy. Both girls got silently to their feet and pulled a sheepskin on their backs, woolly side inside so the dark skin would hide them in the dark. They tied them round their necks like cloaks with Raff's wool rope, looping it through holes they'd made in the skin, and Kita slung the food bag over one shoulder. Then they crept outside and scurried towards the rock face.

Raff was already there, in the black shadows at its base. "Let's go," hissed Kita. "Raff, you follow me and make sure Quainy can see where you put your feet. It looks sheer but there are footholds. Just put your hand exactly where I've put my foot, then follow that with your foot. If you think you're falling, lie flat against the rock, hug it. Understand?"

They nodded.

"All right, let's *go*." She set off. There was a dim light from the cloud-covered moon, but she could have made her way in the pitch dark, she knew the route so well.

She went slowly, leaving each foot in place until she was sure Raff had marked it. She had to trust he was doing the same to Quainy.

Slowly, they ascended. Up, up, until the bare rock gave way to welcome scrub at the top, scrub that could be got hold of. Before long Kita was hauling herself on to the familiar flat near the gorse and brambles, and Raff was right behind her, then he too hauled himself up.

But Quainy was clinging to the steep bare rock below, motionless. "I'm sorry!" she whimpered.

"She's frozen!" gasped Raff.

"Quainy, *please*," hissed Kita, "you have to move!"

"I'm sorry!" Quainy croaked, again.

Kita felt panic rising in her, rising like a storm – then the panic seemed to solidify inside her, dark, strong and powerful. She lay flat and wriggled her shoulders over the edge of the rock. She could see that Quainy was gripping a jut of rock very tightly with her left hand. "Sit on my legs!" she barked at Raff.

"*Kita—*"

"Sit right up high, the top of my legs. Hold me, and hold the gorse. *Do it!*"

He obeyed, sitting on her thighs, holding on to her shoulders with one hand, a thick gorse branch with the other. Then Kita stretched down, and down a bit further, stomach muscles hard and straining. She focused all her energy on her friend, linking with her, willing her courage. Then she said, firmly, "Quainy, reach up with your right hand. I'm here. You don't have to let go of that rock. Just your right hand."

After what seemed an age, Quainy's hand, shaking badly, came creeping up the rock face towards Kita, who stretched some more, then seized it with both her hands, and said, "OK, I've got you. We've both got you." Kita felt her hands grow warm; she felt as though she was sending strength into Quainy. "Open your eyes, dearling," she ordered. "See that rough bit of rock, just above your left hand. Let go, and get hold of it. *Now!*"

Another terrible, dragging, shaking age.

"*Quainy! Now!*" cried Kita, putting all her force into the words. And Quainy lurched, and Kita, tugged violently, thought for a horrible moment that they'd both hurtle down, then she breathed again as she felt Raff steady her, secure her. Anxiously, she peered past Quainy, down at the central yard. It was still cloaked in darkness; no one was moving; there was no sound.

"Now your left foot on that jutting bit, where your left hand was," she said. "Nice and steady. . . Up, up. . . *Yes* . . . now I can. . . *Pull,* Raff!"

A sudden desperate scramble from Quainy, a huge, muscle-tearing tug from Kita and Raff, and Quainy was collapsing safe beside them, trembling all over.

"Oh, *thank you,*" she croaked. "*Thank* you. Oh, Kita . . . I'm sorry, I can't do this, I'm *so* sorry, you go on, go without me—"

"*Shut up!*" crooned Kita, as she hugged her close.

"Just shut up, you've *done* it, you idiot, you've done it! Well done, Quainy!"

"Well done *you two*. . . Oh, I was a mess . . . a terrified mess!"

"But you overcame it! Now let the panic die down and then, trust me, a very good feeling will come in. I remember that from the first time I climbed up here."

Raff was crouched on the edge, scanning the hill fort below. "No movement," he whispered. "No sound. We've got away with it."

"Hear that, Quainy? No one heard us. No one saw us creeping up the rock face like sheep turned inside out."

Quainy giggled, and Kita gently let go of her, and said, "We're fine. Really fine." She grabbed the food she'd hidden in the brambles and crammed it into the woollen bag on top of the other provisions. "How you feeling, heroine? Look at all this food you've got us!"

"Better," croaked Quainy, and she sat up.

"Take it slowly. Raff, you grab the knife – see it?"

They all saw it, sharp in the weak moonlight. Raff stowed it in his belt.

"Right, next stage, if you're ready, Quainy," said Kita. "And I promise this is easier. Follow me."

The three of them crawled through the tunnel of briars and brambles, and came out on the flint ledge. "Your high place," breathed Quainy.

"Endless space," gasped Raff, gazing out.

"Here – look down," said Kita, standing right on the

edge. "We're going down in that channel, where the rock butts up against the wooden barricade. Just slither down, brace yourself against the wood as you go, stop when the rock drops away."

Then before anyone could argue, she set off, sliding and scrambling down the narrow channel. The rock face was sheer, almost vertical, but the wooden wall abutting it at an angle gave something to wedge herself against and a feeling of security. She could hear her friends following her. When she reached the section where the rock fell back, she braced her legs against the wood, and halted. She could just see the bramble bushes underneath her in the dark, a dense mass a long drop below. They'd be painful to fall on, but they might save her bones from smashing. Carefully, she untied the wool rope round her neck, held out the sheepskin, and let it drop to the brambles below where it shone palely like a stranded sheep.

Quainy had arrived just above her. Panting hard, she too wedged herself against the wood. "Hand me your cloak," Kita whispered. Trembling, Quainy untied her sheepskin and handed it down to Kita, who dropped it to land just overlapping the other one.

"Here's Raff's," hissed Quainy. Kita took it and dropped it on top of the other two.

Then came the moment Kita had truly dreaded. She'd lain awake admitting to herself that she had no way of knowing what lay beneath the brambles. It could be a great hole – it could be rocks, sharp as spears. She could vanish – or be mutilated, blinded, killed. She'd got past this hideous thought by telling herself that if she died or disappeared, the other two could shout and be rescued and taken back into the fort.

It was with that bleak consolation that she smiled up at Quainy, turned – and jumped, arcing into the night, the white woolly skins rushing to meet her . . .

. . . and landed. A great crunching and cracking filled her ears, a thorn tore into her neck. . . Then she was motionless and winded . . . but still alive. She stretched her arms, they still worked, she scrambled to her feet, legs unbroken. . .

Still alive.

She fought her way out of the bushes, on to the grass. Then she reached out and arranged the sheepskins back over the brambles and, waving furiously, called softly up to Quainy, *"Jump!"*

Chapter Thirteen

Kita, Quainy and Raff ran fast and silent down the dark, sloping grasslands. No one had been hurt in the jump; a few scratches, that was all. They'd tied the sheepskins back round their necks and they felt the itchy heat of them as they raced along. But the discomfort didn't matter. The clouds had cleared; the huge night blared above them, full of the noise of wind and sight of countless stars. They'd never experienced such space before. No bars, no walls, no barricades. It was intoxicating.

"Goodbye, sheep!" Kita called, softly.

"We're not going to miss you!" giggled Quainy.

"Oh, I love this," panted Raff. "Just . . . *running!*"

On they pounded, as freedom filled their veins and the hill fort drew back behind them and their muscles, accustomed only to grinding hard work, discovered the joy and power of speed. Kita led them in as wide an angle as she dared, eastwards towards the forest. As it loomed up ahead of them, they all slowed, instinctively. They were barely jogging as they reached the first trees and slipped into the shadows.

"I'm exhausted," gasped Quainy. "But that was amazing. We were running so fast."

"We were," panted Kita. "And no one saw, I'm sure – no one's followed us."

They paused, awed into silence, absorbing the absolute strangeness of it all. The wild night rushed in at them. Then, some distance away, a group of trees began threshing and flailing, as if a wild, invisible spirit was stirring them; then, terrifyingly, it came towards them, bending and stirring the trees in its path, rushing towards them—

Kita let out a laugh, exhilarated. "The wind," she breathed, "a zephyr of wind!"

"Oh, lord," muttered Quainy. "That was spooky. That *scared* me."

"Me too," murmured Raff. "We're out in untamed nature now all right. We're *here*." Then he turned and looked straight at Kita and said, "Mad one, I salute you. This is all down to you. You . . . you *dared to think* this. To think the unthinkable. And then you planned our escape, and led us out."

Kita's cheeks glowed with pride and pleasure. Raff's good opinion meant so much to her. And now Quainy was throwing her arms round her, saying, "Yes, *thank you*, dearling! You're so brave, so clever! And whatever happens – I'll be glad I came with you."

"Me too," said Raff.

Kita couldn't speak. Raff nudged her jokily. "OK,

leader. What's the plan?"

"Go into the trees a fair bit further," she mumbled. "Find somewhere to rest until dawn. Then go on when we can see where we're going."

"Let's have a little breather here," said Quainy. "My mouth's so *dry*. . ."

There was a horrible pause then, as they all looked at each other, ashen faced.

They'd forgotten to bring water.

"Oh, I'm an *idiot*," wailed Kita, the pride and pleasure evaporating. "I didn't even think—"

"Kita, *don't*," begged Quainy. "It's not your fault – *I* should have thought. I was the one getting supplies – I could've stolen some kind of container. . ."

"What, like a bucket? It would have knackered us carrying it," soothed Raff. "Look – don't panic. We'll find water. The dogs and the birds survive – there must be water. Maybe it'll rain tonight. We'll be OK. Shall we eat something now, get a bit of energy up?"

Kita took the woollen supplies bag off her shoulder and pulled it open. They peered inside. The stodgy grain cake, the fatty meat. . . it would only make them thirstier. In the end they each nibbled a bit of honeycomb and, fortified by its sweetness, they started to walk through the dark trees heading away, always away, from the hill fort.

It was very dark in the forest. The stars and moon couldn't be seen now. Overhead great branches sprouting new leaf creaked and sawed against each other. Twigs cracked underfoot; the undergrowth rustled and stirred. Raff led the way, his hands out to hold back brambles and branches; Quainy followed, and Kita, eyes constantly over her shoulder, brought up the rear.

"What's that?" hissed Quainy. "Over there — something slithering."

"Keep walking," urged Raff. "Keep close, and keep walking, and keep your eyes peeled for water."

The wind had got stronger. It moaned in the trees above their heads, whisked dead leaves round their ankles. There was a sudden low, violent commotion in the undergrowth nearby. They stopped, hearts pounding; heard a snatching and snarling, a shrill shriek as some small creature died as food. "Come on," said Raff, and they trudged nervously on.

After a while, Kita said, "Look, I know we're parched, but I think we should stop soon. I'm getting disoriented . . . I need the sun to be sure of the direction we take. We're going too deep into the forest — we could be going round in circles."

"You're right," agreed Quainy. "I don't think we'll find water tonight."

But none of them wanted to stop with the creaking darkness all about them. In the far distance, a thin, eerie howling started up; wild dogs, gathering. It felt safer to be on the move; they walked on.

Kita's head was spinning with tiredness, thirst and

adrenaline. After a while, the ground sloped up, and the trees seemed to thin; they could see the moon and a scattering of stars above them. "We really need to stop," she said. "We could be way off course."

Raff halted, and pointed. Ahead of them was a little clearing, with three great trees seeming to stand guard over it. Their thick trunks would give shelter; somehow, the place had a feeling of safety about it. "Here," said Quainy, thankfully. "Let's rest here."

They settled down around the base of the largest tree, laying the sheepskins on the ground and curling up on them. No one mentioned how thirsty they were; how if they didn't find water soon, their lives would be seriously at risk. What mattered now was to rest. As Kita stretched out her legs on the soft sheepskin, her longing for cool water was so fierce she thought she'd never fall asleep. But soon exhaustion overcame her and sleep began to claim her. She dimly heard Raff say, "Shouldn't someone keep watch?" – then she was gone.

In her dream, she was still in the forest, but it was bright morning. She was alone, wrapped in her sheepskin against the chill air, walking, her throat burning with thirst. A shaft of sunlight filtered down through the trees, lighting up leaves and bark, dancing on motes in the air. She smiled and walked into it, held out her hands and admired the sun sparkling on her fingernails.

A twig cracked ahead of her and, startled, she looked

up. Her blood froze. A girl in a red cloak was floating towards her through the trees. The witch, the witch Drell had slit. Terrified, Kita turned and started to run, blundering, low branches tearing at her, when a voice called, "Don't you know me, Kita?"

She realized she did know the voice – knew its kindness. She turned, and there was Nada, her old nurse, standing there in the shaft of sun, smiling at her. Only Nada wasn't an old woman any more, she was ageless somehow, strong, and beautiful in her red cloak.

"You've done so well, my little one," Nada said. "So clever, so brave."

"Are you . . . are you a ghost?" Kita asked.

Nada laughed. "You're dreaming me, dearling. Because you know I'm proud of you. You've done it, you've escaped, you're all set to make a new life for yourself."

Kita hung her head. "I'm afraid," she said. "So much could go wrong. We're just at the start."

"Yes. It's the *start*. A whole night of freedom. Add a day to that, then another night . . . go slowly, Kita! You always did rush ahead, even as a little girl."

"But I've messed up already," said Kita. She longed to run to Nada, to throw herself into her arms, but a fear that she might disappear stopped her. "I forgot to bring water."

Nada smiled. "You're thirsty now, aren't you? I always knew when you were thirsty. You'd lick your lips just like that."

Kita sniffed, and two tears slid from her eyes. Nada's kindness – it was almost unbearable.

"Come on," said Nada. "Follow me." Then Nada turned, stepped nimbly over a fallen tree trunk all covered in glistening ivy, and set off down a little track beyond it, not looking to see if Kita was following. Kita scrambled over the tree trunk too, and hurried after her.

Soon, they were in a clearing. The air smelt fecund, alive, and the earth beneath Kita's feet was rich and moist. Ahead of them, shining in the morning light, was a great swathe of flowers, cool green-white flutes growing low on their dark green leaves.

"Dew lilies," said Nada. "They collect the dew each morning and absorb it. Now watch."

She picked one of the lilies, pinching its base together, then she came over to Kita and said, "Open wide."

Kita opened her mouth automatically, obeying just as she'd done as a child. Nada held the flower to her lips and tipped it up. A cold liquid trickled into Kita's parched mouth. It was sweet, fresh, soothing. She savoured it, deliciously – it tasted of nectar. Then she swallowed greedily, crying, "More!"

"More *please*!" laughed Nada, and Kita laughed too, and they each picked a lily, Nada handing hers to Kita, and Kita drank those, then another two, then she cried, "I'm so selfish! I must tell Raff and Quainy, they must drink too before the dew disappears. . ."

*

Then she woke up, on her sheepskin rug. Dawn was breaking, filtering through the dense trees, and it was very cold. Her dream was still vividly with her – she even felt a little less thirsty. She scrambled to her feet, clambered to the top of the tree they'd slept beneath, and looked around. To her horror, the hill fort was still very close. Her instinct last night had been true, they'd been going round in circles through the dark trees. They still hadn't got beyond the grasslands.

It would be all right now, though, she thought – now she had the sun to guide her. If they walked fast, rested late and rose early, they'd reach the outskirts of the ruined city in two days, maybe three. . .

The thought of drawing close to the old city terrified her. All she knew of it was nightmare tales of depraved cannibals, people too decadent to have made a new start after the Great Havoc, living in wreck and decay, preying on the weak to survive. . . But it was still safer to stay under cover of the forest and skirt the city than cross the wasteland's plains. She remembered Nada telling her to take it a day, a night, at a time, and felt comforted. Her friends were depending on her to lead them. They'd deal with the old city when they needed to.

"Kita?" murmured Quainy, drowsily, from her bed on the ground. "How long have you been awake?"

"Not long."

"Did you sleep?"

"Yes. I feel better. Do you?"

"Yes, except. . ." Quainy broke off, before she could mention water.

"Raff," Kita called, prodding him with her foot. "Raff – wake up!"

Raff stirred, and got slowly to his feet, yawning and stretching. Kita explained what she'd seen from the treetop, and laid out her plan before them.

"Could be worse," muttered Raff. "At least the sun is bright to guide us."

Quainy opened the woollen bag and pulled out some grain cake. "Let's have a couple of mouthfuls before we set off," she said.

They ate it standing up, stamping their feet to get their circulation going. The cake was made with sheep fat so it tasted rank, but the grease made it easier to swallow.

"We'll find a stream," said Raff, in a low voice. "We're bound to."

"Bound to," echoed Quainy. "If there's no water, how do the dogs survive?"

"Drinking blood?"

"Shut up. Lord, their howling really scared me last night. Did you hear it start up again as we went off to sleep?"

"No. Too knackered."

"They were a long way away, thankfully, but they still

95

sounded terrifying."

"Come on," said Kita. "We'd better make a move."
She set off, the others following. The sun broke
through the trees and made walking easier than last
night, but their longing for water was agonizing. "Listen
hard," said Raff, "listen for trickling noises. And keep
your eyes peeled. If the vegetation suddenly looks more
green. . ."

He broke off, because Kita, right in front of him,
had stopped abruptly. She was staring at a fallen tree
trunk covered in vibrant ivy. Without saying a word,
she stepped over it. Raff and Quainy followed her
as she sped along the little track on the other side.
Then she came to a halt in a clearing, gripping her
hands in front of her, breathing fast.

"What is it?" asked Quainy. "Kita, what is it? You've
gone all pale."

Wordlessly, Kita pointed to a swathe of flowers, little
green–white flutes growing low on their leaves. "I . . .
I dreamed this," she said, then she stooped and picked
one, squeezing it together where she'd plucked it, and
lifted it to her mouth.

"Careful!" breathed Raff. "How d'you know it's not
poisonous?" But Kita, laughing, had picked another lily
and was holding it to Quainy's mouth.

"Oh, it's heaven!" cried Quainy, swallowing.

"It's dew," said Kita. "The flowers are shaped like that
to collect the dew. I . . . I dreamt about Nada last night,

and she showed me."

Quainy and Raff stared at Kita, then at each other. Then, without another word, they stooped, and picked, and drank, throwing the broken flowers down. They didn't stop until their thirst was quenched with the fresh sweet water, and every single lily had been plucked and drained.

Quainy looked at the scattering of bruised, discarded flowers. "It seems awful to have done that," she said. "We've destroyed all of them."

"I think we'll be forgiven," said Kita.

CHAPTER FOURTEEN

The forest was far less terrifying in the day. They walked steadily southwards, taking it in turns to lead and choose the way through the undergrowth. Five great crows followed them for a while, clattering on to the treetops above their heads, but the branches were so interlaced they couldn't swoop lower. They saw no sign of dogs, or anything worse.

"D'you think they've discovered we're missing yet?" asked Quainy.

"Bound to," said Raff. "There'll be a right old hue and cry."

"Will they come after us?"

"They'll search the woods all round the grasslands, for sure. But we're way past them by now."

"It's you they'll be hunting, Quainy," said Kita. "Vanished trade. Those old horsemen bridegrooms will be livid."

Quainy shuddered. "Let them be," she muttered.

"And Arc will be mad," said Raff. "The night of passion was planned for tonight, wasn't it?"

"Shut up!" barked Kita, and he laughed.

Then Quainy, leading the way, stopped. "D'you hear that?" she whispered.

"What?" said Raff, impatiently. Quainy was too ready to be startled by a rustle or the crack of a twig.

"It's like . . . it's like. . ."

"Drumming," said Kita.

They stood stock still staring at each other, breathing fast, frightened.

"*Footsoldiers*," gasped Raff.

It was the sound of footsoldiers running in time, like they'd been trained to do when they went to battle. The ground seemed to vibrate with it. The drumming grew louder.

"They're close," hissed Kita, white faced. "Out on the wastelands. Follow me. Deeper in."

Then she froze. Someone was shouting. A young man, loud, full of authority. She knew that voice.

Arc.

"*Move*," urged Raff, and Kita stumbled forward, blundering through the trees with the others close behind her.

The shouting grew louder. This time, they could hear the words.

"*As before!* Into the trees, split up, keep to the line, cover all the ground!"

A huge crashing and thrashing noise followed, as the footsoldiers fanned out into the trees, beating the undergrowth with staves, probing, searching. Kita quickened her pace, but the noise from the footsoldiers only seemed to get louder, closer.

"Kita, *stop*!" hissed Raff. "They'll hear us!"

"*What* then?" she gasped.

"Here. This bush. *Here*." And he darted into a thick, tangled, sprawling mass of dark leaves. Kita blinked. There was suddenly no sign of him at all – he'd disappeared.

Quickly, grabbing Quainy's hand, she followed him into the bushes.

"Get behind me," Raff muttered. "And try not to breathe." There was just room in the dense greenery for the three of them to crouch close together. Raff faced the invisible gap they'd slipped through. Kita heard a thin rasp, and saw the glint of Raff's stolen knife as he drew it.

The terrible crashing and crunching drew closer, as the footsoldiers in their long line tramped further into the forest. "Keep your eyes *skinned*!" roared Arc. "Search!"

Then like an awful tidal wave, the stamping engulfed them, surrounded them. A stave slashed at the bush they were hidden in, inches from Raff's face; branches bucked and cracked behind them. Quainy had her eyes squeezed shut; she was trembling wildly. Kita took hold of her hand.

This was the end, it was coming. Poor brave Raff would be cut down as he tried to defend them – Quainy would be seized – and as for *her*. . .

Then, unbelievably, the noise lessened, withdrew, as the footsoldiers passed on. Huge eyed, motionless, Raff put a finger to his lips, and the three stayed as still as they could, the girls gripping each other to earth their shaking.

Minutes passed, drawn out and dreadful. Then, from deep in the forest, another yelled order. *"Turn around! Retrace your steps! Cover the ground again! I want her found!"*

"No," moaned Quainy, as once again the army swarmed towards them, crashed all round them. *This time they'll get us*, thought Kita, desperately. *This time. . .*

Quainy had collapsed; Kita propped her against her side. Raff crouched, gripping the knife, coiled to spring, trembling visibly now too.

The thick bushes shook to their roots as the army swept on to them, slashing, probing, stamping . . .

. . . and went on past.

The three waited, hardly daring to hope. The horrible tramping withdrew, the leaves settled, the ground stopped shaking.

The terror somehow felt worse now it was over – now they could let themselves feel again. Kita crumpled to the ground with Quainy, and Raff slid down too and put his arms round both girls, and the three of them hugged and sobbed and waited to recover.

Rabbits who've escaped a fox, Kita thought – they must feel like this in their burrows. Weak, waiting for the terror to abate, waiting to come back to life again.

After a few minutes, Raff sat back on his heels and exhaled, long and low. "They're well away now," he said. "Running hard."

"But going in the same direction as us," muttered Kita.

"Far into the wastelands. Far further than when they looked for the horsemen brides."

"And found the witch."

"They'll be lucky to get back to the hill fort before nightfall, searching as far as this."

"Arc won't care if the moon's bright."

"Should we stay here?" breathed Quainy. "Hidden? At least until they've got a lot further away from us."

"No," said Kita. "We can't waste the daylight, and we need to find water. I think we need to go deep into the forest, deeper than the footsoldiers would go – then make our way south again."

"Deeper in," shuddered Quainy. "Nearer those howling dogs."

"I know," said Raff. "But I don't think we've got a choice. You heard Arc. He won't give up. *I want her found.*"

"Except I don't think he meant me," murmured Quainy.

Abruptly, Kita scrambled to her feet. "Come on," she said. "Get going."

Chapter Fifteen

Water, water, water. The silent, yearning pulse in all three of them. The terror they'd experienced had made their thirst far worse. But there was no point in talking about it.

Kita made them walk steadily into the forest, much further than Arc and his men had penetrated. The forest changed. It grew darker, denser, older, more ominous. It was hard going, much slower than walking on the outskirts. They trudged through tangled undergrowth and drifts of decaying leaves, and ducked under branches. Strange vines coiled in the trees above their heads like huge snakes.

Then, at last, Kita said, "OK. That's far enough. Now we head south."

She was still navigating by the sun, but it was growing gloomier by the minute. They didn't stop to rest, just gagged down a few dried berries for energy as they walked. They seemed to be going downhill now, and the ground beneath their feet got harder, stonier. Kita stumbled like a sleepwalker. Hope had left her and she was weighed down by the knowledge that she'd failed her friends. Muzzily, she thought they'd probably die soon, die of thirst. She thought maybe they should turn back, give themselves up, to prevent this, but she was unable to act on that thought or make any change to just walking, walking.

But then she became dimly aware that something had changed; something in the heavy, muted noise of the forest was different. She slowed, listening. Quainy drew up close behind her, saying, "You all right?"

"Shhhh," warned Kita.

"Oh, no – what can you hear, what—"

"*Shhhh!*"

Raff had stopped too, and all three listened intently. Then Kita gave a little wail and rushed forward, hurtling on through the undergrowth that grew thicker, lusher, the others following, and soon the noise they were making wasn't enough to drown out the gurgling, trickling, beautiful sound of water flowing. . .

Kita pushed her way through thick ferns, and stopped. She was staring at a little spring. It forced its silvery way up past several smooth, worn boulders, then flowed down a pebbly track to pool under a great, overhanging tree.

Without a word, they threw themselves down flat, side by side, and pushed their faces into the stream. Then they lapped, like animals, laughing and spluttering with pleasure, drinking, drinking. Kita felt as though every molecule in her body had been shrivelled and shrunk and now they were all swelling and flexing, coming back to life. When she'd drunk so much her stomach felt like a drum, she rolled on to her back and said, "Why don't we stay the night here? We're knackered. And it's nearly dark."

"Oh, yes," breathed Quainy. "I was thinking the same but I didn't want to sound soft if I suggested it. Oh, *yes* – we can wake up and have another long drink before we set off. . ."

But Raff was pointing towards the pool, and the mud surrounding it. "Animal tracks," he said. "Look – paw prints. Dogs."

They got to their feet, and examined the mud. "There's bird prints here too," Kita said. "And rabbits. Maybe there's a truce when they all come to drink."

"We don't have to sleep right by the water," said Quainy. "Just near enough to drink when we want to."

"I'll make a fire," said Raff, decisively. "That'll scare any dogs away."

"And signal to Arc where we are!"

"He's well gone, Kita. And we're so far in now – a little fire won't show through this dense forest."

"What about the smoke?"

"It's dusk, it's misty . . . by the time the smoke's made its way out through the tree canopy, you'll hardly see it."

There was a pause, then Kita grinned. "Looks like we all agree," she said. "Let's camp for the night!"

Raff, grinning too, moved away from the stream, the girls following. "Here's good," he said, kicking away moss and leaves from a level stretch of ground. He found a flat piece of wood and placed it in the middle, then made a nick in it with his knife. Then he pulled his fire-making kit from his belt, looped the wool string on the little bow round the straight stick, and set the stick upright in the nick on the wood. He palmed the stone, fitting it on top of the stick.

"OK," he said. "Pull up some of that dried grass, there. When you see smoke at the base – feed the heat."

He began to saw the little bow back and forth rapidly, and the stick wedged between the wood and the stone whirred.

Quainy raised her eyebrows at Kita, and they smiled. They weren't at all sure that this would work but it was enough that Raff was animated and happy, like he'd been years ago, before the bullying had crushed him. He was unfolding – stretching out again. He sawed furiously and the stick whirred.

Then there was a smell of charred wood, and a wisp of smoke rose. Hastily, Quainy dropped a few strands of dead grass on to it. Raff blew on it, and the tiny burst of flame that followed made them all cheer, then *shhhhh* each other, laughing. Quainy added more grass, and soon there was a bright blaze. Raff stowed his fire-kit away, saying, "Get some twigs – dry as you can. And wood. This fire is officially alight!"

"Well done, Raff," breathed Kita, pushing twigs into the flames. "First you protect us from the footsoldiers, then you create fire!"

"Protect? I was cowering!"

"You had the knife drawn. I saw it. You were ready to fight!" cried Quainy. Then she reached her arm round his neck, and pressed a kiss on to his cheek.

Raff, blushing, scrambled to his feet. "I'll get more wood," he muttered. "Keep the fire fed, won't you." And he disappeared into the low-branched trees.

"I think you scared him off, Quainy," said Kita. "Grabbing him like that!" But she was thinking, *he's never fazed when I get hold of him.* She wasn't sure what she felt about that.

Raff was gone for quite a while. "What's he up to?" murmured Quainy, nervously. "There's plenty of wood right nearby. You don't think he's got lost, do you?"

"No. Maybe he needed to take a dump."

"Charming," said Quainy, but she seemed consoled.

A few minutes later, Raff appeared, and practically swaggered up to the fire. Three pink, raw-looking shapes swung from his left hand.

Quainy gasped. "Are those—"

"Rabbits," said Raff, proudly. "They'd come to drink on the other side of the stream, further up. I lay in wait and grabbed 'em."

"They're very small," said Kita.

"They're young. That's how I could catch them.

I skinned and gutted them over there so the smell of blood wouldn't be near our camp. And so you two could bear to eat them. They did look very sweet. Before they died."

"Monster!" cried Quainy, as Raff, laughing, found a long stick, spitted the three little corpses, and propped them over the fire on some stones.

As they lay back on their sheepskins on the soft, earthy forest floor and relaxed, firelight flickering across their faces, it seemed incredible that only twenty-four hours ago they'd been at the start of their escape. They felt good – victorious. They'd eluded Arc and they'd drunk as much water as they could hold and they'd staved off hunger with a piece of grain cake each. The dull food had tasted better with the smell of roasting rabbit in the air – with the promise of that to come. Quainy had collected two large handfuls of watercress from further down the stream; its fresh peppery taste would be perfect with the meat. It was going to be a proper meal, and then a proper long sleep, and then tomorrow, recharged, they'd forge on.

Kita rolled on to her side, and sighed contentedly, full of affection for her two friends. Pride and pleasure were filling her once more. "I need to pee again," she said. "It feels wonderful. A few hours ago I seriously thought I'd never pee again."

*

The roast rabbit was tender and delicious. They sat round the fire cloaked in their sheepskins and ate as slowly as they could, savouring it, interspersing meat with watercress. Then they gnawed at the bones. Raff was letting the fire die down – they'd be asleep soon.

"Wonder if you'll dream again tonight, Kita," he murmured. "That was such a useful dream."

Kita shifted uncomfortably. She hadn't thought about her dream since they'd drunk from the dew lilies – about the weirdness of it spilling into her waking world.

"Do you think . . . do you think Nada contacted you?" whispered Quainy. "From the dead?"

"I don't know," muttered Kita. "I just know, when I saw that log, the ivy-covered one – I knew it was the one in my dream. I can't explain it."

"Maybe it wasn't a dream," said Raff, and he opened his hand. Lying on his palm, gleaming palely in the firelight, was a tuft of sheep's wool. "I found this caught on a thorn," he said. "By the dew lilies."

"So?" said Kita. "We were all wearing our sheepskins, remember?"

"Yes, but I found this when we first arrived. On a thorn none of us had been near." He paused, then went on. "By four or five lilies crushed on the ground – already drunk from."

There was a silence. "You're scaring me," mumbled Quainy. "Why didn't you say anything at the time?"

"I don't know. All that mattered was to drink. And it . . . it disturbed me. It was too much like—"

"Witchcraft," croaked Quainy.

"Maybe I sleepwalked," said Kita, indignantly. She felt suddenly, weirdly, as though her friends were ganging up on her. "I dreamed about meeting Nada, and I sleepwalked, and just happened to find the lilies . . . reality and my dream were all mixed up."

"Or Nada came to you," said Quainy. "From the dead."

"Is there more you can tell us, Kita?" Raff asked, quietly. "About what happened?"

"No!" cried Kita. "Nothing! Why are you asking? Stop looking at me like that! Like you doubt me, like you're . . . like you're *afraid* of me. . ." She broke off. Quainy was no longer looking at her but beyond her, and her face showed absolute terror.

Kita spun round.

From the dark shadows of the forest, five pairs of eyes glinted.

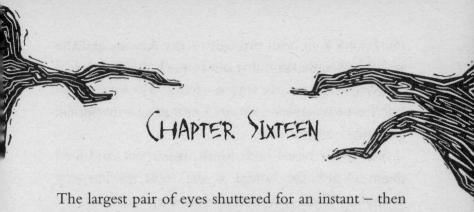

CHAPTER SIXTEEN

The largest pair of eyes shuttered for an instant – then floated forward. Slowly, dreadfully, a great black hound came into view in the light from their dying fire.

Then four more wild dogs materialized behind it. Crouched, menacing, they grouped behind the huge hound.

And everything waited. Held its breath.

Kita, frozen, suddenly understood that her mind was her only weapon. It had saved Quainy on the rock face; it would save them now.

She stared unblinking at the hound, mastering it, silently telling it how powerful she was. The hound stared back. She knew that if she let her mind wander, even for an instant, if she let doubt in – the dog would be on her. She gazed at it, holding its stare. Then slowly, she got to her feet and, half crouching, took a single step towards it.

"*Kita!*" breathed Raff, horrified.

"*Shhh,*" she hissed. "Trust me."

The great dog didn't move. Its eyes were locked into Kita's, unwavering, a battle of wills. Kita filled her mind with a sense of herself – with who she was and how much they'd all been through to get this far, and she sent this thought streaming out towards the dog. *You're not going to hurt me*, she told it, silently. *I'm too strong for you. I'm not going back — you are. You're going to turn around and go back into the trees.*

Slowly she raised both hands, palms out, and held them towards the hound as she took another step towards it. Then, in a calm, almost sing-song voice, she said, "It smells good, doesn't it? The roast rabbit. Well — you can have the bones. Raff is going to pick up the bones and give me the biggest one. Then he's going to throw the rest to your pack."

There was a tense pause; she and the dog continued to stare each other down, unmoving. Behind her she heard Raff gathering up the bones from around the fire; the pack shifted as the smell of meat strengthened in the air. Wordlessly, Raff put a small backbone and skull into her hand. "Throw the rest, Raff," she chanted. "Behind the hound."

Raff's aim was good. The lesser dogs leapt on the bones, snarling and fighting over them and, at the noise, the great hound dropped its gaze at last, and turned.

But Kita summoned it back to her. "Take this!" she commanded, holding up the backbone and skull.

The dog gazed at her. She threw the bone and it caught it deftly in its huge jaws. Then she took another step towards it, arms still raised, and said, firmly, "Now go. There's nothing more for you here. *Go!*"

There was a terrible frozen moment, everything hanging in the balance. Then the dog turned and melted into the blackness of the forest, its pack obediently following.

Kita stayed where she was, looking after it, looking at the black trees it had vanished into. She felt astounding. Free, full of power. Somehow, she'd known she'd subdue the dog, and that knowledge had given her power. She waited for her friends to speak, to express their wonder, to praise her – but all she heard was silence.

"Maybe you're right," she said, loudly, angrily, still not turning round. "Maybe I am a witch. Now let's get some sleep."

No one mentioned the dogs the next day, or what had happened. Kita waited for questions, acknowledgement – maybe even congratulations – but none were forthcoming. So she felt her friends had somehow joined forces against her, and now there was estrangement within the little group. But it was too risky to talk about it. They breakfasted on grain cake and honey, and drank deep and long from the bubbling spring. Raff tried to fashion a water carrier from a lump of wood, scraping out the centre with his knife, but the wood was crumbling and rotten and it didn't work. They'd just have to trust to finding another water source before nightfall.

Kita climbed a tall tree to see if she could get her bearings, but saw nothing but forest. As far as she could tell, though, from the position of the sun, they were on track for the ruined city. She couldn't be sure exactly where it lay – she knew it was to the east of the wastelands around Witch Crag, that was all. If they walked steadily and didn't meet any trouble, they might reach its outskirts by nightfall.

They set off walking, Kita leading as usual. Except it wasn't as usual. She knew that behind her Quainy and Raff were exchanging glances, whispered words – wondering about her and her strange powers. She wanted to tell them that the dream and the broken flowers and the way she'd mastered the hound baffled her just as much as it did them, but something steely and silent – something she couldn't put a name to – stopped her.

Once, going over some rocky ground, she looked back and saw that Raff had taken Quainy's hand to help her, and jealous rage gripped her, so fierce it frightened her. *I mustn't do this*, she told herself. *I mustn't feel this way We'll talk tonight. Once we've camped, we'll talk and clear the air. We'll be friends again.* Because they had to stick together to survive. To evade Arc and his determinedly searching footsoldiers, to avoid the city cannibals, and keep on to reach their goal. *Unless my friends don't trust me any more,* she thought sourly. *Unless they think I'm in league with the witches, luring them to the crag to trap them there.*

To her horror, the idea made her smile. She quickened

her pace, and Raff and Quainy quickened theirs, too.

After a few hours, thirst haunted them once again. They ate on the move, just enough to keep their energy up. Then, a couple of hours after midday, they had some luck – it started to rain. Lightly at first, then huge drops fell, thick and fast. Raff, laughing, positioned himself under a large vine leaf and tilted it into his mouth; the girls did the same. The rain pooled on the wide leaves and streamed down their dry throats. In minutes, the ground was sodden and they were soaked through, but they felt refreshed and so much better. Then the rain stopped, as abruptly as it had started.

"I wish we'd had something to collect some of that rain in," mourned Quainy.

"I know," said Raff. "But look at all the puddles about – look at the fork in that tree, it's full, dripping. We'll be able to drink again when we want to."

Fortified, they set off once more, walking quickly. The sun had gone behind clouds, but Kita kept to as straight a line south as she could, and walked quickly. She was determined to reach the edge of the ruined city by nightfall. She wanted to know what faced them there.

It was late afternoon when the trees ahead of them began to thin out, and the brambles and giant hogweed grew thicker. "I think we might be getting near," Kita muttered.

They walked on and came to a strange and frightening space. Huge, alien objects, like crazy sculptures, lay about, half buried in the long grass.

"We can't go through that," breathed Quainy. "We'll die. Something'll get us."

They stood in silence, gazing in terror at the harsh, brutal shapes. Then Raff said, "OK, look at that one, there. That red thing, close to us."

It crouched malignantly on its black wheels, its monster's eyes glaring at them. Quainy shuddered. "What on earth is it?" she breathed. "There's lots of them. An army of them."

"I – I think I know," said Raff. "When I was a child, I heard one of the oldies talking about them. It's something from before the Great Havoc. Men used to travel in them. I don't know what made them move, what kind of life."

"Or if it's gone from them," said Kita. "The life."

"No, *look*," Raff went on. "See the way that flowering vine's twined all over it. And the grass growing up through its centre – that great fern, right up against it. It hasn't moved for a very long time. It's useless. It's no threat to us at all. None of it is."

The three stared on. And it was true. Nature – grass, leaves, plants and vines – was slowly, inexorably engulfing all the ugly man-made metal shapes. Rubbing them out.

"You know what this is, don't you?" said Quainy,

unexpectedly. "It's the road – the road into the city."
She pointed ahead. The space in the forest continued.
Scattered with more harsh, disintegrating shapes, it
curved away through the trees as far as they could see.

"You're right," said Raff. "The great road from the
south. I've heard the headman talk about it."

Quainy walked into the middle of the cracked,
white-grey road with its invasion of grass and nettles.
"Why don't we follow it?" she said.

"*What?*" cried Kita. "And take ourselves straight into
danger?"

"We only need to follow it till we see the city in
the distance," Quainy said. "Then we can skirt round
behind as we planned. If we don't, we might get lost
again. The sun's not coming out again today. Can you be
sure we'll keep heading south without it?"

"I agree with you," said Raff. "It makes sense. Kita?"

Kita shrugged. "You two say yes," she said. "I'm
outvoted, so what does it matter what I think?"

Raff and Quainy exchanged a glance, but said
nothing.

Kita was uneasy, following the old road, but the other
two sped ahead, dancing round rotting metal shapes,
jumping lumps of concrete, congratulating each other
on how easy going it was compared to struggling
through the close-set trees.

The dull light was waning fast. Kita was worried that

the road might take them all too abruptly up against the city – that there wouldn't be a chance to pull back and hide, that they'd be seen – but she sulkily didn't share her fears.

At first, she ignored the noise coming from behind them. Low, insistent – a swarm of bees, maybe. Only she knew it wasn't bees. It was like growling, like drumming, like thunder, growing louder, louder by the instant—

She knew that noise. "*Horses!*" she screamed, but Quainy had already started running, racing forward along the road at breakneck speed.

"*Quainy!*" yelled Raff, in panic, sprinting after her. "Get off the road! Get *off!*"

But now dense brambles flanked the road, banning entry to the forest. Quainy ran on like a startled hare; Raff couldn't catch her. There were no metal shapes or lumps of concrete to weave through now, just a clear, cracked surface to race along. Kita, last in line, was racing along too, wildly hoping that Quainy would see a gap to swerve into and hide. . .

The horses, hooves thundering on the derelict road, grew nearer. The road curved, the terror-stricken runners swerved with it. And then shockingly, hideously, they were running at a towering, ugly ramshackle wall of shattered jagged metal, a wall that stretched wide on either side, no way to go round it. Behind them the horses were closer yet.

As they drew closer they saw that the road led straight

through a gap in the nightmare wall, and now there was no way to go but forward.

Through grotesque piles of metal, into the heart of the ruined city.

CHAPTER SEVENTEEN

No guards on the gateway. No one watching. They sped through. Raff at last managed to catch up with Quainy and seize her arm, pulling her behind a low wall of crumbling concrete, metal poles sticking out of it like beetle legs. Kita dived after them.

And then six horsemen thundered through the gateway, and came to a jangling, snorting halt. "*Who's here?*" bellowed the leading man.

Silence in the rotting city.

"Come out, *show yourselves!*" he roared. "Thieves! Sneak thieves! *Show yourselves!*" No movement. The horses danced in place with their riders' rage. Frozen, the three friends watched and waited as the leading horseman paced closer, peering from side to side, eyes swivelling as he searched the ruins for movement. The three shrank back, breathing as faintly as they could.

These horsemen were not the long-haired warriors from the tribe the sheepmen had their pact with. They had shaven heads, decorated by three dark slashes spaced from the base of their skulls to their crowns. Their clothes were crude, ill-matched, and ragged. But they held weapons – clubs, long knives – and there was a feeling of discipline and power about them.

The leading rider suddenly let out a roar, and pointed beyond a great pile of rubble. Three of the men sprang down from their mounts and swarmed over the pile, disappearing from view. Kita's blood froze at the squeaking and scuffling that followed. Then the men climbed back again with a struggling child gripped in each hand. The children were thin and filthy – the oldest perhaps ten, the youngest half that. Quainy let out a low, desolate moan at the sight of them, and Raff seized her hand.

"*We have your young!*" roared the lead rider. "*Show yourselves!*"

Silence still, except for the cursing and whimpering of the children and the stamping of the horses.

"*Scum!*" yelled the man. "Unnatural *scum*! We take them as slaves to pay for your thievery." He nodded to the men, who tossed the children up like bundles, one to each horse, then remounted. With harsh efficiency, the riders wheeled around and cantered for the gap in the monstrous wall of metal. As they reached it the leader reined his horse in once more and turned, his face twisted with rage, and yelled, "*Stay away from our fields!* Go near them again – *steal our food* again – and we'll be *back* again, more of us, an army of us, we'll smoke you out, we'll *destroy* you!"

Then they galloped off, back along the long ruined road.

And slowly, very slowly, heart pumping with dread, Kita turned around in her hiding place. She'd known someone was behind her — very close behind her — ever since the children were dragged out. She'd felt a zephyr of breath on her cheek, smelt a sickly, rotting odour.

A face thin as a skull with wide red lips was very close to hers. A simpering smile was on the lips, but the dirty-yellow eyes were hard and wary. A white plait sprouted from just above the left ear, balanced on the right by a long, jangling earring.

The lips parted. "Hello, strangers. *Mmm*, he was cross, wasn't he?"

Kita glared at the extraordinary man (she thought it was a man) hunkered down in front of her. His arms and legs were thin, but he had a comfortable little belly resting on his thighs. His clothes were a mad cross-hatch and patching of hundreds of different shreds of material. Some bright, some shiny, some smooth, some furry.

Quainy stared in disbelief, then blurted out, "Why did no one stop them taking those poor children?"

The man shrugged. "You don't argue with the farmers. They defend their fields with blood. In fact — a lot of folk say that's why they grow such good crops. Blood being a wonderful manure, as it were. Sweetcorn and squash and taters, they grow. We can't keep away from them."

He thrust a bony hand towards Kita, as if he wanted

122

her to take it. She didn't, so he spread his fingers and paddled them lightly down her arm. "My name's Geegaw," he said. "And you are. . .?"

"Strangers," said Raff, gruffly. "Like you say."

"Oh, now. You're annoyed with me, aren't you? Don't feel too sorry for those kiddiwinks. They'll work the fields alongside everyone else, they'll get fed, they'll be fine, they'll be fine. Better than staying around here to be—"

"Eaten?" demanded Raff.

"Oh, you've heard the stories. Eating kiddiwinks! I don't know about that. Where are you headed?"

Geegaw hadn't taken his eyes from Kita's face for a moment, even when answering Raff. It made her skin crawl. "Straight out through that gateway again," she said, firmly.

"Well now, I wouldn't advise that," Geegaw said, softly. "It's nearly dark, isn't it? And after dark . . . let's just say that some of the things the city is notorious for tend to take place *outside* its walls. The roastings, the feastings. You're safer off in here, with me. I'm known, you know. No one will threaten you while you're with me." With that, Geegaw stood upright, and strode out into the open. He glittered like an ugly exotic bird in the dusk. "Come along. I'll take you to my Manager. He's one of the main men in the city. You know, you're lucky I've taken a liking to you, because you're going to be all right."

"What should we do?" whispered Quainy, urgently, as the three stood up too and emerged from behind the wall. "Make a run for it?"

"Where?" said Kita. "Outside? I've got a feeling he's not lying about what happens out there at night."

"But is he lying about liking us? Maybe he likes the thought of eating us. Maybe his Manager is just code for some horrible great fire pit they're going to roast us in. . ." Quainy tailed off. A group of five youths were cavorting noisily towards them; each wore a tight black jacket with silver chains fantastically looped across it. One of them had an eyepatch; one of them limped; one of them had an arm severed just below the elbow. They reminded Kita of the wild dogs that had come out from the forest the night before, only they looked a lot meaner. And somehow she knew she'd never be able to reach minds as shut down and brutalized as theirs.

"Hey, beauty!" the youth with the eyepatch called. "You with the yellow hair, you going to come with me?"

"We like the black-haired lady. We like her a lot," said a second boy. He was linked by a chain to a boy of the same height, with the same green-white hair.

"Oh, lord," muttered Raff. "Quainy – Kita. Get behind me!"

"Say something, you boy?" said the first youth. "They your girls, is they? Not any longer."

"We can waste him *easy*," a third crowed.

They were converging on the friends as they spoke, spreading out like a pack about to pounce, two of them darting behind Quainy and Kita to cut off their retreat. Raff drew his knife.

The gang paused – laughed – and each one of them drew a knife too.

There was a brief stand-off, blade flashing murderously to blade. Then Geegaw, who'd been watching this with interest from a short distance away, clapped his hands three times, and did a kind of capering skip towards them. "Not good!" he cried. "Not good at all! They were just coming with me to see the Manager!"

The gang stopped in their tracks.

"Hoop-la!" cried Geegaw. "*Off* you go!"

And to the friends' absolute amazement, the gang sheathed their knives, and melted away.

"Follow me!" carolled Geegaw.

So they did.

CHAPTER EIGHTEEN

Hearts hammering with terror, they followed Geegaw in his crazy harlequin costume through the wreckage of the city. At first sight, first sense, it seemed deserted. Shattered buildings, heaps of rubble, piles of rusted and jagged metal. But Kita's quick eyes caught a movement here, a rustle there; glimpses of people disappearing like rats into their holes. A kind of miasma of horror lay over everything; of despair and bleak, rotting depravity.

Nature was absent. There was no plant life at all, no fresh-growing green to lift the bleak, bleached deadness of it all. No birds or insects flew above them – even the hungry crows were absent. The sterility of the place made Kita's skin crawl. The hill fort was bare, the sheep people quick to hack down creepers and plants that encroached on their living space. But here it seemed that nothing could grow.

Geegaw turned round and grinned at them, his plait and earring swinging. "Nearly there!" he announced.

"That gang," said Raff, "are there lots of gangs like that here?"

"Oh, boy gangs, girl gangs, yes, lots of them. But stay with me and you'll be safe."

Kita exchanged anxious glances with her friends. It seemed they had no option but to keep following Geegaw, who continued, "They fight and skirmish, the gangs. Over food, usually. There's never enough food. That's why we have to take the farmers' taters and squash. But the farmers are getting better at fighting us off."

From somewhere close by, a terrified scream severed the air; the three stopped, frozen, as a horrible bumping and scuffling followed; then silence.

"Hard times, hard times," muttered Geegaw, shaking his head. "Something will have to be done. The Manager says he has a plan. Maybe you can be part of that plan? *Hoop*-la! Here we are!"

They'd reached another wall of junk metal, with a gateway in it. But unlike the gap in the outer wall, this gateway had a design. On top of a pile of oil drums either side of the gap, two dragons with saw teeth perched, their spiky steel wings half-folded. Raff was staring at them, mouth open. "Is that . . . is that *art*?" he breathed.

"Indeedy," said Geegaw. "Real art. Made from the tools and debris and bobs and bits from before the Great Havoc. Steel, tin, nuts, bolts, screws, rivets . . . all the old stuff. The Manager is a very cultured man. He had a fine sculptor who would weld them all together. But the sculptor's recently been wasted." Thoughtfully, Geegaw twirled his earring round a long forefinger nail, adding, "Shame, really."

"They're awesome," said Raff.

"More inside!" said Geegaw, and he went through the gap, beckoning to the three to follow. As they reluctantly went through, two thin dark shapes on either side uncoiled threateningly from the floor.

"Search them!" Geegaw barked.

"*Search* us?" cried Raff. "What – are we your prisoners now?"

"Just a precaution, silly boy," said Geegaw. "I'm responsible for the Manager's life." The two guards seized hold of Raff and Quainy, and he turned to Kita, saying, "Permit me, my dear. What do you have in that bag?" He peered inside, scraped a fingernail along the honeycomb, tasted it, and said, "Mmmm!" But then he gave the bag back to her, contents intact.

The guard searching Raff seized his knife and fire-making kit and handed them to Geegaw. Raff and Kita locked anguished eyes for a moment, but there was no point in protesting. Geegaw tutted, and tucked the knife into his multicoloured robes. Then he handed the stick, string and stone back to Raff, and flapped his hand at the guards, who subsided on to the floor once more.

"Now. What skills do you have?" Geegaw asked, as he led them through a ramshackle courtyard. More fantastic sculptures were all about them: louring monsters, a huge bird with a beak made from an ancient machine gun, insects with nail legs crawling the walls. . . "You must have skills, or the Manager may not . . . take to you." There was a silence. Geegaw turned, and his skull eyes raked into them.

"I'm a sculptor," said Raff, firmly. "I can make stuff like this."

"Amazing! Really? Well − you will be tested. And you, blonde girl?"

"I can . . . I can weave," said Quainy, faintly.

Geegaw sneered.

"And . . . *dance*."

"Ah," he said, approvingly. "The Manager likes a party, now and then."

Kita's mind raced. What could she say? Sheep tending? Child minding? That wouldn't impress anyone here, where no resistance was made to children being carried off as slaves.

But Geegaw had come up close to her, and was looking yearningly into her eyes, murmuring, "I think I know what your skill is." Then he turned back and stalked on round a corner, where a curtain of chains all of different sizes and lengths hung. He stopped, and in a wheedling sing-song voice that made Kita's flesh crawl he called, "Man-a-*ger*! Man-a-*ger*!"

There followed a wheezing, flubbering noise, like six sheep rolling over in unison. Then a gurgling voice said, "Enter!"

The three friends followed Geegaw through the clanking curtain, and stopped, aghast. In the centre of the room, surrounded by yet more scrap-metal sculptures, illuminated by four oil lamps on spindly stands, an immensely fat man sprawled on a wide, cushion-laden bed. He was dressed in a purple and red kaftan, and his long greasy hair was wound into a knot on the top of his head.

Geegaw pranced forward, shadows from the lamps prancing eerily with him, and said, "How are we this evening, Manager? No more bad dreams, I hope?"

"A few," the Manager grumbled. "Daytime dreams are bad." Thick rolls of flesh around his face undulated as he spoke.

Geegaw dropped on to his hunkers beside the bed, then reached out and stroked the side of the Manager's face, who gazed at him like a fat, trusting baby. "Fewer tonight," he soothed. "Promise."

"You promised before," groaned the Manager, then he turned and gazed at the three friends. "Who have you brought me?"

"A sculptor. A dancer. And. . ." Geegaw leaned forward, and whispered something into the Manager's fleshy ear.

Kita, straining her ears, caught only one word, and could not be sure she'd heard right, because the word was *vision*, and how could that belong to the violent, depraved world they'd entered?

Geegaw continued to whisper for a while, while the Manager nodded. Then Geegaw sprang to his feet and clapped his hands three times, calling, "Hoop-la! Food! A feast! Bring it in, bring it in!"

Almost immediately, the chains parted, and a thin boy all in black carried a tray inside, which he laid reverently on the end of the bed, then withdrew. On the tray were three ancient battered cans, five tin plates and five spoons. Kita, Quainy and Raff stared in bemusement as Geegaw hooked a spindly finger through the can rings and deftly decapped them. Then they watched in fascination as he tipped them up and a white, creamy gunk flopped on to the plates.

"Delicious," Geegaw simpered, handing the largest plate to the Manager. "Chunky Chicken. Whoever would have thought it would have lasted quite this long, quite these many, many years, beyond its sell-by date? A testament to food science, I call it. Our glorious Manager has a whole warehouse of this kind of stuff. Although it's getting emptier and emptier – you're privileged to taste this. Baked beans, sardines . . . flavour's mostly gone but it feels good on the tongue and it never poisons you."

The three friends exchanged a glance. The Manager was already gorging himself on the creamy mess, and they were salivating with hunger, despite their great fear. Kita picked up a spoon and took a taste. It was bland, tasteless, but she felt her body craving its nourishment.

Soon all three of them were eating fast.

"Look at the weight of him, hey?" murmured Geegaw, nodding towards the Manager admiringly. The huge man had cleared his plate and was now licking it with a vast, pale tongue. "Look at the flesh on him! What a successful, devouring man, hey?"

"Certainly is," choked out Kita.

Geegaw clapped his hands again, and the boy re-entered, this time with water in a tall clear bottle and a bowl full of apples.

The three eyed the apples covetously. At the hill fort, apples were gathered in the wild in the autumn – but there was only enough to have two or three each every year, and never enough to store, as these had been. At a nod from Geegaw, they fell on them, sinking their teeth into the wrinkled, sweet flesh. Then they passed the water bottle around.

"Now," gurgled the Manager. "You've eaten my food, drunk my water – time to sleep. Take them to a side room. Then tomorrow – time to work."

CHAPTER NINETEEN

"The Manager relies on me," Geegaw confided, as he escorted them early next morning through a warren of derelict walls and filthy spaces. Kita tried not to look too closely at the piles of rubble they passed. She'd spotted a thick hank of hair sticking out from under one of them. "He needs me to calm him."

The three had slept surprisingly well for prisoners in a place of horror, curled up on piles of rags with their sheepskins for covers in a small room with no windows, just holes in the ceiling for air. Throughout the night, two young guards were slumped in the doorway, but their presence was a comfort rather than a threat, because it meant none of the hungry citizens of the city could creep up on them while they slept.

"Only I have the skill," Geegaw went on. "For the Manager's nightmares, for his terrible depressions and rages. Rages that sweep over him like a black storm, when he'd waste you soon as look at you. My skill . . . is a *mind* skill." His eyes slid sideways to Kita as he said those last two words, but she was looking at her two friends, trying to assess how they were. Quainy was pale, she seemed anxious and scared, but Raff looked determined and focused. When Quainy stumbled on some of the rubbish that was everywhere on the ground, he took her hand to help her, and they walked close. Jealousy flicked at Kita like a snake.

"*Mmmm*," sighed Geegaw, and this time Kita did meet his eyes. He had a knowing, sympathetic smirk on his face, as though he understood what she was feeling. She glared down at the ground again.

Geegaw stopped in front of a large metal door leaning against two collapsing walls, and rapped on it three times. Almost immediately, the door quivered and rattled, then it was lifted bodily aside, and two more boys dressed in black appeared. When they saw Geegaw, they stepped subserviently aside, and he strutted through the gap, beckoning the three to follow.

They were in a long ruin of a room, crammed as a junkyard with disintegrating machines and chaotic heaps of scrap metal. Geegaw led them through the wreckage into a space in the centre. Light from a great gash in the ceiling shone down on a large sculpture of a strange creature – copper coloured, with four very long, oddly bent legs, and a crude, blunt head. Nearby, a long, scoured table had an arrangement of tools, like the ones the original sheep people had brought with them to the hill fort, but finer. Raff stared at them hungrily.

"The tools of our last sculptor's trade!" Geegaw

announced, with a theatrical gesture towards the table. "He was making, as you see, a horse."

"A *horse*?" scoffed Raff. "It looks nothing like a horse."

"The Manager agrees with you," said Geegaw, grimly. "Which is why the sculptor no longer works for him."

Quainy went paler still. "But you said . . . you said he'd been *wasted*. Did the Manager—"

"The Manager threw him out into the city," said Geegaw loftily. "Withdrew his protection. The wretch could still be alive – but it's doubtful."

Kita cleared her throat. "How do the city people know if someone is under the Manager's protection?"

Slowly, Geegaw turned to face Kita, a menacing smile on his face. "Oh, clever," he breathed. "Clever, clever, clever. You're still thinking of making a run for it, and wondering if there's some token, some badge, that will keep you safe? No, my dear. Alas, no. Word gets around, that's all. Gossip spreads like wildfire. Within a few hours, the whole city knew that the sculptor was disgraced. Very, very soon, the whole city will know about you. The Manager's new employees. So you're safe. While you work for him." He clapped his hands, three times, and one of the black-clad boys came running over. "Hoop-la! Breakfast. Breakfast for our guests."

Soon the boy was back with water, apples and a large green tin with orange marks on the side. "*Baked Beans*," spelt out Geegaw. "I can read, you know. I've taught myself."

The three stared at him, impressed, as he preened and smirked. They'd heard about reading from the oldies, but never expected to witness it being done. Then the four sat on the floor, and as they ate, Geegaw talked, often with his mouth full.

"I want *you*, boy sculptor, to finish that horse. The Manager's latest fad, his latest love, is the horse. Ever since the farmers have taken to riding through our city gates on the backs of them, demanding their food back, taking our offspring, he's admired the horse. Do you think you can do it?"

"Yes!" said Raff, firmly. "But I'll need to dismantle it first. It's all wrong. Everything about it is wrong."

"H'm. That will take time. The Manager isn't patient. He—"

"But I have two assistants," said Raff. "That means I can go a lot faster."

"Assistants? You mean the girls? Oh, no, you can't keep the girls. I have plans for them. The blonde girl says she can dance, and my little dark-haired one and I, we need to have some conversation, we need to—"

"I can't work without my trained assistants," interrupted Raff, loudly. "It's impossible, especially with a sculpture of that size."

Geegaw lowered his head, and his mouth moved fast and ugly, little growling noises coming from it. Kita drew back from him in distaste.

"Think how pleased the Manager will be if I fix the

horse quickly," Raff went on. "And how *mad* he'd be if he knew I was prevented from working as fast as I can."

Geegaw threw down a half-eaten apple and scrambled to his feet. "You're right," he snarled. "Of course you're right. Get to work. I'll be back tonight to see your progress." Then, in a multicoloured flurry, he sped out of the door, and the two guards wrestled it shut behind him.

The three drew together over the empty tin of beans. "Brilliant fast thinking, Raff," said Quainy, fervently. "You kept us together. But can you do it? Can you improve the horse?"

"Look at it!" said Raff. "*Anything* I do will improve it. You know what, I'm itching to begin. See those thin strips of metal over there? I can make a mane from them. It'd be stunning—"

"Oh, yes," enthused Quainy. "And you need to shorten the legs. . ."

"You *amaze* me," snapped Kita. "We're here in this *hell*, this *sewer*, and you're chatting about legs and a mane—"

Raff turned to her. "You've forgotten our training, Kita," he said. "*Survive, survive, survive?* My sculpting will help us do that. No virtue in not enjoying it too, is there?"

Kita sat back, impressed by the new note of strength in his voice. "OK," she muttered. "But let's not forget our main purpose, ay?" She glanced behind, at the two guards lounging by the door, and lowered her voice. "We need to work out how to get out of here."

"I know," murmured Raff. "But I can buy us some time. And in the meantime, we're safe and we'll get fed."

"Anyone want the rest of Geegaw's apple?" asked Quainy, nodding towards it as it lay on the floor.

"*No!*" said Kita and Raff, in unison, and they all laughed.

For the next few hours (Kita said to herself silently and somewhat sourly) an onlooker would have thought that improving the metal horse was all that mattered to the three of them. Raff examined the horse, then the tools – then like a magician, he seemed to know just what to do. He discovered that it was relatively simple to unbolt the legs, shorten them, hammer them out to look more horse-like, then reattach them. Simple it may have been, but it was also very hard work, needing both girls to lift and hold while Raff adjusted the bolts or shaped the metal with a heavy hammer. Even the two guards got involved, holding up the body while the legs were reattached.

But the muscle-straining work was a success. By the time another meal was brought in on a tray, the sculpture looked far more like a horse.

"It's amazing," breathed Quainy, as they sat down to eat. "You've made it look like it's *running*. Geegaw will be thrilled. The *Manager* will be thrilled."

"So thrilled they'll guard you even closer, to make sure you don't escape," grumbled Kita.

"Those guards are to keep people out, not us in," said Quainy. "They think we'd be mad to escape from the Manager's protection."

"But that said, it will be easier to make a bolt for it if they're not expecting us to," said Raff. "Try to look more grateful, Kita – smile more! Now come on – tuck in."

The food in front of them was fresh, raw vegetables, stolen no doubt from the farmers, with a handful of nuts. They ate it with relish. When they'd finished the water, Kita slid the bottle into the woollen food bag. She'd held the bag close to her the whole time they'd been in the city.

"Won't that get us into trouble?" Quainy asked, nervously.

"They have thousands of them, they won't care," said Kita. "I asked one of the guards when he was helping with the horse. They're made of something called plastic – from before the Great Havoc. Plastic lasts for ever, he said."

"Brilliant, mad one!" said Raff. "A water carrier at last!"

Kita felt a spurt of happiness at Raff's praise, the use of his old nickname for her. Then she told herself not to be soft. "We need to get our bearings in the city," she muttered, "find out the fastest way out of here. I hope we're taken off somewhere else to sleep, not just left here – then we can get a look around."

"Yes," said Raff, quietly, glancing at the guards. "We need to find out if there are any exits not watched. The guard you spoke to – he liked you, Kita. You were good at pulling the wool over Arc's eyes. Maybe you can chat the guard up, and—"

"I'll do my best," she snapped. She didn't like being reminded of what had happened with Arc. She felt she wanted to run away from it.

"Shhhh," hissed Quainy. "They're looking this way."

They got back to work soon after that, perfecting the angle of the horse's legs, then making a start on the mane, cutting and straightening the thin strips of metal and attaching them to a single band. Raff kept considering the horse's head, wondering how he could improve it, running his ideas past the girls. Kita knew it was part of being convincing as the Manager's new protégé, but it was also obvious how much Raff loved the work just for itself. He was more energized, more alive than she'd ever seen him.

When she was working alongside him she muttered, "How strange that that huge evil lump of lard likes sculpture. How can you be so ugly and full of rage and in such a hideous place and want this *art*?"

Raff shrugged. "Maybe that's exactly why," he said.

CHAPTER TWENTY

Dusk was falling; soon, it would be too dark to work. "I'm knackered," murmured Kita. "If we just down tools and stop, d'you think the guards will lay into us?"

"I don't know," answered Raff. "Better not test it." The truth was, he didn't want to stop. The horse, which was growing more stunning with every hour that passed, had become his obsession.

The decision was taken from them, however, by Geegaw sweeping in, followed by two more guards, one carrying a tray of food, the other a pile of bedding. Kita's heart sank. Bedding meant they were sleeping here, that there would be no chance to reconnoitre.

Geegaw halted theatrically in front of the sculpture, hands raised. Then he circled it, fluttering his hands in the air, emitting little soft cooing noises. Quainy was right – the horse now looked as though it was running, its new mane flying behind it. Raff had started creating wonderful silver hooves; one was half-attached.

"I need to work on the head, sir," said Raff, humbly. "I think that will be hardest."

But anyone could already see that when it was

finished, the horse would be beautiful, powerful. Elemental.

At last, Geegaw tore his eyes from the sculpture, and turned to Raff, plait and earring swinging. "Hoop-la, extraordinary, boy sculptor!" he said. "You have done wonders here. The Manager will be pleased. I can paint a good picture for him of how that deformed lump of tin is becoming a real horse."

"Thank you, sir," said Raff, like a grateful employee.

Geegaw pointed to the food and bedding. "Now eat, and get some rest. But before I go, I must have some conversation with my little dark-haired friend here." And he sidled closer to Kita, smiling his skull smile.

Kita backed away a little, trying to smile back.

"It's all righty, all righty," he murmured. "I'm not going to take you away from your friends. Come, let's sit over there, in that corner." He cavorted over and sat down on an old steel pipe, patting a place beside him as he nodded at her, still smiling. Kita turned to her friends, shrugged, and went to sit beside him. They were still in eyeshot, though too far away to hear.

"Now, pretty lady," Geegaw said, "it's admirable that you support the boy sculptor, travelling with him to find work. And how glorious that you've found such rewarding work in the city!"

Kita said nothing. *How people create their own reality*, she thought.

"But you must know you have talents of your own,

142

maybe more valuable even than his. You have the *vision*. I know it, because I too have the vision, and I recognize one of my own. I recognized it as soon as I saw you. It's like a mist, an aura around you – the power of it."

There was a pause. Then Kita said, "I don't know what you mean."

"No? Have you never had strange dreams – strange knowings of things?"

She remembered her dream about Nada and the dew lilies. "Maybe," she said.

Geegaw sat back importantly. "The vision came to certain people after the Great Havoc. It was as though that great wrenching time – when everything was torn out of kilter, out of joint – gave birth to something new. Another sense in human beings, to add to hearing, smelling, sight. And it has lasted – inherited son from father, daughter from mother – or sometimes just appearing with no link. Few in the city have it. Lots of the witches have it, though it seems to make them very angry."

Kita looked up at him. "The witches?" she breathed.

"Yes, those wild hags who live up on the crag. The bitches won't cooperate with us, though." He leaned forward, and spat on the ground. Kita flinched back, as though he'd spat at her.

"I've never heard of the vision," she said.

He patted her knee patronizingly. "You come from ignorant people – sheep people, I guess, from your clothes?" Kita nodded.

"They're too stupid to recognize vision. Or see the boy sculptor's talent. That's why you fled, isn't it? That's why it's so wonderful you've come here, isn't it? Because now you can be *valued*."

She nodded again, eyes down so he wouldn't see she was lying.

"I can help you develop your vision. And *use* it. The Manager needs people like you. To help we city dwellers come together and work together and survive into the future. We're running out of food. We need to . . . make plans. Plans which will not be liked by others. You can help there, too, with your vision. When it comes to a war."

Kita hunched forward, her arms round her knees. She felt chilled, fearful. "How will the vision help in a war?" she croaked.

"Oh, in a multitude of ways," said Geegaw, airily, waving a scrawny hand. "We'll talk about this again. Now, you need to get some sleep."

Curled up on the rough bedding, covered by their sheepskins, the three whispered in the dark. Kita told them what Geegaw had said about the vision, the new intuitive sense that had been wrenched into life during the turmoil of the Great Havoc. But something, some resentful pride, stopped her telling them that he thought she possessed it. And they didn't ask if she knew why Geegaw had singled her out to talk to.

"He says it's coming to a war," she said. "So the city can survive."

"Grim," muttered Raff. "But I think by war he means the city will increase its efforts to steal what the farmers and sheep people have created by hard work. They're despicable scavengers. It's what they do."

"You're not tempted to stay here among them, then?" asked Kita, snidely.

"What?" exclaimed Raff. "What are you *talking* about?"

"Geegaw thinks we're delighted to be here. Where your sculpting talent is appreciated. We'd be welcome to stay. And you love doing that horse."

"Kita, you're crazy," said Raff, bewildered. "Of course I don't want to stay."

"We don't know what's waiting for us at Witch Crag. This may be better."

"Kita, we all *agreed*," said Quainy, fervently. "We're going to Witch Crag. This place is a cesspit. Full of horror and cheap death. Even the horsemen's fort is preferable. But we're trapped in this room, and outside it's a concrete labyrinth. Even if we can get past the guards I'm scared we'll get totally lost, circling round and round. . ."

"And the sky's shut out," said Kita. "So we can't navigate by the sun."

"Did you manage to get anything helpful out of that guard, Kita?" asked Raff. "I saw you chatting to him."

"Only a few new words and bad news. He only knows the main gate, the one we came in through. It seems all the citizens keep to their own little patch, and straying out of it is death. The Manager only heads up a part of the city, though he's expanding his territory. There's all kinds of gang leaders, some of them sound really horrific. Someone called . . . Dreg? He's a serious cannibal. With a liking for kidneys."

"Brilliant," muttered Quainy. "So we circle round and round until we're eaten."

"Well, I think we just focus on making a break for it, out of this room," Raff said. "I'm not thinking about what comes next."

"Because you think death will come next," whispered Quainy.

She sounded so forlorn that Kita spontaneously shunted close to her and put her arm round her, exactly as if they were back in the old sleeping hut on the hill fort again. "Don't say that," she murmured. "Have some faith, ay, Quainy? We've got this far. Trust me, dearling. We're going to get out of the city."

Quainy was silent, but she nestled into the warmth of Kita's arm.

Chapter Twenty-One

They were woken next morning by a tray of breakfast, and a pail of water to wash in. Then the guards withdrew back to the lopsided metal gate, leaving them to eat and wash at their leisure.

Raff was the first to set to work; he was busily perfecting the horse's silver hooves. The three friends had little to say to one another. Kita found herself wondering how long this state of things would go on – *could* go on – if no chance to escape presented itself. Weeks, months? As they got fat on tinned food and forgot what the outside world looked like and gradually lost the will to escape? She kept looking up at the gash at the ceiling, watching the light change, but she couldn't see the sky through it. The day passed with more food, more water – then darkness and rest. Geegaw didn't make an appearance. The great door remained shut.

That night, Kita dreamt about Nada again. She was unsmiling as she told Kita to leave the old city. With or without her friends, she had to leave.

Kita was snivelling, a little girl again. "I don't know how to," she sobbed, in her dream. "Can't you show me how to?"

"No," said Nada, firmly. "I can't. But you'll know, when the chance comes. You'll *see*. Just be ready." And then she walked off, and Kita cried after her, but she didn't turn round.

The dream clung to Kita like cobwebs the next day. She felt unsettled, tearful. Raff, on the other hand, was buoyant. He finished the hooves, and made a start on the head. There was little for the girls to do; it was small, intricate work. They rested, and that and the canned food and water nourished them, would make them ready, Kita told herself anxiously, for what was to come. At each meal she squirrelled away in her wool bag an apple, a carrot, a handful of nuts, and she stole another plastic bottle, and gradually filled both of them with water.

Late that afternoon, Geegaw paid them a second visit. He pranced around the horse, grinning, then – weirdly – ran out without saying a word. The three friends looked at one another, shrugging. "Quainy, next time the door opens, jump up, rub at the horse's legs or something, make it look like we're working," said Kita. "We don't want to be taken away from Raff."

"No," said Quainy, fervently.

"And we must be *ready*," Kita went on. "If we see a

chance to bolt – like if he takes us off to see the Manager again – we must seize it, yes?"

"We must all act together," said Raff, and he clambered back up on to the horse's neck again, absorbed in shaping its nostrils.

A little later, a strange, rhythmic noise broke into the half-silence of the junkyard. It was a beat of metal on metal, with voices chanting low, and the wailing subtext of a flute. The friends all looked up, scared by what this could mean, and waited; then the great metal door rasped as it was lifted back.

A grotesque cavalcade filled the doorway. Twelve thin black-clad men carried a gold-swathed bier on their shoulders, their faces grim with strain. Lolling on the bier was the vast bulk of the Manager, undulating in purple silk, a gold turban coiled on his head. Geegaw skipped in front, playing on a bent flute; then he halted, crying, "Hoop-la, great honour, my young friends! Great honour to you! Hearing my description of the horse, my Manager insisted he would see it now! *Now!*" Then he blew on the flute again, and waved the cavalcade forward.

Kita froze. Something like a dozen tiny lightning bolts zipped up her spine and filled her head with hot, white light. She stared, dazed. Then, as if she'd darted forward in time, she saw the open doorway blocked by the fallen bier, the Manager sprawling, chaos, shouting – and the three of them running, running away. . .

This was it. This was the chance that Nada had spoken of. This was when they could escape, and she would lead them.

The cavalcade moved through the doorway, the twelve men inching slowly and painfully on, stepping in time. Kita backed towards the wall where the bedding was heaped and, with her foot, drew her food bag towards her. Then she stooped swiftly, and picked it up.

She turned to Raff and Quainy, standing huddled together, and willed them to look at her. She felt as though the hot white light was leaving her eyes, striking them – they looked up, startled. She nodded down towards the bag, looked back at them – and knew they'd understood.

"Behold the horse, my Manager!" Geegaw proclaimed, his plait and earring trembling visibly. "A horse such as the farmers ride – only more godly. More wild. More better!"

"Closer!" rumbled the Manager. "Take me closer!"

Then, as the thin men quickened their creeping march, Kita bounded forward. Straight at the bier she ran, then she jumped, like a fox – leapt up off the ground and landed on top of the great purple mound of the Manager. She shrieked all-out into his blubbery startled face while with both hands she seized his monstrous arm – and dug all ten nails in, hard.

The scream he uttered was high pitched and hideous, and as he screamed, he bucked and rolled, and the bier lurched sickeningly, tipping, falling, the bearers collapsing as they tried to steady it. Kita and the Manager fell with it. She threw herself sideways as the Manager hit the floor with a reverberating thud; then, with a crack, the bier landed half on top of him.

For a full two seconds there was a vacuum of pure silence as though the world had ended. Then the bearers and Geegaw and the guards all wailed, panic-stricken, and surrounded the Manager and seized the bier, lifting it, and Kita shrieked, "NOW!" and darted out of the open doorway.

And *ran*.

She heard feet running behind her but she didn't dare look round, she just had to hope it was her friends. She pelted down a derelict alleyway, then straight across a rubbish-strewn wasteland and into a reeking slum, where ragged people slunk out to stare. Then she heard Raff calling, "We're behind you, Kita! Keep going!" and in relief she quickened her pace, darting, ducking, weaving, knowing that speed alone would keep them safe. On she ran into the rotting city, scanning doorways, corners, checking for danger, trying to sense which way to go. Swerving, doubling back, hoping she was heading more or less in one direction, a line that must, surely it must, eventually take them to a wall, to the boundaries . . . to the outside.

Darkness was coming. The stale light that leached in through the cracks and splits was lessening. Maybe that would help keep them safe – but the gloom added to the fear. They had to keep running – no point hiding. With every minute that passed the news of the outrage committed on the sacred body of the Manager would spread further throughout the city. There'd be a big price on their heads.

Then, suddenly, straight ahead of them, a long, high wall. Kita's heart leapt in hope and, for the first time since she'd sprung on to the bier, she stopped running. The wall stretched in either direction as far as the eye could see, and had been shored up where it had disintegrated.

"Do you think we can go over?" gasped Quainy. The wall was rough with poor repairs, giving lots of footholds. The girls scrambled up and peered over the top.

And looked down on lines and lines of large, ancient, metal boxes, at least a hundred of them, every size, all colours, and all facing the same way. Terrified, Quainy uttered a low wail and dropped down again. "Those . . . *things*," she said, to Raff, "that we saw just before we got chased into the city – that you said men used to travel in—"

"They can't hurt you," Raff said, putting his arms round her.

Kita dropped down from the wall. "They're called *cars*," she announced. "The guard told me. He was very keen on them. He said if he played his cards right with the Manager he'd get a job doing them up."

Raff frowned. "Why would the Manager want to do up cars?"

"Who knows. Who cares. What matters is, we can't go through there. I saw three guards in there, roving about. Come on. This way." And she darted off to her left, racing alongside the wall because there was nowhere else to go, hoping it wouldn't take them too far back into the city. Before long, the wall bent sharply to the right, and Kita ran alongside it, then off into a dismal slum where you could hear breathing and whimpering but see no one, and out the other side.

"Kita," panted Raff, from behind, "is this. . .?"

The narrow alley they were speeding through was changing – opening out. Walls looked as though they'd been knocked down deliberately – the rubble had been piled to the side. And then, abruptly, they were out in a huge space. No roof – the dusk rushed in, damp and fresh and invigorating. Underfoot, cracked concrete – and the ground was clear, no rubbish or rubble on its surface. There were broken, ruined walls to either side, facing each other, and you could just see more walls at the far end, too – all of them a long way apart across the vast concrete field.

"What d'you think?" she breathed. "Straight across the middle?"

"I'd feel safer by the walls," muttered Quainy.

"But we don't know what's crouching behind them. *Come on!*" And Kita started running, racing across the wide long space to the other side, so fast she'd almost reached the end of it by the time they were surrounded.

CHAPTER TWENTY-TWO

There were eleven of them, nine men and two women, all ages, all sizes, but they had in common a muscly, brute strength and grins like hungry dogs sensing sport before they gorged. The three friends huddled close, back to back, faces out, faint with fear, full of grief that their escape had been stopped.

Kita had been aware of a dark, terrifying surge to her left for only a split second before they'd been surrounded. They hadn't stood a chance.

"Come to play?" a ferocious-looking woman sneered. "Where's the rest of you?"

"They're not fighters," a man growled. "Too pretty."

"Pretty, pretty, pretty," repeated the woman, and she picked up a lock of Quainy's hair, and sniffed it.

"What you got in that bag?" said another, reaching out to Kita – but he got no further. There was a sudden, raw shout from far over to the right. The gang's focus shifted entirely; they faced the right and stiffened, like dogs on the attack.

The shout was repeated. "*Who you got there, Bluejack?*"

A man with blue paint zigzagging his bare, muscled

chest marched defiantly towards the centre of the concrete field, flanked by three others.

In response, five lean, broad-shouldered shapes stepped out from behind the crumbling walls on the far side, and took several menacing steps towards them.

"No one here to concern you!" yelled Bluejack. "They're strays, not fighters. We'll get our gang ready for next big moon. Like we pledged."

"And then we'll spray the walls with your guts!" his adversary shrieked.

"*Your guts first, Reddog!*"

Tension, adrenaline, rage — it sucked out all the air in the great space. A horrible, sub-animal growling and snarling mounted louder on both sides. The men and women shifted nearer each other, footsteps like blows.

"This is a battlefield," breathed Raff. "A space just for fighting."

"Between those two gangs," muttered Kita. "The left and the right."

"And the poor sods they drag into it. Like us."

"What you going to do with those?" yelled a woman on the right. "Strays belong to both sides!"

"Strays belong to whoever gets them," roared Bluejack. "And they is ours."

"But this one's all for *me*," shouted the ferocious woman, and she made a grab for Quainy's arm.

Quainy desperately wrenched free and whirled away

under the force of it, losing her balance, regaining it again, and went on spinning into the battlefield, right past Bluejack and his men, into the middle of the great, fearful space.

"Quainy!" wailed Raff, in anguish, but Kita gripped his arm, stopping him from following her.

"Watch her!" she breathed. "Wait!"

"Girl!" snarled Bluejack. "Get back here or I'll throw my dagger, stick you like a rat!"

"You throw, and you're dead, Bluejack," yelled Reddog.

"*She's ours!*"

"No, you come to me, corn-head, blondie," leered Reddog. "We'll keep you nice."

Both sides surged, shifted, wanting to seize Quainy, but neither dared move closer.

There was a pause, violent with waiting. Then Quainy raised her hands above her head and started to move, to dance. Swaying, dipping – she didn't need music, it was as if she made her own, as if the battleground was filled with it. Both sides watched, entranced, greedy, wanting her. Raff exhaled – then he stepped forward and started clapping his hands, steady, suggestive, and the tension increased, and Quainy moved to that beat now. Tossing her hair, swaying her hips, hands swooning above her head, a parody of the women she'd seen dancing at the horseman fort.

Reddog could bear his desire no longer. With a roar,

156

he rushed at her – to be met full on by Bluejack and the woman, knives out, metal crunching on bones—

Quainy's face was splattered with blood. She turned and ran, Kita and Raff right behind her, racing through the fight, ducking the blows, on across the great space, no one seeing them go because battle lust had taken hold and that was all that mattered to the two gangs now.

They reached the far wall, ran beyond it, down alleys, and as she ran, Kita realized that it was still all open to the sky, and a light rain was falling like bliss on her face. Then the ground changed, it became earth, soft earth, and soon, ahead of them, there were trees.

They raced into them. Then Quainy stopped, seized hold of a low branch, leant forward, and vomited up a thin stream of half-digested Chunky Chicken.

They walked on into the woods. It was getting darker all the time. "I think we should stop," Raff said. "Get some sleep. In the morning, we can work out where we are." Before long they'd found a low group of trees that felt safe, and provided good shelter.

Kita squatted down, drew out one of the water bottles from her bag, and handed it to Quainy. "It's a shame we had to leave the sheepskins," muttered Quainy, drinking gratefully. "But you were so clever to hang on to that bag."

Kita smiled, while she thought, *What about the way I*

jumped up on to the Manager? Or is that too scary to talk about?

"And *you* were clever, Quainy," said Raff, lovingly. "You were inspired!"

"I . . . I didn't plan it," Quainy mumbled. "I saw a fight over a dancer, at the horsemen fort. It came into my head when I saw the look on that . . . *Reddog's* face."

Raff shuddered. "If he'd got his hands on you . . . if I'd still had my knife. . ."

"Shhhh," sighed Quainy, and she stroked his arm. "If he hadn't rushed me, I was going to cross over to him. To make Bluejack attack."

"Thank the lord you didn't have to," Raff croaked. "Quainy, you were so brave . . . unbelievably brave. And beautiful, the way you danced. No wonder they were set to kill each other over you."

"I don't understand why the city just . . . petered out like that," said Kita, louder than she'd intended. "No walls, no nothing."

"No need for walls," said Raff. "That concrete killing field would stop anyone going in or out, wouldn't it?"

"I suppose."

"Word would get round. People would avoid it like the plague – or get used as fight fodder."

"D'you think they're still fighting?" said Quainy. "How come they don't just wipe each other out?"

"Maybe they have rules for the battles," said Raff. "Maybe they use slaves. I don't know, I don't care. I'm just glad to be out of that place."

"But aren't you sad to leave your horse unfinished?" Quainy murmured. Their faces were only inches apart. "It was brilliant. It was true art. And it saved us."

"Like you saved us, back then," breathed Raff. "With *your* art."

Kita wrapped her arms round her body and made herself as comfortable as she could on the ground. *I s'pose all I've done is hang on to the stupid food bag*, she thought, bitterly.

Hours and hours later, a shaft of sun woke Kita, warming her eyelids. She'd slept well – she felt a little stiff, but good. It was morning, and they were free again, and alive, and they must all make a new start. She resolved to talk openly to her friends about the changes that were happening to her, the *vision* – they'd listen, she thought, and lose their fear as they began to understand, they'd support her, encourage her. . . She sat up, squinting at the sunlight as it filtered its way deliciously through the trees. Now she knew which way Witch Crag lay – over there, to the west. They could start out as soon as they'd had breakfast.

She twisted round, looking for Raff and Quainy, resolved on behaving better to them. They were nowhere to be seen. Her heart started shuddering – her mouth dried. What had happened – had someone from the city seized them in the night, had some wild animal dragged them off? But why only them and not her, and surely she'd have woken?

"Quainy?" she called softly. "*Raff* – where are you?"

No answer. She scrambled to her feet, circled the group of trees they'd camped by – and saw them, at the back of it. In the shelter of a drooping hazel tree, curled up together on the ground, twined round each other, sleeping like babies.

Sleeping like lovers.

A moment's relief as she saw them – then a horrible stew of feelings invaded her. Grief, resentment, anger . . . jealousy. *Jealousy.* She'd never felt it as savagely, as cruelly, as this before. Just those dark squirmings when Raff looked at Quainy too long, touched her too readily. . .

And that other time. When she'd seen them holding hands the day after she'd scared the wild dogs away with the power of her mind. When she'd felt revengeful, like a witch.

Disturbed, she turned, and stomped back to where she'd slept, where the sun was shafting through. *Stop it*, she told herself. *You knew this was happening. You've seen the way they look at each other, and cuddle up close to each other. You'd have to be an idiot to miss it. Just – let it go. Cut them out. All that matters is to get to Witch Crag.*

She heard rustling behind her, and turned round to

see Raff and Quainy coming towards her. They had their arms round each other, but they let go when they saw Kita.

"Morning!" Kita called, hoarsely. *Don't let them see how you're feeling*, she thought. *Keep that hidden, keep that down.*

"Morning, dearling!" called Quainy, dancing towards her. She looked more beautiful than ever. Happiness was pouring out of her like liquid honey from a jar. Raff was shining with it, too. And Kita couldn't be glad for them, she couldn't, it just made her feel more bitter and alone. "Did you sleep well?"

"Yes. Let's eat, quickly, and get going, shall we?" Kita had her head down, as she pulled the last of the mutton out of her bag. "I've no idea which side of the city we came out of, but if we keep the sun behind us we'll be going the right way."

She knew Raff and Quainy would be exchanging glances over her brusqueness, but it was too bad. It was how it was going to be from now on.

Soon, they were trudging through the woodland. They'd been too disoriented last night to be sure now which direction the city was in, but the woodland was dense, the trees comfortingly old, and they hoped they were heading away from it.

Kita led the way, and the other two followed her. They didn't speak to her, but sometimes she could hear them whispering to each other, and it made her heart harder. They walked on into the evening, then stopped and camped for the night. Raff made a fire but there was nothing to cook on it; they ate the food Kita had stolen from the city, and rationed the water from the two plastic bottles.

When Kita woke she couldn't remember her dreams, but she felt them darkly cling to her. She shinned up a tree to see if she could see anything; but all she saw was more trees. So they started off again with the sun at their backs, trudging along silently as before. Then, in the late afternoon, the trees thinned, just as they had done on the outskirts to the city.

"Oh, no," muttered Quainy. "Are we going to come across another great road?"

"If we do, we'll turn right round again," said Raff.

"No, I think this is different," said Kita. "Look down, it's weird." Their feet had begun to sink a little with every step. The ground was increasingly marshy, boggy; streaks of virulent green-yellow algae were threaded through it, pooling occasionally in strange shapes.

"It's sinister," said Quainy.

"And getting warmer," added Raff.

"But let's keep going," said Kita, sharply.

They hurried on in silence. The trees continued to dwindle; large-leafed, fleshy plants had colonized the land here, and plump cushions of moss. The ground began to slope upwards; they waded on through lush greenery.

Then they reached the top of the slope, and Kita pulled up short, and pointed.

Ahead of them, on the close horizon, ringed by dark pines at its base, loured the stark, black shape of Witch Crag.

Chapter Twenty-Three

"Oh, lord," muttered Quainy. "Now we're so close I'm. . ."

"Not so sure?" snapped Kita.

"Just – all those stories. The bones in patterns, the corpses—"

"Are made to scare the fainthearts away. If that's you, Quainy – well, don't come."

Quainy didn't snap back. Raff didn't tell her off for her mean words. Their silence was somehow worse, set her further apart from them. They walked on towards the pine trees.

The landscape changed yet again. The earth underneath them was clayey and moist, and few plants had taken root in it. It gave off a strange heat as they walked. Then a ring of rocks barred their way; they scrambled over them, heading for the base of the crag. The light was fading fast; they'd been walking all day.

"Maybe we should rest here for the night," said Raff, "in among the rocks. Start the ascent fresh the next morning."

"We're running out of water," said Kita, shortly.

"I know. But we won't find any in the dark."

"Shhh," said Quainy. "Can you hear that?"

It was a faint sucking, bubbling sound, like soup in a great cauldron. "It's coming from over there, behind that clump of ferns," muttered Raff. The ferns were lush, tall and unexpected, among the dark rocks. Raff walked guardedly towards them. The girls followed.

All three of them stood in silence, staring. In among the rocks lay a perfect oval-shaped pool, quite large, about the size of one of the old sleeping huts at the hill fort. It was fed by a little waterfall that gushed down from the rocks behind it. The water swirled invitingly, and steamed in the cool evening air. Around the edges of the pool was clay-coloured mud – mud that moved, and steamed, and gurgled. Ferns flourished where the mud turned to earth again.

The air was moist, and smelt mineral-sharp and wonderful. Kita felt better just breathing it in. She longed to climb into the pool, subside into its depths, sit under the waterfall and let it pound on her head and wash all the sweat and suffering of the last few days away. . .

"I've never seen mud or water behave like that before," said Raff. "It's . . . hot."

"It might be poisonous!" blurted out Quainy.

"How could it be?" said Kita. "With those ferns there."

"Maybe they like poison."

"Nada used to tell stories about hot springs. How wonderful they were. Maybe it's a hot spring."

"Well, I'm not going to risk it," said Quainy, but all three of them continued to stare longingly at the water. A giant crow clattered down and landed on a rock at the edge of the pool. It glared at them, head cocked, out of one eye; then it flapped on to a flat rock that was lower in the pool and had water flowing over it.

It took a deep drink, head tipped back to swallow. Then it started to bathe. It flipped water up in the air with its wings in great sparkling sprays, throwing them over itself, a great joyous flurry of black feathers and diamond waterdrops. They laughed just to see it.

"That proves it," said Kita, and she pulled her old woollen tunic over her head and dropped it on the rocks.

"Kita – *don't!*" begged Quainy. "S'pose it's a witch's trick, s'pose the crow's just part of the spell, s'pose—"

"Quainy, if you think that scary tale crap from the infants' pens is true, what the hell are you doing here?" Kita retorted; then she stepped, defiant and naked, over the rocks and lowered herself into the pool.

And forgot Quainy, forgot everything. The warm, silky, mineral-rich water flowed over her tired dirty body, covered every inch of her. She sighed out in absolute, animal bliss, spreading her toes and fingers, feeling the water cleanse every atom of her. She scooped up water with her hands and drank it; it was warm, but alive, and it slaked her thirst perfectly. Then, crouching, she waded over to the waterfall and, closing her eyes, sat right underneath it. The rushing water, colder than the pool, pounded on her head, massaging her neck and shoulders, then her back as she leaned forward. Her muscles felt deliciously sore as they tightened and relaxed. Sweat and grime streamed from her hair as she was washed clean of all the foulness of the ruined city.

When she'd had enough, she moved away from the waterfall and opened her eyes, and saw that Raff and Quainy had joined her in the pool. They grinned at her through the steam, and Raff called out, "OK, mad one – you were right! This is *heaven!*"

She smiled back but didn't say anything; she gathered up handfuls of the hot bubbling mud and rubbed it on to her arms and feet, even her face, using it to scour her skin cleaner still. Then she pulled her tunic into the pool with her and washed it, too. She didn't care about putting it back on wet; it was warm by the pool and she couldn't bear to put a stale, filthy garment back on her shiny new body.

The evening meal was a mostly silent affair. All three of them relaxed on the rocks as the steam drowsed over them, eating grain cake and honey with two-thirds of an apple each. There was nothing to discuss; they could make no plans; they had no idea what lay ahead of them.

But anxiety about what the morning would bring was beginning to lap at Kita's mind. And she wanted to be away on her own, away from Raff and Quainy – she felt horribly in the way. *Anyone would want to make love,* she thought, *after they'd bathed in that pool.*

"I'm turning in," she announced. "There's a nice little hollow there, all sheltered, and I'm marking it for me – just room for one."

They said goodnight to her in soft, almost pleading voices – but they didn't ask her to stay.

That night, wrapped up in four huge fern leaves, she dreamt about her old nurse Nada again. They were sitting together by the pool, the waterfall splashing deliciously behind them, and Nada was smiling and feeding her sweet brown fruit she'd never tasted before, telling her well done, well *done* to have escaped the rotting city. Kita felt soused in happiness, completely content. Then Nada told her she should bathe, and enjoy the water once more, so she pulled off her tunic and slipped naked into the water.

She waved to Nada from the pool, but her old nurse stood up and, laughing, started to walk away. "Where are you going?" Kita called out, but Nada didn't answer.

Kita turned round. There was a statue under the waterfall. A man, a warrior by his looks, water cascading all around him, beautiful, elemental.

She moved closer. The statue came to life, blinked, looked at her.

It was Arc.

Kita gasped and stepped back; Arc threw himself forward into the water, and in seconds he'd surfaced right in front of her. The vividness of his face shocked her; then shock changed to absolute desire.

"I've found you, tree rat," he said. "I've found you at last."

CHAPTER TWENTY-FOUR

When Kita woke in the early light she was trembling with the power of her dream. She sat up and immediately set about rationalizing it. Bathing in the hot spring had been so sensual, and she'd been sure Quainy and Raff would make love . . . *and I thought of Arc because he's the only boy who's ever kissed me, if you can call that mauling a kiss.*

She was silent as they all got themselves ready for the day, eating a few mouthfuls of grain cake and nuts, and filling the plastic bottles from the waterfall.

"So," said Raff, "I guess we just – head into that pine wood and then start climbing? And see what happens?"

"And see who comes to meet us, yes," said Kita.

"I'm scared," muttered Quainy. "What if we find skeletons? Or corpses hanging upside down?"

"Oh for *goodness'* sake!" Kita erupted.

"Don't yell at me like that! The city was everything the sheepmen said it was and worse – what if they're right about Witch Crag too?"

"That's the risk we agreed to take," said Kita, grimly, and she stalked on.

Raff put his arm round Quainy, and followed Kita into the pine forest, following a little rough track that ran from the pool. It was silent and calm in the forest: no birds, hardly any wind. The pine needles on the ground gave off a fresh, astringent smell as they crushed them underfoot.

After an hour's steady uphill walking, Quainy left Raff's side and caught up with Kita. "Are you excited?" she murmured. "To meet the witches?"

Kita didn't answer.

"Do you know what you'll say to them?" Quainy persisted.

"No idea," Kita snapped.

"Oh, dearling, please don't be cold with me," Quainy burst out. "I can't bear it. It just – *happened*, me and Raff. Because of nearly dying. Because of getting out of the city. And because we've *really liked* each other for ages. It just seemed so *right*."

"Well, that's all right then, isn't it?" retorted Kita.

"I know you feel left out. But you mustn't. We're still your friends. We're—"

Kita wanted to scream at her to shut up, but instead she gritted out, "Quainy, it's *all right*. I just don't want to talk about it. Not now. Let's just keep focused on getting up on the crag, shall we? On doing what we set out to do."

And she marched on, and Quainy fell back to join Raff again.

After a while, the pine forest began to thin, and the ground got stonier. Then the uphill slope got steeper. Here and there, huge boulders jutted out; in the stark terrain, there was something comforting about them – you could take shelter there. Kita with her skill in climbing led the way. She was just considering a group of three great rocks, thinking it would be a good place to rest for a while, when something red flashed between two of them. She quickened her pace, heading for the rocks, but when she reached them, there was nothing there.

"Do you think there are foxes here?" she asked. Although the red hadn't been fox-fur red. It was berry red – blood red.

"Dunno," said Raff. "Could be. There are rabbit holes enough. Keep your eyes peeled – we could nab a couple and roast them for supper."

"Won't the witches see our smoke?" Quainy blurted out.

"So what?" snapped Kita. "We want them to find us, remember?"

"I suppose. It's just – I hate that feeling they could come upon us at any minute. I'm so on edge with it."

"Let's stop for a bit," said Raff, soothingly. "This is a good spot."

*

After resting, they climbed on, into the evening. "How far do you think we've come?" asked Quainy. "Are we halfway up yet?"

"Hard to tell, but I doubt it," said Kita — and then she saw another flash of red, behind some stunted thorn bushes clinging to the rocky slope ahead of them. "I think someone's following us," she whispered. "Well — not following. More like going ahead of us."

"Oh, lord," groaned Quainy.

"I think I've seen it too," said Raff. "Just a glimpse of something red, disappearing . . . I've been wondering if we should call out—"

"No," said Kita, firmly. "If it's a witch, we must wait till she comes to us."

They trudged on for another hour, but the steepness of the crag made it very slow going. As darkness fell, they found a huge boulder that gave shelter, and Raff made a fire with the dry brushwood that was all around. He tried to catch a rabbit, but they were too canny for him, and Quainy wouldn't let him go far from the fire. So they settled down for the night, but no one could sleep. They were hungry and full of apprehension. Kita had gone completely into herself; she seemed to the others to be coiled up like rope. *Or a snake*, Quainy muttered to Raff sadly, when she thought, wrongly, that Kita wasn't listening.

*

The next morning, a grey, foggy dew covered everything. The three got to their feet with barely a word to each other and started again on the slow, dreary scramble upwards. Rocks and sparse thorns loomed spectral and eerie in the mist, and the damp clung to them; they licked their hands to ease their thirst. Kita's thoughts gnawed at her; she was sure now that the other two were deeply regretting agreeing to her plan, believing that the witches would leave them to starve in this desolate place. But she told herself she didn't care about that; she was resolved to climb on to the top of the crag, and demand an audience.

"Do we have any food left at all?" asked Quainy, faintly, after a while.

"A bit," Kita croaked.

"I think – I'm sorry, but if I'm to go on – I need some food."

Kita stopped, sullenly, and pulled the woollen bag off her shoulder. Then stared. The three rocks ahead of her, shrouded in mist, had moved, had disintegrated, two of them splitting in half. . . She peered harder, heart thudding. Something red was drifting into the fog, swirling closer. And something green.

Kita waited, barely breathing. Then through the fog materialized five women, coming down towards them.

Quainy let out a low moan of fear; Raff seized her hand. Kita waited.

The women moved with animal ease as they sped down towards them, footsure, jumping or sidestepping rocks. Two had red cloaks, three green, wrapped round them against the damp. Their faces were vivid – super alive, somehow naked. Kita made herself meet their gaze. Each of them had a slender blackbow held in front of her, arrows aimed at the friends.

They came to a stop a short distance away. A broad-shouldered woman with long, wild black hair tied loosely at the nape of her neck took a step forward and said, "Kita."

"Yes," gasped Kita.

"My name is Wekka."

"Yes," said Kita again.

"It's taken you a long time, to get here."

"Yes," said Kita, once more. "We got trapped in the old city."

A hissing sound went from witch to witch; they raised their black bows menacingly. Something yellow-green oozed from the arrowheads. "You were *inside* the city?" demanded Wekka.

"Yes. For some days. Then we escaped."

"How interesting. Who are your friends?"

Kita shrugged. "Friends," she said.

"We've been watching you. Since the hot pool. We wanted to see how determined you were. We let you get most of the way up here before we showed ourselves."

"And now what?" demanded Raff – then wished he hadn't. As one, the five witches all turned towards him, eyes hard, appraising. Arrows aimed.

"And now – come with us, please," said Wekka. And she set off up the crag, her red cloak flowing. The four remaining witches motioned for the three to follow her, and then they came behind. They still hadn't lowered their blackbows.

CHAPTER TWENTY-FIVE

They climbed for another hour, with no more conversation. The crag got steeper, barer, harsher, devoid of plant life. Kita passed Quainy the last little piece of honeycomb, to give her energy, and Raff helped her climb. The mist cleared; the sun came out.

Then, at last, they arrived.

Kita's heart sank. The domain of the witches looked disappointingly like the sheepmen's hill fort – a stark wooden barricade surrounded the summit. The gate that led into it was different, though; intricately woven of willow wands, some of them still sprouting, it looked graceful and magical. Wekka led them through it.

And there any similarity to the sheepmen's home ended.

They walked into a vast, craggy, undulating, free-flowing space, full of colour. Colour on the people moving confidently about; colour stretched in great, billowing lengths of cloth on wooden hurdles. Orange, blue, green, red and yellow shone against the black rock. Large russet and gold birds stalked the ground, or soared overhead. The air was full of sound – laughter, chatter and, at a distance, pipe music and singing. And *scents* – Kita inhaled greedily, as her heart pounded with wonder. A sweet warm fragrance rose from the huge bunches of herbs and flowers tied to poles, drying. Rich spiciness came from a great stone dish that a young girl was pounding with a wooden pestle. And the freshest of scents came from the banks of lush green plants, some flowering, that flanked a large part of the outer walls, growing in great wooden trenchers.

All the women, children and men who were near enough to notice the newcomers stopped, and gathered round, gazing at them. The five warrior witches sheathed their arrows, then retreated, melting into the crowd, which parted, to let a woman through. She was wearing a long orange shift; she had a child balanced on her hip; a leggy grey dog padded beside her. Her white hair was piled wildly on top of her head; her bare arms clinked with bangles made from metal and bone. "Ah," she said, looking straight at Kita. "I congratulate you. You made it here at last."

Kita bowed her head, unable to speak.

"Food," the woman said, "urgent food, and a bath, and hot sweet drinks, and fresh clothes. Then we can talk."

Minutes later the three friends found themselves sitting on a curved bench in a warm, steamy building, whose wall coiled like a snail's shell in on itself. A smiling girl brought in little bowls of a hot, spicy distillation and a dish of delicious pasties. "Rabbit and onion," she said. "Eat and enjoy. I made them and I know how good they are. The bath is through there – I'll bring you drying cloths and fresh clothes. Take your time. And if you're too tired to talk this afternoon, Vild says to show you where to sleep, and it can wait till tomorrow."

"Vild," echoed Kita, wonderingly.

"Yes," said the girl. "The white-haired lady who greeted you. She was one of *your* people." Then she smiled, and left.

The three friends silently swallowed the frothy, sweet drinks and devoured three pasties each before they said anything. Then Raff muttered, "I've got so many questions. Millions of them. Like – how did Wekka know your name? Why didn't we ask her any questions?"

"Because we're half starving?" said Kita.

"There are men here – did you see? Not many, but there are. And children. So the witches give birth?"

"It's good here," said Quainy fervently, wiping her mouth. "Oh, it's good, isn't it? Weren't we right to come?"

"Yes, dearling," said Raff. "Especially as I haven't been slaughtered on sight! Here, have the last of my drink. Oh sweetheart, your colour has come back. . ."

Kita got to her feet. She felt distanced from her friends, separate, everything in her focused on the witches and what was to come. "Can I bath first?" she said, bluntly.

They looked up, surprised. "Of course," said Quainy.

She followed the snail-shell wall round into its inner section, which was perfectly circular and filled by a vast, sunken tub that could hold perhaps six people, sitting upright. The water steamed and gave off a delicious lavender scent. She dropped her old woollen tunic on the floor and lowered herself into the bath, gazing up at the curved walls, amazed that a barrier could be so flowing and beautiful. Then she slipped right down under the water, and lost herself to the warm pleasure of it.

Moments later she surfaced out of breath to see a slim brown arm reaching through the door gap and hanging a length of cream-coloured cloth and a purple shift on a peg on the wall. Immediately, she stepped out of the bath, dried herself on the cloth and stepped into the shift. It slinked down to her ankles, fresh, soft and wonderful on the skin. She left her old tunic on the floor – she knew she'd never wear it again. Then she walked out to join her friends. They were cuddled up, close and happy, on the bench. "You were quick!" said Quainy.

"I want to talk to Vild," Kita answered. "Like you said, there are so many questions."

"Shouldn't we all talk to her together?" asked Raff.

Kita raked out her wet hair with her fingers. "I don't see why," she said. "Enjoy the bath, it's wonderful." Then she left.

She felt curiously confident as she crossed the compound. She'd used great ingenuity and courage to get here. She'd suffered and endured. At some deep level she knew she was entitled.

As she walked, she looked around. The black uneven rock that the witches had made their home had been adapted with graceful ingenuity. Here, a slab had been hacked out to form a group of benches, where people sat and chatted. There, a huge jagged spike had been carved into a tracery of shapes – leaves, faces, strange creatures with wings and webbed feet. And here, a natural pit had been filled with earth to grow a lush swathe of plants with bright, nodding flowers.

People smiled at her, but no one stopped her or questioned her. They moved with confidence, and ease. There seemed to be no rigid order to the place, not like the sheep hill fort, where there were regimented spaces and times for eating and working. But the flow worked, here on the black rock. Children ran free or played on the ground, and the singing in the distance grew louder, and the bright birds hopped and soared.

Kita stood still, suddenly overwhelmed. The colour and the beauty and the grace – it was too much, too powerful. *It's bewitched me*, she thought, gulping back tears – then she laughed. Was this what the sheep people meant when they talked about the seductive sorcery of the crag?

Then, from a distance, by the masses of plants flourishing in the wide wooden trenchers, she spotted an untidy white bun of hair, and hurried over.

Vild turned to her, smiling. "Just doing a bit of weeding," she said. "You wouldn't think weed seeds would make their way up to the top of this mountain, but they do."

"These plants look so beautiful," said Kita.

"Aren't they? It's restoring just to be near them. And they're so useful! For food, medicine, sweet scents, and cloth dyeing."

"How do they grow so well?"

"Ah," said Vild. "It's all part of our clever, simple system. Come and see."

Kita followed her along a path between the plant trenchers, and up a short flight of steps to a wide platform, where a variety of short, sturdy trees grew in huge tubs. Perched in the trees and strutting about the ground were more of the large, boldly coloured birds. "Pheasants," said Vild, with satisfaction. "Or a kind of hybrid pheasant, anyway. We managed to breed them after the Great Havoc. There's where they lay their eggs." She indicated a long, low, straw-lined hut, with many entrances. "A very good addition to our diet. As are the poor pheasants, occasionally. Their bones make tasty soup stock."

"Don't they ever get attacked, by the crows?" Kita asked. "And your children – they run about unprotected. . ."

"Oh, they're protected," said Vild, firmly. "The crows don't dare land here. Now – see that channel? We sweep the pheasant droppings into that, and it all gets washed down to the plants. It's the best compost going. The water is dirty bath water, drained from the bathhouse where you had your soak. Nothing is wasted."

"The bath was wonderful. How do you heat it?"

"We don't. We managed to divert water from a tiny hot spring near the summit of the crag. That took some cunning, trust me! When we first settled on the crag, we discovered a fissure with steam coming out of it . . . with a lot of clever drilling and redirecting and blocking to build up the pressure, we got the water to follow. In a very thin stream, but piping hot. We cool it and drink it too, but not out of the bath, of course."

"Ingenious!"

"As are so many of the sheep people's methods," said Vild. "We copied their ways of using our dung to grow corn for bread. On the gentle slopes on the south side – I'll show you later. Now. You look better, Kita. Refreshed. And purple suits you, with your lovely dark hair! Shall we go somewhere quiet, to talk?"

So once again Kita followed Vild as she climbed higher, crossing an open space filled with people spinning and weaving, calling out greetings as she passed. The leggy grey dog trotted over, and Vild patted him and said his name was Moss. Then she slipped behind a tall bank of rock to where several boulders made natural seats. "Here," she said. "We won't be disturbed." She subsided down on to one of the boulders, indicating to Kita to take the one facing her. Moss curled at her feet, sighing peacefully.

"So," Vild said. "You must have a hundred questions. And I have too. We'll take it in turns. What's your first?"

Kita scuffed at the black rock with her foot. "Is all this – for real?" she asked. "The harmony and happiness and everything, what I feel all about me – is it real?"

Vild laughed. "You think we might be putting on a show just to fool you? What a mad waste of energy that would be. You're just afraid to trust it, Kita. Yet."

"But the *fear*, the terrible stories about you—"

"Are just that. Stories. Back in the time of the Great Havoc, men fighting for control wanted to crush the free-thinking women among them – they were afraid of their power. So those women fled to this crag. And decided – everyone thinks we're evil, fine, we'll continue that myth. And stay safe."

"Aaaah," breathed Kita.

"Soon, other women joined them. Then some men. Breaking through the fear that surrounded the place, *trusting*. Just as you did, Kita. And now you're here, I hope you understand why we go to such grisly lengths with our wheels of skeletons and dangling corpses to protect how we live? We feel it's acceptable propaganda. Don't you?"

"Yes. Yes, of course I do. Witch Crag is – so *much more* than I hoped. I felt mad, hoping even my little thoughts. It felt like an insane leap in the dark, hoping them. The horsemen, the sheep people – they're all convinced you're hugely dangerous."

"Good. Our propaganda works. And of course we *are* dangerous. To their way of living."

"The only other person who saw beyond it all, beyond all the fear, was. . ." She broke off. Arc had no place here. Just the thought of him sent the strongest sensation through her – it got in the way. "But it's not entirely propaganda, is it?" she went on, hurriedly. "Those arrows aimed at us – what dripped from them?"

Vild laughed. "Poison. Oh, we defend ourselves, and what we've made. And we kill, when we have to. Too many people in this new world hate us. Now, Kita, a question for you. What made you so desperate to escape the hill fort and come here?"

Kita was silent. She thought of the witch Drell had slit, her long intense stare before she'd died. She was the real reason Kita had come here. But she couldn't bring herself to talk about it. She felt the guilt of the death on herself. "You lived there," she mumbled. "You must know."

"Mmm. Sheep life is rather pared down to the bone, isn't it? Nothing that isn't part of survival allowed to survive. Love, pleasure, friendship, laughter, chatter – all frowned on. Beauty is a distraction; hair is shorn; even

185

the wild flowers are hacked down."

"Yes. *Miserable*."

"And unnecessary." Vild raised her hand to tuck a stray lock of hair behind her ear, and her bangles clinked. "The sheep people don't need to be so joyless. They're efficient; they grow food and collect water. They rear sheep, and children, and keep them all safe. They weave cloth, like us. They could let themselves feel pleasure in it all. They could live far richer lives than just those of survival."

"That's what I want to do," said Kita, fervently. "Live a richer life."

"Of course you do. And you shall."

"*Here*," Kita blurted out. "I want to live here! It's – I feel as if I was cramped in a bucket, all shrivelled and starving, and now I'm here I'm. . ."

"Free," said Vild, smiling. "And nourished."

"You'll let me *stay*, won't you?"

"Yes. You can stay. But there's a lot more at stake than just your happiness. That's why we helped you to come to us."

Kita shook her head, bewildered. "Helped me?"

Vild looked at her intently. There was a long silence. Moss got to his feet and growled softly, in warning – then wagged his tail.

"I think we have a visitor," said Vild.

Kita looked up. To see Nada walking towards her, round the black bank of rock.

CHAPTER TWENTY-SIX

The colour drained from Kita's face. She scrambled to her feet and backed away. "This is wrong, this is *weird*!" she gasped, rounding on Vild. "How have you done this? Is this necromancy? Have you called up her *ghost*?"

"Calm down, dearling," said Nada, smiling. "Here, take my hand. Feel its warmth. *Oh*, it's good to see you."

But Kita wouldn't take Nada's hand. She backed further away, trembling. "You're *dead*," she muttered. "I saw your funeral."

"Oh, Kita, come," said Vild, briskly. "Do you really think they're always dead, those bodies the sheepmen carry out beyond the gates to be left for the dogs and the crows? *Completely* dead?"

"No," croaked Kita. "I'm sure they're not. But they are as soon as the dogs come—"

"Unless the witches get there first," said Vild.

Kita stared. She was remembering the day of Nada's funeral, when the crows had wheeled up into the sky again, and the yelping dogs had streamed back to the forest. . . "You scared them off?" she breathed.

"We did. We have some power over dogs and crows.

We came to get Nada. She wasn't dead. Just tired, worn out – it was time for her to come to us."

Kita looked at Nada, at her dear face. She looked younger, plumper. "Why not come for her earlier," she murmured, "why on earth leave her in that dreary fort for so *long*?"

Nada smiled. "Because I had work to do. With several of the young ones, and with you, dearling, above all. And how well my work paid off. Look at you. I'm so proud of you."

Kita's eyes filled with tears. She felt dazed, bewildered – she didn't understand a thing. But at last she came forward and reached out to Nada, and took her hand, and then Nada pulled her in and enfolded her in a warm hug.

"I dreamt about you," Kita whispered.

"I know you did, sweetheart. I meant you to. I focused on you – I tried to send you energy. I could sense when you were scared, when you needed my help."

"Witchcraft?"

Nada laughed. "If you want to call it that. Or just the flow of my mind, linked in to . . . well. I don't like to name it, but I think of it as the greater good. I knew the night you'd escaped – I felt the shift. And then I knew something happened that needed all *your* strength . . . I tried to send you energy then."

Kita flinched. "Quainy," she breathed. "That was when Quainy froze, climbing up to my ledge, and I

suddenly knew I could calm her, by focusing on her —
sending her mind strength."

"That's how it works, dearling. And then you were
thirsty — oh, I felt how thirsty you were! I tried to send
you knowledge of the dew lilies, they grew near the hill
fort. . . I just kept visualizing them, focusing on them. . ."

"I dreamt about them! And about you . . . I
sleepwalked, and picked some — then the next day,
I found the place again. . ."

"And then there was another time," Nada went on,
frowning as she remembered. "Real immediate danger.
It was at night — the shock of it woke me up. But I knew
you could deal with it, your mind had grown so much
stronger—"

"The dogs," gasped Kita. "I stopped them — dominated
them. I sent them back into the forest."

"Ah, excellent," laughed Vild. "Communication with
beasts and birds. So you're really one of us."

"You mean I'm a witch?"

"If you want to call it that," Nada said.

They talked on and on, and Kita's narrow experience
from the world she'd come from began to crack all
along its edges and let new understandings in.

"I was struggling in the dark," Nada explained, "just
like you, dearling. As a girl I longed for something richer
and happier than life on the hill fort. I couldn't accept
that that was all life could be. And then one day, out on

the grasslands guarding the sheep in the summer, a voice called to me from the forest. It was a sweet, light voice – you couldn't be scared. I drew closer, intrigued, and there was a girl, a little older than me. She wore a green cloak that blended in with the leaves. She beckoned me to follow her and I kept losing her in the foliage, she was so well camouflaged. She took me where some herbs were growing, and told me they were good for pain relief. Then one of the sheepmen yelled my name. I ran back, said I'd had to pee, and got a belt round the ear for being prim and prudish. "Squat on the grass next time," he said. But I didn't care. I'd grabbed a handful of those herbs before I ran back. I smuggled them back with me up my sleeve. I dried them – I sniffed them and crushed them. I longed to see if they worked – I knew I had to try them on myself before I used them on anyone else."

"Weren't you afraid the witch had tricked you?" Kita demanded. "Weren't you afraid you'd be poisoned?"

"Yes, all that. Although it was only when I'd got back to the fort that it dawned on me that the girl had come down from Witch Crag. And therefore according to the sheepman's creed, was evil. I wrestled with it all for days, Kita! Why would that lovely young woman kill me just for the sake of it? I couldn't believe that the way of things could be that . . . perverted. But I was too scared to test it out. Too scared to try the herbs. Until one day, I hurt my arm, badly. I wrenched it shifting sheep fodder. I was in agony, and very low. I couldn't sleep for the pain. I felt like I didn't care if I lived or died. So I chewed a few of the leaves."

"*And?*"

"And the pain subsided. I relaxed. I felt wonderful. So peaceful. I slept. The next day, my sprained arm was a lot better. So the next time I was out sheep watching again, I slipped into the forest, to look for more of the herbs."

"You found them?"

"Only with help. I honestly know I had help. I was blundering about, looking, risking a beating for leaving the sheep, and then I just stood still and shut my eyes and waited. I stood still and cleared my mind − and waited. Then I knew which way to go. I found the herbs again. That was the first of many secret gatherings of shadewort, as I now know it's called. I experimented − I crushed it and boiled it and mixed it with other herbs. Raw crushed shadewort is best for bad wounds, applied like a poultice. A tincture for childbirth, sipped slowly . . . I used shadewort in many different ways."

"And risked getting slit for a witch every time you did," said Vild, lovingly.

"I suppose so. But it was worth it. Pain degrades. And people knew − they knew I helped them, they protected me."

"I remember," said Kita, wonderingly. "I had a fever, my head ached, you gave me something sweet to drink—"

"Shadewort mixes well with milk and honey, it's a good disguise."

There was a sudden chinking sound; a woman with dark hair in a beautiful long plait came smiling round the steep rock bank, carrying a woven tray with three wooden bowls on it. "Excuse me," she said, "for interrupting you. But we felt you really needed some refreshment. Such important talk going on."

"Daria, thank you!" said Vild. "I smell peppermint tea. How kind."

Daria set the tray down on the boulder beside Vild, and asked, "It's getting dark – would you like fire too? Shall I bring a brazier? Maybe something to eat?"

"Thank you, my lovely, but no. We'll be out soon, to join everyone for dinner."

Daria nodded, still smiling, and left.

"That," said Vild, handing Nada and Kita a bowl each, "was a perfect little example of 'witchcraft' as you call it, in practice. It's not all grand and stunning and spooky, Kita. Sometimes it's just sensing that important talk is going on, and that the talkers may need fuel. Anyway, Nada. Please finish your story."

"I never met that kind lady again," said Nada. "Or indeed any of the witches, until the day they came to get me. I just had a growing . . . sense of them. I dreamt of them, dearling, like you did me."

"Dreams can be powerful," said Vild. "It's the subconscious at work. Asleep, you can connect with things you're already open to. Nada was open to Witch Crag – so she dreamt of it."

Kita had a sudden, shocking recollection of her dream of Arc in the hot spring, and pushed the thought down.

"One of my dreams was escaping to the witches," said Nada. "But I just wasn't bold or brave enough to try – not like you, Kita! So instead – I tried to *live* differently, following the things I dreamt. I helped the children. I whispered them stories, loved and encouraged them. Carefully, always in fear. And some responded strongly, stood out for me – like *you*, dearling, and Raff with his art, and long before that, Vild—"

"Nada was as important to my childhood as she was to yours, Kita," said Vild. "And when I escaped. . ."

"*Aaaah*," breathed Kita. She felt it was all dropping into place . . . dropping beautifully into place. "How did you escape?"

"*Aaaah*," teased Vild. "That's not part of this story. I reached Witch Crag and told them everything they'd already sensed about Nada. The good she was doing, with her herbs and storytelling and freethinking. We all sensed when she'd reached the end of her work with the sheep people – when she was bone tired and ready to die. We sent her very strong energy for her dreams that night."

"They told me simply to sleep," continued Nada, "to sleep, to trust and wait and *be still*. So I shut myself down. Why not? I was tired of living. I lay as still as death and hardly breathed. It hurt me, dearling, to send no word to you, but the dream was so powerful and real, I had to follow it. The next day, two men carried me out on a stretcher, and tipped me off. Lord, it hurt when they tipped me off – I thought all my bones had cracked. But I kept still, with my eyes shut. I heard the crows – I felt their wings beating in my face. I smelt the slaver of the wild dogs. And then. . ."

"And then. . ." echoed Vild, tenderly.

Nada was weeping. Kita hesitated, then put her bowl down and threw her arms around the old woman, and hugged her.

"Oh, it was terrifying, when they came to get me," Nada sobbed, laughed, "far more terrifying than the crows and the dogs! I thought I'd die of shock. And then . . . they smeared something on my lips . . . and I woke up here. And the . . . the *joy*, Kita. To have everything you've hoped is real but never known – the *joy* to simply step out into it. Like a dark curtain being torn aside, and brightness behind it."

CHAPTER TWENTY-SEVEN

Kita, Vild and Nada sat silently on the boulders in the dusk until a strange, haunting note sounded, three times. "The dinner horn," said Vild, with satisfaction, getting to her feet, the dog Moss copying. "Come – I'm famished."

Darkness had enveloped Witch Crag. Jagged shapes loomed through the blackness. But Vild strode forward, sure-footed, and Nada took hold of Kita's hand, and they followed close behind.

They were heading to the far side of the summit, where Kita hadn't been before. They followed Vild through a narrow gap in two great banks of rock, on to a wide, open space with wooden huts of all sizes arranged around the edge. "Where we sleep, and cook, and eat," Vild explained. "Although we always eat in the open unless the weather is really foul."

In the centre of the space, a great oval of fire glowed from a deep pit in the rock. Shadowy ranks of the witches, nearly a hundred of them, and a dozen or more large, gentle dogs, were grouped noisily around its edge. "We keep that fire going all day in the cold weather,"

Vild explained. "Just ticking over, with chunks of dried peat. So people can warm themselves when they want to."

"How lovely," said Kita, wistfully.

"Different to the hill fort, eh?" said Nada. "The headman couldn't wait to douse the flames. When I first got here, I'd spend hours just sitting at the edge, gazing at the glow."

"Let's sit here," said Vild. "Here's a space."

As Kita subsided down she scanned the faces around her for Quainy and Raff, but she couldn't see them. And she couldn't form the words to ask about them, she was so absorbed in watching the life crackling and fizzing all around her. Laughter and tenderness and astonishment and deep conversation – it was all there, all going on. Two women heaved a great metal rack covered in roasted squash and sweetcorn up from the fire pit; another two shifted a rack of loaves that smelt of rosemary. A man emerged from one of the huts with a steaming cauldron of soup. And soon, smoothly and democratically, the food was passed from hand to hand, and everyone began to eat.

"You grow this squash, too?" asked Kita, her mouth full. "It's wonderful."

Vild looked at her steadily. "We trade for this," she said.

"*Trade. . .?*"

"Oh, who'd trade with the evil hags on the crag, ay? The farmers, that's who."

"The *farmers?*"

"You've heard of them? I'm surprised. They don't have much to do with the sheepmen, which is why they're thankfully ignorant of the worst of the tales about us. Oh, they were suspicious when we first approached them – but a few herb remedies put their minds at ease. Especially shadewort, of course. Now we trade healing for vegetables. They're straightforward people, vigorous and pragmatic. We enjoy their company! They're teaching us about the soil and what it can grow. And as they trust us more, we can do better work with them – why are you looking like that, Kita? Did you swallow a seed?"

"I've met them," she said bluntly. "On the way into the old city. They steal children."

There was a beat of silence, then Vild said, "Yes. I know. Some things that seem hideous on the surface can be excused, Kita. The farmers are rough, but kindly. Those children do far better as slaves than living in the city."

"That doesn't make it right."

"No. Some of the younger children that they've snatched – or the ailing ones – they're up here with us. With Nada. We promise the farmers we'll raise them fit and strong to be better slaves. We get heaps of squash for that, I can tell you."

"And will you send them back, as slaves?" demanded Kita.

"No. Something's going to happen before that."

197

There was a long silence. Kita knew she should ask Vild what she meant, but she couldn't frame the words. And then a girl sitting straight across from her suddenly sprang to her feet, laughing, and threw a shower of dark powder into the fire pit. Tall purple flames shot up, roaring, and everyone clapped, and then a young boy scrambled to his feet and threw in more powder, and the flames turned green, shooting exquisite purple sparks into the air.

"This is what we used to see," breathed Kita, amazed, "from the hill fort – flames of green and purple. They'd warn us not to look, they said it would bewitch us, make us come to you. . ."

Vild laughed. "It worked then."

"What's the powder? Sorcery?"

"No. Dried fungi. The inedible kind."

Music was starting. A man was playing a flute; a girl beside him kept the beat with a little drum, and swelled the notes with her voice. "No storytelling tonight," said Nada. "Dancing instead, to welcome our guests."

"Storytelling?" asked Kita. "For the grown-ups, too?"

"Of course," said Vild. "Without stories, how do we know who we are? How can we imagine who we can be? And storytelling keeps our language rich."

Kita didn't answer. Her head was spinning. She felt tired, stretched – too full of all the amazing new things she'd been faced with. She wanted to creep away from the fire, fold herself into darkness. Sleep.

Two young women had got to their feet. One slender, one curvaceous, both beautiful, with long, chestnut-coloured hair. Giggling, they raised their hands above their heads and started to dance, as the witches clapped and sang.

"Our horsemen brides," said Vild, with satisfaction. "They dance for themselves now, and not their masters."

"We heard about their escape!" said Kita. "How did they – how did you. . .?"

But Vild had nudged her, nodding towards the girls, who were beckoning another girl to join them. She was laughing, waving them away – but the curvy one seized her hand, and pulled her to her feet.

It was Quainy. Her thick, blonde hair, now almost shoulder length, swung and shone in the firelight as she spun around and started to dance.

"They met Quainy when she went as trade," said Vild. "I saw their reunion earlier. Delicious. They were sharing their pleasure and astonishment at their new freedom. Ah, look – the men are joining in."

A lanky, leggy boy had jumped to his feet – he cavorted extravagantly between the girls, both teasing and reverential. Then Raff jumped up, and Quainy danced straight into his arms.

Kita felt as if she couldn't bear the beauty of it. It was as if, in this wild, open atmosphere, they could throw off all restraint and become who they really were. Which was in love with each other. They danced on, and the witches clapped and applauded.

Kita scrambled to her feet, mumbled an apology, and slunk off into the shadows.

"Ooof!" complained Vild, plumping herself down beside Kita on the hard ground a short while later. "You didn't make it easy to find you!"

"I didn't want to be found," muttered Kita.

"Well, too bad, you are," Vild said, firmly. "Now, what's up? As if I didn't know. It's all too much, isn't it? Overwhelming."

"Yes, partly. Although that's not the main thing. It's wonderful here, thrilling. And I know you have more to tell me – about what's coming, about why you helped me come here. And I have things to ask you, so many things, but . . . right now I'm just feeling awful. About Raff and Quainy. I know how that sounds. Like I'm mean, small, jealous. Well, I am. I can't bear to see them so happy together. I feel so *shut out*."

Oh, the relief. The relief to spew out some of the hurt and sourness. She didn't stop to think how Vild might be judging her, might be disappointed in her. She simply rattled on.

"When we left, we were the best of friends. And *I* was central – I was. I never doubted it. Closest to Quainy, closest to Raff. Without me we wouldn't be here. I led the escape. And I *want* to be happy for them, but I just can't be! And I know I've driven a wedge between us by being like this. By acting all bitter. I'm so far away from them now. And I miss how it was. I'm . . . I'm *lonely* for them."

Vild covered Kita's hand with hers, and said, "You didn't drive a wedge between you and them, Kita – it existed anyway. You're made from different metal altogether. Be glad for what you had for a while – and let them go."

"Let them go? They're the only friends I ever had. I can't just *let them go*. I – I want to go back to how I was."

"That's impossible."

"You don't understand. I'm . . . I'm horrible now. I've been feeling . . . such *rage*, and *hate*. . ."

Vild stood up, put a firm hand under Kita's arm, and hauled her gently to her feet. "Bed," she said. "You're raving. Come, I'll show you where to sleep."

A short while later, Kita was cocooned luxuriously in a kind of patchwork sleeping bag, in a warm tent on the far edge of Witch Crag.

"Comfy?" asked Vild, as she stretched out beside her, wrapped in her cloak. Moss's nose appeared through the tent flaps, then he crawled in too and curled up between them. "I prefer this tent to the huts to sleep in. I like my solitude. But tonight, I'll share it with you."

Kita looked around her, eyes adjusted to the dark now. She felt wide awake, but much calmer. There was something so safe and soothing about the small space, the soft folds of the tent, the low breathing of the dog.

"Kita," said Vild, quietly. "I know what you've been feeling. And I know how terrifying it is to be overtaken by rage and fury. A lot of us go through it. Witch rage, we call it."

"So lots of you people feel it?" Kita murmured. That thought, the knowledge, seemed to fill her with hope.

"Yes. The last time I felt it was when I heard about the death of one of us. Our lovely Finchy. Slit by one of your footsoldiers."

Kita felt herself grow cold. She couldn't speak. The silence grew, intensified. "I'm . . . I'm so sorry," she croaked, at last.

"You're not culpable, Kita. But my lord, the rage I felt then. I could have frozen the blood of the whole sheepmen army. Turned them to stone."

Another silence. Kita was afraid; she slid her eyes sideways. Vild's white hair burned like frost in the darkness. Then she mumbled, "I'm ashamed. Feeling what I feel . . . just because I'm jealous. How petty. *Pathetic.*"

"It is as it is," said Vild. "Don't be so harsh on yourself."

"It feels . . . *awful*. Really awful. And I'm scared where it will take me – what I'll become."

"Don't be scared of it, Kita. It's a bit like birth pains – the slow birth of the power that's grown inside you. At first this power is in its crudest, most violent form and you can't just *select* what you feel strongly about. You can't be fierce enough to frighten off the wild dogs, but calm when jealousy invades you. It doesn't work like that. But gradually you learn to channel it. It becomes less about anger and more about a strong desire to make a change."

Kita lay with her hands behind her head and stared at the folds of the tent above her. "Please, Vild – tell me more."

"About?"

"About witch rage. About everything."

"You wanted my story. Are you awake enough to hear it?"

"Oh yes," said Kita.

Chapter Twenty-Eight

"When I was a young girl on the hill fort," said Vild, nestling down into her cloak, "I longed for a better life, just like you and Nada. I never fitted in – I was always in trouble. And freakish things would happen – I scared off two huge crows, once, just by the power of my mind, although afterwards I doubted that I'd done it. Nada looked out for me, loved me. She used to tell me to be quieter, less stroppy, or they'd think I was a witch. *Anyway*. One day, out by the dung heaps, I found a tiny puppy scavenging, separated from her pack. She was shivering, starving. I smuggled her into the hill fort and tended her." Vild stroked Moss's head, gently. "We loved each other. I hid her in my bedding and clothes at first, then she grew too big and boisterous and the headman, just a young man himself back then, he saw her and seized her and – crushed her to death. In front of me."

"Nada told me," whispered Kita. "Horrible."

Vild wrapped her arms tightly round her body, as though she was feeling again what she'd felt all those years ago. "It unleashed a mad torrent inside me. *Witch rage*. I scared myself, I scared *him*. I railed at him and cursed him and he wouldn't come near me. If I'd been less terrifying I think he'd have killed me, too. He made five men grab me and tie me up in one of the sheds. That night, I had a vivid dream. I saw myself sawing through the ropes using a jagged stone embedded in the ground. Then climbing out of the tiny window, running across the compound, and slithering under the great gates like a snake. When I came to . . . the ropes were already sawn. Maybe I'd done it as I dreamt it. To be honest, I felt as if I was still dreaming. The tiny window looked impossible, but I pulled myself up there and somehow, contorting my whole body, I squeezed myself through and dropped to the ground. I ran to the gates – no one saw me."

"Those gates," Kita murmured, "they're right down to the ground, only a snake could get under them. . ."

Vild laughed. "Then that's what I am. I flattened myself until my sinews screamed. I pushed the hard earth away . . . I scraped and scrabbled my way under the hard wood, inch by inch. Then suddenly hands seized my hands from the other side, and I thought I was done for. I thought it was footsoldiers. They hauled me out, too fast to resist, and I came face to face with my first witches." She turned towards Kita, her face eerie in the darkness. "They'd connected with me. Unleashed my strength, my ability to shrink and contort. They'd sent me my dream. Then they came to get me."

Kita's heart was thudding. "Quainy called me a snake," she whispered. "She said I was all coiled up like one."

"I'd take that as a compliment, dearling. Witches aren't sweetness and light. We need our power, our hard core."

"Nada's sweetness and light."

"Yes. But she didn't fight to escape. Not like you and I did."

"Why didn't they come to get me, like they got you? Aren't I worth as much?"

"Things have got more dangerous for us; our resources are more stretched. And we knew the journey would educate you for what is to come. *And* – most of all – we knew you were capable of making it on your own. I'd take that as another compliment, Kita, if I were you."

Then Vild rolled over, and went to sleep.

The next morning, a meeting was called, round the glowing fire pit. Kita, Raff and Quainy were called on to be present; Vild and Nada were there, and about thirty others. There seemed to be no hierarchy – anyone who could get free from their necessary chores could attend. Those who knew their presence was important gave their chores to others, who took them on willingly. Children, though, were gently steered away – Nada insisted. She felt they'd be alarmed by what was to be discussed.

Vild opened the meeting simply, by asking the three

friends to describe what had happened to them in the rotting city. "That place troubles us," she said. "A while back, some of the city dwellers were skulking on our lower slopes, and when we challenged them, they asked to parley. They wanted to employ us to 'do magic for them'. They wanted poisons, potions, anything that could harm. Oh – and they were after our 'vision'. To predict the action of the enemy, they said. They talked about joining forces."

"We declined, of course," said a witch, loudly. "They're scum, thieves – carrion eaters!"

"Living on the waste from the Great Havoc!" cried a witchman.

"But since then," said a thin witch, "a great many of us have seen the old city in our thoughts and dreams. There's one powerful presence – he comes to me – robed in fantastic colours, with uneven horns either side of his head. . ."

Kita clapped her hand over her mouth. "That's Geegaw!" she cried. "They're not *horns* – it's a greasy plait, and a long earring. He went on about 'the vision' to me, too. He said he had it – and some of you did – and he said I had it, too." From the corner of her eye she saw Raff and Quainy turn to stare at her, astonished, but she ignored them, and rattled on. "He told me the Manager needed help from people like me to help the city come together and survive into the future. Because it was going to come to—" She broke off.

207

"What?" Vild pressed her.

"War," said Kita.

A crackle and rustle went round the witches, like wind in a cornfield. "We *said* this," hissed the loud witch. "We've been dreaming of war. . . War! They mean to invade us, invade all the tribes."

"They've built nothing themselves, so they grab what others have worked to build!" cried another.

"*Devour* what we've created. Devour *us*."

Vild leaned towards Kita, face strained. "What did you tell this Geegaw about the sheepmen's hill fort?" she demanded. "Defences? Weak spots?"

"Nothing," said Kita, eyes wide. "He didn't ask."

"There's so many of them," wailed an elderly witch. "So many hungry soulless creatures in those ruins. . ."

"I've been seeing an advance of . . . of monsters," said a young witch, shrilly. "Great ranks of them, all colours . . . great gleaming eyes. . ."

"Ah," said Raff. "I think they're called cars."

Over the course of the next few hours, with breaks for hot, sweet drinks and crumbly scones flavoured with herbs, the three friends told the story of their time in the decaying city. They talked about Geegaw and the Manager, the ruthless gangs, the raids on the farmers' lands, the dwindling stocks of canned food. They described the ranks of cars they'd seen, all lined up and facing out of the city. Raff told how they'd escaped, and how they were nearly slaughtered in the killing arena. The witches listened attentively, asking questions, filling out the friends' words with their dreams and sensings, their scant knowledge of the city, and the tales that the farmers' young slaves had told them.

Before long, an undeniable vision of war was seen by all.

"They mean to come out, in those *cars*," said a witchman. "They'll be invulnerable. They'll overrun us, seize our resources. . ."

"It's happening too soon," sobbed the elderly witch. "Years too soon, for the tribes to unite against this. We've not finished our work — the sheepmen and the horsemen, they fear and hate us more than ever. . ."

Vild stood up, crossed over to her, and hugged her. "We'll find different ways," she soothed. "We have to."

Now all the witches were standing up, stretching their legs. It seemed that the meeting had come to a natural end, but Kita's mind was still crammed with questions. The thought of an invasion from the city terrified her, but she needed to know more — and she longed to learn about the *work* that Vild and the others kept mentioning. What had Vild said, about her flight from the sheepmen hill fort? "We knew the journey would educate you for what is to come." What was to come? And what part had she to play in it all?

But Vild had disappeared, and now Daria, the witch with the beautiful dark plait of hair, was approaching her, smiling.

"Tired, Kita?" she asked. "Or can you help me prepare the evening meal? This long meeting, it's put us all behind."

"Of course," said Kita, reluctantly. "Are Raff and Quainy. . .?"

"Oh, someone else will have claimed them. We love new people, here."

The kitchen on Witch Crag was not so different to the one at the sheepmen hill fort – basic, clean, efficiently run. But the atmosphere inside was worlds away. Rumours of the invasion hadn't reached the kitchen yet, and the workers inside were carefree. They laughed, talked, teased each other; one young boy broke off chopping root vegetables to juggle with three of them, while others applauded and urged him on.

Kita was asked to strip long wiry plant stalks of their leaves. "The stalks are bitter," Daria explained, "but reviving. We make tinctures from them, with honey added. The leaves are tasty eaten raw."

Kita was halfway through her task when there was an uproar from the far end of the kitchen. "Sessa, *what* on earth d'you think you're up to?" a portly witch barked. "Those flatbread buns should be in the baking pit by now!"

Kita stared uncomfortably, waiting for Sessa to whine out an apology. But Sessa, who looked a couple of years younger than Kita, stood her ground. "I'm making flower shapes," she said. "It's taking longer."

"And why are you making *flower shapes*?"

"To welcome our guests tonight."

"We welcomed them last night."

"Not properly we didn't, because we didn't all know they were coming!"

"Well, it won't welcome them to have uncooked flatbread, will it?"

"No," said Sessa. "I suppose not."

"So what do you propose to do about it, *h'm*?"

"Well . . . if I put these flowers in the oven now—"

"Ah. And roll out the rest of the dough in thin leaves?"

"Yes. They'll bake quicker, they'll bake in time."

"And look very festive," said the portly witch, "leaves and flowers together. Well, get to it, then!"

Kita turned back to her task, amazed. So the witches argued, they fought. But—

"We sort it out, as calmly as we can," said Daria, as though she'd heard Kita's thoughts. "We hear each other. But of course we disagree! What intelligent people don't? It's only by exploring our differences that we can grow."

Chapter Twenty-Nine

Another evening meal, more music, a tale of the witches' long-ago arrival at the crag. As if by agreement, no one mentioned the old city. Instead, they danced under the stars, everyone joining in this time, snaking around the fire pit, laughing and singing in time with the flute and the drum.

Another night in the warm tent for Kita, curled up beside Vild and Moss. As she got up the next day and breakfasted on dried fruit and flatbread laid out on tables for all to take, she felt herself beginning to unfold into Witch Crag. Maybe, she thought, she'd find the answers to her questions spaced out along the way. She wandered over to the pheasant huts and offered to help, and this was gladly accepted. Suggestions were made, rather than directions given, on the best way to go about the work. Sessa toiled alongside her, collecting eggs, sweeping droppings, and plied her with queries about her life before she'd come here, and no one told them to work more and talk less. Then, in the afternoon, a sturdy young witch with long loose auburn hair appeared, introduced herself as Comfrie, and wondered if Kita would like to help her mix herbal potions. This was something Kita was eager to learn about, and she agreed happily. Then it hit her – she was happy.

She said goodbye to Sessa and followed Comfrie down the steps to the apothecary, as Comfrie called her place of work. It was situated on the far north side of the crag, where a steep and jagged rocky outcrop formed part of the outer barricades. Halfway up between two jutting spurs of rock, a low roof of dried ferns had been hung, creating a deep cave.

"No door," Comfrie explained, beckoning Kita to follow her inside. "We need the air to get in or the infusion fumes might overcome us."

Kita followed her slowly, eyes wide, into the gloom of the apothecary. And felt a deep thrill of fear at what she saw. Every section of the rock face, on all three sides, was covered in strange necromantic shapes, hanging from hooks. Crows' wings, birds' beaks, dogs' skulls. Hanks of hair, twists of fur, bunches of strange-looking plants, bundles of dried fungi. And on the ledges, lower down, piles of bones, bundles of sticks, and strange, dark, spiky seed pods.

"Is this where you mix the poison, too?" Kita asked, trying to keep her voice steady. "For the arrows?"

"Oh, yes," said Comfrie. "Everything is done here." She picked up a thin bone from a ledge with one hand and with the other, deftly wound her long, silky hair into a knot on the top of her head, then skewered it with the bone. "Right," she said. "First thing – we must get the fire going under that pot. Then we pour in some of *this* –" she held up a bulbous bottle that glowed red and sinisterly – "crack those seed pods, crush the seeds, and add them."

Kita licked her lips; her throat felt very dry. "What are we making?" she whispered.

Comfrie giggled. "Your face!" she cried. "The face of a true sheep girl, thinking she's been lured into a witch's lair to brew up evil. It's a gentle sleeping infusion, Kita, nothing more. Nada's asked me for one. Rumours of the invasion have stirred everyone up and fear is contagious – it's spreading fast among the more nervous of us. The sleeping draught will stop the nightmares, keep things calm at night."

Kita let out a long *phew* of relief. "Sorry," she muttered. "Just – you're right – you did look like a sheep girl's worst fear. Just for a bit. With that bone in your hair and that bottle of blood."

"It's whirtle berry juice," smiled Comfrie. "Now, are you going to help me or not?"

The next few hours passed wonderfully for Kita. As she stoked the fire under the little cauldron and deseeded the pods, she listened to Comfrie describe the magical and amazing world of plants and living things, and all the ways they could be used to enhance life and help with its pain, and she saw that this was a great part of the witches' work, and she felt that she was part of it all, helping too.

When it grew dark in the cave, the little fire allowed Comfrie to see the "set" of the draught, as she called it. It wasn't until the dinner horn sounded across the crag that Kita realized she was hungry.

"You go along without me," Comfrie said. "I need to see this right, then cool it and decant it."

"But, Comfrie, you must be starving—"

"Don't worry, they'll save me some food. Go!" Then she held out her arms to Kita, who slid into them, and hugged her tight.

Kita felt as though she was flowing along the top of Witch Crag, as she followed the crowds to dinner in the dusk. She felt so good, so relaxed, so much herself, that she wondered if she'd inhaled too much of the steam from the cauldron. People smiled at her, and reached out warmly and touched her arm or her back, and some called out, "Liking it here? Glad you came?"

And she called back, "Yes! Yes!"

Then she saw a face she recognized, lit by a little oil lamp burning on the ground. Stooped in concentration over a large black spindle of stone that jutted out from the ground at the side of one of the witches' social areas. Raff, doing what he loved most. Carving and scraping at the rock, creating something, making art.

She went over and stood beside him. "What's it going to be?" she murmured.

"A tree," he said, decisively, glancing briefly at her to smile, and getting back to his carving again. "A sculpture of a tree. So many of the witches say they miss tall trees more than anything living up here. They love to go to the forests."

"H'm," said Kita, doubtfully. "That's great bark you're carving – really real. And I love that snail. But don't trees have branches?"

"And this one will have. There's a load of crude pikes and weapons stacked behind the cook house, taken from marauders they defeated—"

"What, the ones whose bones ended up in a daisy chain?"

"Probably." Raff shrugged. "They were stripping them down to burn the wood – I earmarked them just in time. They'll make perfect branches, and I can beat the metal into leaves. I just need to work out how to attach them. It's going to be shady, this tree. And *beautiful*, Kita."

"I bet," she said. Then, "How's Quainy?"

"Oh, happy as a lamb. The weaver witches found our old wool tunics, they've taken them apart, unpicked the threads. They're working out how best to weave the wool in with that hemp stuff they use, for warmth, and Quainy's helping them."

"She was always good at weaving, wasn't she. She'd have done that if she hadn't been worth more as trade."

Raff straightened up then, and looked straight at Kita, and between them was all they'd been through to get here, and how good it was to be here, but there was also the space, the gap that had opened up between them. "Come on," he said, at last. "Let's go to dinner. I said I'd meet her there."

As they made their way over to the great fire pit, Raff pointed to a line of little huts. "Couples' huts," he said, simply. "Privacy. That's where we sleep – the third one along."

"How lovely," Kita answered.

At dinner Kita asked Vild if she shouldn't find somewhere else to sleep that night. "I could move to the girls' hut," she said. "Only I've been with you for two nights now, and you said you like your own company. . ."

Vild looked at her, considering, then she reached out quickly and stroked Kita's cheek. "Time enough for that," she said. "You're welcome in my tent. You'd be badgered to death with questions in the girls' hut, and you need a good rest tonight, because Nada wants you to help with the children tomorrow."

That night's meal was more subdued. Rumours of the invasion from the rotting city had circulated and spread; uneasiness lapped at everyone. There was lots of talking, but no singing or dancing, and little laughter. Comfrie appeared with her sleeping draught, and everyone who felt they needed some took a sip from the bulbous bottle.

Kita didn't have any.

Unlike the happiness of the day, her dreams were full of battles, of fleeing and fighting. She woke once screaming to find Vild soothing her, cradling her in her arms.

Nada called for her very early the next day, and there followed a morning of wonder for Kita. She'd only ever thought of babies and children as weeping, needy, sullen things. Not the exuberant, spontaneous little individuals who jumped and rolled around her like healthy puppies, or stood very still, eyes wide, as she told them all about sheep and drew a crude picture of one in the dust. Some of the older kids had collected feathers from the pheasants' pens, and were making headdresses from them. As Kita helped fasten one under the chin of a solemn little girl, a sob suddenly gripped her throat, and she tried to stifle it but failed. She turned away, arm over her eyes, as the tears started to flow.

And Nada was there beside her, like she'd always been when most needed, taking her arm gently and steering her away from the children. "It's all right, sweetheart," she said, "it's all right. Come this way, come and sit over here. We don't want to frighten them."

"I . . . *ooooh* . . . oh, I'm sorry. I don't know what happened then, I just—"

"I know," soothed Nada. "They're just so different to those poor little tykes in the pens at the hill fort, aren't they? And so different to you, when you were that age."

Kita gulped in air. She felt like sudden grief had engulfed her. She felt if she didn't stop herself crying now, she'd never stop.

Nada rubbed her back, and waited. Another witch had appeared, and was leading the children in a skipping song.

"*I want to save them*," Kita grated out, at last. "I want . . . *somehow* . . . to spare the sheep children what I went through. To let them be loved, free. To *open up life* for them."

"And if that's your aim, dearling," said Nada, "you'll find a way to do it. I know you."

"*How?* Transport them all here? I want them to have *this* life! *How?*"

"Be patient, Kita. Go slow. You always did rush ahead, even as a little girl. Now. Why don't you take a wander? Soak up more of Witch Crag."

So Kita wandered, and as she did, the grief left her and she felt instead a kind of deep, restful calm. She saw an old man making bracelets out of delicate scrap metal. He called her over and presented her with one, a chain with large thin links, and they talked for a while about what fun it was to adorn yourself. She wandered on and saw the cloth dyers treading in their great tubs; she waved to Quainy at the looms. She moved through all the witches, chatting, smiling, stopping to watch their work. Then she spotted Vild's white topknot at a distance, standing in a ring with a group of the other older witches round a large patch of ground. They were all staring intently down at something, not talking. Intrigued, she started to head towards them when young Sessa darted up to her and seized her arm.

"*Wheeesht!*" hissed Sessa. "Don't interrupt, don't go too close. They're salad–spell–making!"

"*What?*" laughed Kita.

"Salad–growing. Spell–making. That patch of earth – it nearly *cost* the earth, trust me. They carried up soil from the lower slopes – mulched and manured it – and they sow fresh greens in it every spring to keep us going all summer. And when they sow, they spell–make, to make the salad grow. Can't you almost *see* the energy?"

Kita stared. Maybe she imagined it, but there seemed to be a slight haze, like the shimmering around a fire, above the dark earth, in the middle of the witches.

"Now," said Sessa, happily, leading her away by the hand, "I've got you again. Go on with your story. Tell me about the night you escaped."

Kita laughed, and began, but sudden shouting interrupted her. Shouting from lower down on the crag. Angry, frightened shouting, interspersed with yelled commands.

Everyone around stopped what they were doing. The noise was shocking; utterly unlike the usual harmonious buzz and hum of Witch Crag. Sessa sped towards it, Kita following. They merged in with a great crowd of witches, all hurrying in the same direction. The dogs of

226

the crag ran with them, barking.

On the lower slope where the spinning and weaving took place, a group of five warrior witches were aggressively herding a man forward. Three of the witches had blackbows, aimed at their prisoner; two had him clasped by the arms.

The man was young, strong, and struggling violently. The witches screamed and threatened as they lurched forward.

Kita recognized Wekka, the warrior witch who'd come to meet them when they first arrived. "Look at our *quarry*!" she yelled.

"Caught him climbing the sheer face of the crag!" shouted the witch who had hold of the young man's right arm. "*Spy!*" Then, with a huge thump, she spun him forward, so that he sprawled on the ground.

He raised himself on his hands. Kita gasped. There, on the black rock, his face a mask of defiance and rage, was Arc.

CHAPTER THIRTY

"Stay down! Move and I'll spit you!" Wekka cried, aiming her blackbow at Arc's head. "This poison kills in seconds. Doubt it and it'll be the last thing you doubt."

"Wekka, be calm!" cried Vild, as she hurried over. "Don't let fly!"

Wekka lowered her weapon slightly. "There were three others," she said. "Sheepmen footsoldiers. This likely lad was ahead of the rest of them, scaling the north face. His three friends scarpered when they saw us swarming down towards them." She grinned with satisfaction. "We made sure we looked wild and witchy, like we'd have the flesh off their bones. But laddy here –" she cuffed Arc, who snapped his head away, furiously – "he didn't stand a chance. We climbed down and got him."

Furtively, Kita stepped back, and hid behind some of the others. She was frozen; dreading Arc seeing her.

Another of the warrior witches spoke up. "Tell us what you were doing. *Spy.*"

Arc was silent, glaring.

"Kill him!" shouted someone in the crowd.

"Put an arrow in him!" screamed another voice.

"*No!*" cried Vild. "Since when have we behaved like them?"

"Since they started slaughtering us!" A witch in a faded yellow cloak darted out from the crowd. "I was there, remember, gathering red saffrey with Finchy in the forest. I saw them seize her. I was helpless to help. And *he* –" she pointed with a shaking, hate-filled finger at Arc – "he was the leader of their little troupe. He ordered her seized! And then she was *slit*!"

The crowd of witches keened and growled. "Shoot him dead!" shrieked someone, and the cry was taken up, a murmur first, then a grim chant, *shoot him, shoot him*, growing in intensity. Wekka stepped away from Arc, and slowly and deliberately raised her blackbow, aiming at his face.

Before she could think or even know what she was feeling, Kita pushed her way through and ran towards Arc. She stood right in front of him, facing down Wekka and her dripping arrow. "He didn't slit Finchy!" she cried. "I saw it. He – he disobeyed the headman. He tried to *stop* her being killed."

Arc had raised his head; he gazed at Kita. "*You!*" he breathed.

She wouldn't look at him. She continued to look steadily at Wekka, who snarled, "Get back, newcomer. If the majority of witches say he dies, he dies. That's how we work here."

"But not on mad impulse!" cried Vild, coming forward, standing beside Kita. "Not in the white heat of the moment. We don't know what help he can be! Don't act in haste."

"*Well?*" demanded Wekka, of the crowd. Finchy's friend and a few others shouted, "*Kill him!*" but from the rest there was only muttering.

Wekka waited for a full minute. Then she said, "Truss him up. Put him in the shallow cave. Leave him bound until you've fashioned strong wood stakes to bar it. Until then, guard him."

Arc was hauled away.

Kita was shaking. It was some time since Arc had been dragged off, but she was still shaking. She slunk off on her own, to where she and Vild and Nada had talked the day she arrived on the crag, hoping no one would find her.

Why did he come? she thought, in anguish. *Why did he have to come here?* She kept seeing him pitching forward, sprawling on the hard rock. The sudden violence of the witches terrified her; she dreaded their questions. She'd just announced to everyone that she'd seen Finchy being slit, and done nothing to save her. Where did that leave her? She thought of Vild saying *witches aren't sweetness and light*.

In the distance, she could hear wood being sawn, split. They were making a cage for Arc. She couldn't even look at what had made her leap to Arc's defence. It was like something she couldn't own had grabbed her by the scruff of the neck, and thrown her out in front of him. She wanted to talk to someone – Vild, or Nada, or Raff and Quainy – but no one came to find her. The open, glorious friendliness of the place – it seemed to have vanished. She was scared to go out into the open again.

In the end, in the late afternoon, hunger drew her forth. She skirted round the cookhouse, and was given fruit and bread. Then, head lowered, she wandered down to the main concourse. It was obvious even from a distance where Arc was being held. In front of one of the great outcrops of rock that broke up the summit of Witch Crag, people slowed and stopped in shifting, changing groups. They talked, looked – moved on. Kita edged nearer, joined the group on its outskirts. Over their heads she could just see the hollow in the rock face, the shallow cave – and the fierce line of sharpened wooden staves that had been driven into the ground in front of it. Anxious, angry conversation flowed all around her.

"What's the sense of keeping him alive? He'll have to be killed."

"Maybe he'll tell us something first. Maybe he knows something about the old city that will help us."

"He won't help us! You saw his face!"

"She's right. The sheepmen hate us!"

"He'll have to be killed."

"Shame. He's a fine young man."

"And we're always low on men – maybe we can keep him as stud!"

Cackling laughter followed this last remark. Kita grimaced, and pushed her way closer to the wooden stakes. Something compelled her, though she dreaded Arc seeing her. Then – abruptly – Vild was in front of her, coming the opposite way. "Kita!" she cried. "Come away, sweetheart. Don't add to the crowds round him. He's swearing and snarling. Calling us all foul and evil. I can't get a sensible word out of him."

Kita allowed herself to be towed off to the side. "Can't you just tell everyone to leave him alone?" she mumbled.

Vild looked at her wryly. "No, I can't. Everyone makes their own choices here. Unless there's immediate danger – then Wekka takes control."

"You won't get anything out of Arc while he's treated like an animal in a cage."

"He can signal any time that he wants to parley."

"He won't, he's stubborn."

"Then that's *his* choice. Will you walk with me?" Vild tucked her hand through Kita's arm and steered her towards the far edges of the crag, where the high wooden wall loured. The fresh spring wind flowed over the top to meet them. "Let's walk the perimeter," said Vild. "We witches often do. Some of us run it. When we feel a little penned in."

226

"You feel *penned in*, here?" Kita asked, taken aback.

"Of course we do, sometimes."

"But it's so harmonious, and beautiful, and. . ."

". . . small. That's another reason we're keen to get out into the world and convince it to like us." After a few minutes' strolling, Vild said, "Kita, why didn't you tell me before that you'd seen poor Finchy die?"

"I don't know," muttered Kita. "Because it seemed so horrible, I suppose."

"They should never have gone." Vild sighed. "It was too dangerous, with the horsemen brides just escaped. Men were bound to be out searching."

"Why did they go?"

"To gather red saffrey. It's such an important flower for us — we dry it as a preservative, the best we know. Fresh food sprinkled with it lasts all winter. Finchy insisted she'd pick some. It only grows in early spring, in the woods on the edge of the sheepmen grasslands. She paid a terrible price for it."

They walked on, past the racks of drying dyed cloth which fluttered like huge colourful flags in the wind. "You know, there was another reason for her going," said Vild, lowering her voice a little. "Nada had been telling her about *you* and she hoped she'd somehow connect with you, help you come to us. She'd been dreaming about you, you see. Kita? Kita, what's wrong?"

Kita had stopped; she felt like she could hardly

breathe. "She did connect with me," she croaked. "I was hidden up high – I watched her die. And as she did – she looked straight at me. It had . . . it had a great effect on me."

There was nothing more to be said. They walked on, round the great perimeter, and with every step Kita was aware of Arc in his prison. She was circling him, now close, now at a distance, as if there was a thread fastened between them. She took in a deep breath and said, "Vild, tell me about this *work* you do. What do you mean by it? I can see that you help the children snatched from the old city, and you help girls like me escape, but it seems to be about even more than that."

"Yes, even more." Vild smiled. "It's about – what was it Nada called it? *The greater good*. We think our ways are good. Democratic, fair, happy. *Free*. We're trying to infect people with them."

"But people won't listen to you when they think you're evil."

"Yes, that's a problem. In the beginning we just strove to protect ourselves, and we did it rather too well. What protects us also makes us feared. But increasingly, we're breaking through. We're well on the way to a real bond with the farmers. At heart, they're decent people. They're happy to trade with us and learn from us. And for some months now we've had two subversive witchmen in among the horsemen."

"How did you manage that?" asked Kita, astonished.

228

"Surprisingly easily. They presented themselves at the horsemen fort as wandering mercenaries. The horsemen were glad to take them in. We lost two good fighters — but the subtle influence they're spreading is worth far more. And of course, they helped the brides escape."

"Do you have anyone with the sheep people?"

"Only people who aren't aware that they're working for us. Like Nada. And you, my lovely! The need is more urgent with the horsemen. Some of their ways are vile, not much better than the old city."

"Do you have anyone there? In the old city?"

Vild seemed to subside, as if the thought saddened her. "No," she said. "A deputation of witches went, before my time — only two came back. The others had been killed. Probably eaten. And the decision was made that — the city is beyond help. For all the faults of the new tribes, they're moving into the future, supporting themselves by farming, hunting, trade — the city does none of this. It's like a fungus, surviving on the rot of the old world. And now the fungus wants to spread out and feed off what we've worked to create. What I'd love is—" She broke off.

"What?" asked Kita.

"I wish I could scoop up all the children in the city. I wish I could save them. Before they turn to cannibalism and despair."

"Oh, Vild. So the farmers really do rescue them, when they take them as slaves."

"We think so. Especially the ones they pass on to us. I saw you playing with a few of them, earlier."

There was a silence. Then Kita said, "Go on about the horsemen. They're not beyond help?"

"Oh, no," said Vild, her voice lifting. "They make their own way in the world – hunting boar, fighting and plundering – but mostly only those who would fight and plunder them first. They have an intelligent pact with the sheepmen, and a basic if corrupt democracy. And I'm rather partial to the fermented berry juice they brew! Kita – it's the horse*women* who are driving this change, in subtle, powerful ways – they long for change and increasingly, the young men wish it, too. Only those old warriors glutted on the privileges of power and status fight to resist it. But our witchmen report there are signs that their time is ending. The horse people are easier to shift than you stubborn sheep people! You're impenetrable in your virtuous plainness. Your belief that feeling pleasure is wrong."

"Not my belief, Vild."

"No. Not yours, dearling. I wonder if it's the belief of that young buck we have penned."

But Kita didn't want to talk about Arc. She quickened her pace a little, and said, "So your work is for the greater good. Vild, how do you know? How do you *know* what's good? And how do you know which way to help people?"

· Vild shrugged, smiling. "It's not written in stone, Kita.

236

In fact it's not written at all. The best image I can give you is – you see a stream, clogged with leaves and debris, bogging down the land around it, not running its course. Don't you just unblock it, clear it, let it flow again?"

"It sounds so . . . so *vague.*"

"Maybe. But there's no one way. Everyone's different. We don't preach – no point. We discuss and suggest and encourage and share. And we believe that freedom and happiness will win out in the end, however long it takes. We hope for a unified future, with the flow of trade and discussion and respect and learning between us all. But achieving that open unity will be a long, slow process – and now there's a war coming." Vild stopped walking; she turned and faced Kita. "Somehow, and soon, we must all link together, Kita. The witches, the farmers, the sheepmen, the horsemen. We must make a strong protective chain, or the rotting city will break through and devour us all. And I don't know how that chain's to be forged."

Then they walked on to the upper sleeping area, and Vild halted by her little tent. "I need this to myself for a while," she said, gently. "I've got a lot of thinking to do. But you're welcome to sleep here again tonight." She pulled open the tent flap, then turned and said, "Goodbye for now, Kita. I'm so glad poor Finchy connected with you. It means there was a purpose to her death. She used to say she saw you all the time in her dreams. A spiky-haired girl who climbed like a tree rat."

CHAPTER THIRTY-ONE

Tree rat, tree rat – the words seared through her. It was what Arc used to call her. And now she'd found out that a witch had called her it, too. A link, what link? Vild had talked about links in the chain that must be forged. . .

She sped on, continuing the walk around the perimeter, thinking of Arc cramped in the shallow cave. He'd hate it, he'd loathe being vulnerable. He'd be fighting the fear that must be swamping him. She found herself hoping it wouldn't break him. Why did she care? Why?

She remembered Finchy spinning as she died, looking straight at her, the power of that one intense look. She remembered how, after that look, unthinkable things had clicked into place in her mind. . .

And now, once again, she had the extraordinary sensation of things clicking and fitting together in her mind. Confusing, challenging, terrifying things.

She walked on and on, until night fell on the crag. She paused only to cadge a bit more bread and fruit from the cookhouse. She didn't want to join everyone round the fire pit for the evening meal. She saw Raff and Quainy in the distance, and fell back into the shadows to hide. She didn't want company.

Vild was asleep and Moss was snoring gently when Kita slithered into the tent later that night. The dog wagged his tail drowsily a couple of times in welcome but stayed lying down. Maybe, she thought, as she wriggled into the sleeping bag, maybe an answer would come to her in a dream, like before. Maybe Nada would appear, and tell her what to do.

But she couldn't even get to sleep. She lay staring at the folds of cloth above her, as awake as she could be. And her restlessness grew until at last she couldn't stand it any longer. She shucked off the sleeping bag and crawled out of the tent again.

It was a cold clear night, with a bright half moon casting clear shadows. She started to walk, fast, half running. One part of her mind knew exactly where she was going, and was taking her resolutely there. The other part looked on in doubt and fear at what she was doing.

She hurried on, and soon was drawing close to the solid rank of bars that kept Arc imprisoned. There was no guard on duty. The bars were enough.

"Arc!" she called softly. No answer. She drew closer, peered into the black recesses of the shallow cave. The moon shone through the bars and made more bars on the floor. There was a hunched shape at the back of the cave, but it didn't move.

"Arc, it's me," she said, coming right up to the bars now. "It's Kita. Please talk to me."

The shape moved. Then suddenly, shockingly, it sprang towards her, shot an arm out through the bars, and seized her by the wrist.

"Get me out of here!" Arc snarled.

When the shock had subsided, Kita found herself wanting to laugh. "How am I going to do that, huh? Especially with you hanging on to me."

"Call someone. Tell them I'll break your arm if they don't let me out."

"They're all asleep. No one would hear me call. And anyway, they'd shoot you before you could hurt me."

Silence, but he tightened his grip on her wrist. And Kita realized something momentous. She realized she was no longer intimidated by him. Not after all she'd been through since she'd left the hill fort. "OK, Arc," she said. "Let go of me or I'll sink my teeth into your hand. And we all know how toxic a tree rat's bite can be."

Arc made a noise that could almost have been a laugh, then he let go of her wrist.

"Are you OK?" she asked. He'd moved back again – she couldn't see his face. "Have you got food, and water?"

"Yes, I've got food and water. And *no*, I'm not OK. That's a monumentally dumb question, even for you."

"Arc — please talk to me. Tell me why you're here — why you climbed up here. And then maybe I can persuade the witches to let you out and you can parley with them."

"Parley with those rancid hags? I'd sooner rot in here."

"They're not rancid. They're not even hags. They're brilliant. You'd like them if you'd open that trap of a mind and think clearly. Arc, you were *right* about them. They just tinker about with corpses, like you said, to scare people off. They're not cruel and inhuman."

"Oh, right," he said bitterly. "They've shoved me in here as a big treat, to be kind to me."

"Oh, grow up. You were climbing up the north face of the crag! What were they supposed to do?"

"You're bewitched. They put you under a spell and got you here. I'm not listening to you."

"You *know* you don't believe all that magic crap, Arc. You didn't believe it when you refused to slit the witch you caught, and you don't believe it now. I came here of my own free will because I wanted a better life. Deal with it."

"Fine. Be a hag. You live your way and I'll live mine."

"Arc, listen. If we don't act soon, none of us will live. *Listen* to me! We got trapped in the old city, on our way here. They're preparing for war."

"I know," he said.

"You *know*?"

There was a long pause, as though Arc was wrestling with his desire to stay crushingly silent and his desire to talk. The desire to talk won out. Kita heard him drinking from something, then he said, "When we were out looking for you three pathetic runaways, we saw smoke coming from the direction of the old city. When we couldn't find you, you ungrateful *bitch*—"

"*Ungrateful?*"

"You and I were going to mate together!"

"Oh, *right*. Well, I must've been under a massively strong spell, after all. No one who *wasn't* bewitched would refuse you, right?"

"Right!"

"And be massively *grateful* too, right?"

"Do you want to hear what happened, or not?"

"I do. Go on."

"I will if you'll shut up. When we couldn't find you, I reported back, and was given permission to take four footsoldiers and go and investigate the old city. We got in through a breach in the walls. We ran this way, that way, avoiding trouble – what a stinking *sewer* that place is! After long, sleepless hours we found the source of the smoke. They're forging weapons – great, crude, jagged pikes and poles, out of the broken metal of the city. Hundreds of them. Terrible things. I was trying to get closer to grab one when we were spotted. This gang gave chase – it came to a fight – we lost Ethan. Poor sod. Then we raced over this open space, blood all over the concrete floor . . . and got out. We slept in the forest and the next day discovered we were right near Witch Crag."

"And decided to climb it?"

"The lads were against it. But I wanted to see what went on up here. I wanted to complete our reconnoitre. I thought the hags may be preparing for war too – in league with the old city."

There was a silence. Arc shifted nearer the bars, and the moon shone on his cheekbones and his mouth. Kita gazed at him. He was looking straight back at her.

"Arc," she began, "now you've seen what it's like here – you know, you *must* do, that there's no way the witches could be in league with the old city. They want to be in league with *you*. With the sheepmen, and the horsemen, and the farmers. We all have to stand together, or the old city will devour us all. When we were there, we didn't see their weapons, but we saw their vehicles. Hundreds and hundreds of metal cars, moving armour, to protect them when they attack."

Silence. Arc moved back into the shadows again.

"Arc – think about it," she went on, urgently. "If anyone can convince the sheepmen and the horsemen to join forces with the witches, it's you. You're going to be the next headman. It's *you*."

"That's crazy," muttered Arc, at last. "You're crazy."

"Yes. I was crazy enough to think the witches weren't evil. And you thought that too! You *know* you did! And now you have the proof of it, if you'd just open your eyes." More silence. Then the sound of Arc moving again, right back into the cave. "OK," said Kita. "I'm going. But think about it. Sleep on it. *Dream* about it. And I'll see you tomorrow. OK?"

Then, incredulous at what she'd done, amazed at the way the talk between them had just racketed along, honest and open, Kita started to make her way back to Vild's tent.

CHAPTER THIRTY-TWO

Kita slept deeply that night, and woke feeling calm and confident. She ate breakfast with everyone and chatted with Raff and Quainy, who were bubbling over with how wonderful life was on the top of the crag. They'd battled so hard to get here that the thought of a war wasn't going to spoil it for them. Kita smiled as she listened to them talk of sculpting and weaving; she was warm towards them, and told them she was fine. They didn't mention Arc, which was weird; but then neither did she.

She wanted above everything to go and see him again, to see if he'd come round to her way of thinking. She wandered down to the main concourse, keeping an eye out for Vild, when she saw Nada waving to her over the heads of a bouncing group of toddlers. Daria was there too. Kita hurried to join them. Nada and Daria were singing and the toddlers were jumping up and down, clapping, and loudly joining in. Nada turned to Daria, and asked her to take over. Then she seized Kita's hand firmly, and led her away.

"They look so happy," said Kita. "I still want to cry when I see them."

"Well, you must spend more time with them later, Kita," said Nada. "Tell them all about your adventures in the old city. Suitably toned down, of course. Don't scare them silly! But now – we have rougher fish to fry. We're going to see Arc."

"We are?" gasped Kita.

"Yes. I'm going to reintroduce myself to him. He was a baby in the pens with me, just as you were. You probably don't remember him there. He's a few years older than you – he was on his way out as you came in. But you overlapped."

The thought of Arc as a baby was unimaginable to Kita. She found herself smiling as Nada towed her along. Before long, they were outside his prison. The usual crowd of curious witches were gathered there, some of them trying to get him to talk to them. Nada walked briskly into the middle of them and said, "I wonder if I could ask you all to very kindly let us speak with this unfortunate young man on our own?"

The respect felt for Nada on Witch Crag was unmistakable. Everyone nodded, smiling, and melted away.

"Arc," Nada called, through the bars. "Arc, it's Nada."

At the sound of her voice Arc flinched, and twisted round to look. "Oh, this is foul," he groaned. "This is necromancy, you're dead, your body was eaten by dogs."

"Clearly not," said Nada, firmly. "Use the evidence of your eyes."

"I don't trust my eyes," he said, turning away again. "Or my mind. Not any more."

"Oh dear. Feeling sorry for yourself this morning, ay?"

"Get away from me. *Spectre*."

"Arc," said Kita, gently, "it *is* Nada. She was still alive at her funeral – the witches came to get her and chased off the dogs and the crows. Arc, you need to get out of this cage. Your mind needs to crack open and it can't do it penned in there. Please say you'll parley."

Arc said nothing. Nada took hold of a bar in each hand, and leaned her face against them. "You were such a spirited little boy," she said. "Such courage. And you've fulfilled your early promise. Look at you. I'm so proud of you, Arc. You're still destined to be the next headman, you know. You just need to find your way to it."

Then she took Kita's hand, and led her away.

The morning progressed with chores and talking but it was as if a dark fret of fear lay over the crag now. Few people smiled. Vild stayed closeted in her tent. Wekka took a small band of warrior witches to scour the lower slopes of the crag and observe the old city. They arrived back in the early afternoon, rabbit carcases hung from their belts, accompanied by a band of four young farmers. Word spread fast when the shaven-headed strangers walked on to the main concourse, and soon all the witches were gathered around them.

"We met our four friends on the lower slopes," cried Wekka, loud enough for everyone to hear. Loud enough for Arc, in his prison, to hear. "They were climbing up to parley. What we feared is happening already. Pitch, tell them your tale."

Pitch stepped forward. Like all the farmers, he had three dark slashes spaced from the top of his neck to the crown of his head, and with those and his worn, torn clothes he had a barbaric, brutal air. But his voice, when he spoke, was clear and straight.

"We've come to ask your help," he said. "We won't survive without your help. The city raided us last night. Not in their usual sneak-thief creeping way, the way we've got used to. They . . . *invaded* us. They came with metal wagons, fifty or more, and savage weapons. Dozens of us were slain trying to fight them off. They left with their infernal vehicles piled high with our produce. We have very little left."

A grief-stricken, fearful murmur spread from witch to witch.

"We know they'll be back," Pitch went on. "They goaded us with it. About coming back and leaving some of their worst to enslave us, to farm for *them*. We need to smash them first. Chase them into their rotting holes and exterminate them. But they're working together now — they've unified. They're armed and they're organized. We're afraid they're too strong for us. But *you* – you have ways, you witches. We ask that you use them. Come with us as we invade that sewer – fight alongside us. *Use your powers!*"

More wretched murmuring from the witches. Pitch exchanged an anguished look with the three other farmers, then spread his arms wide in supplication. "Don't you see, this is not just about us? We *all* have to fight back to survive! They'll come for you next, with your herbs and your skills and your weaving. You won't be safe, not even up here on your mountain top. They'll come for anyone who has anything they want."

Wekka walked slowly forward. "It would be madness to follow the raiding party back into the old city," she said. "We'd be surrounded and destroyed."

"But you have *ways*—" Pitch insisted.

Vild raised her hand. "Pitch, we *do* have powers," she said. "We know about healing, we have subtle senses that help us. But we don't have the kind of powers people are afraid that we do – that you *hope* we do. We can't smite with a look, we can't call up fire and lightning."

Pitch and his men stared at the ground, shuffling their feet.

"We'll stand by you, farmers," said Wekka, firmly. "We have no choice. We'll help protect your lands – my warriors with their blackbows are superb. But our numbers are small compared to the hordes in the old city."

Silence, broken only by an undercurrent of fearful whispering of witch to witch, and the downcast muttering of the farmers.

Then a loud, insistent hammering broke through, the hammering of a fist on wood.

"Let me out!" Arc shouted. "I demand a parley!"

CHAPTER THIRTY-THREE

Wekka looked across to Vild, eyebrows raised. Vild nodded firmly, the beginnings of a smile on her lips.

"Break three of the bars!" Wekka ordered. "Enough for the prisoner to scrape through. Keep your arrows trained on him. If he makes one bad move – shoot him."

Kita stood rooted to the ground, mouth dry. She was aware that Vild was now standing next to her, murmuring, "I told you we weren't all sweetness and light."

"What's going to happen?" croaked Kita.

"Wait and see."

A great cracking and smashing followed, as the warrior witches broke down three of the bars. Then Arc stepped blinking into the arena, with two oozing arrows trained on his face by his guards.

"Speak, sheepman!" ordered Wekka.

"Speak," he echoed. "*Speak*. I've had my mind turned inside out and back again these past few days, and now you want me to speak with death dripping in front of me. Lower those arrows, then I'll speak."

The toxic arrows drew closer. "*Speak!*" roared Wekka.

And suddenly it was as if Kita's head was filled with hot, white light and lightning was ripping its way out of her mouth. "*Stop threatening him!*" she yelled. "You agreed to parley – take those arrows from his face! Or you're lost – debased – you're on a level with them, the city scum and the marauders and the horsemen. You're already defeated!"

There was stunned silence. Then Vild whispered, "Witch rage. *Well done!*" And a look passed between her and Wekka, who raised her arm, and the arrows dropped. Arc gazed at Kita open mouthed, trying and absolutely failing to keep a look of awed admiration from his face. Then he drew himself up, and spoke. "I've been in the old city. Wekka's right about keeping away from it. It's infested with human vermin who know every twist and turn and tunnel of the place. They'd pick us off, one by one. We'd be annihilated."

"So what do you suggest, sheepman?" said Pitch.

"We must all stand together," Arc said, and he looked straight at Kita, acknowledging her, acknowledging he was speaking her words. "The sheepmen, the horsemen, the farmers, the witches too. If we stand together, we survive."

A sizzle and hum of excitement answered his words.

"We need to trap them," he went on. "Wait until their metal army makes a second invasion on the farmers – then surround them. Meet them in open battle on the farmlands. Cut off their retreat to the rotting city.

Destroy them. Use our separate skills and strengths, and fight together. And survive."

He looked over at Wekka, whose eyes hadn't left him, and who now nodded forcefully, telling him to continue. "My people were waiting for me to report back," he said, "until my men reported me seized by the witches. Well, I'll report back. I'll tell them what I've learnt about the old city preparing its arsenal, about the attack on the farmers, about the ways of the witches. They may decide I'm mad and slit my throat. Or they may just listen to me. And call the horsemen to a council of war."

There was a tense silence, the witches waiting for Wekka to respond. But Pitch spoke first. "I'll go with you, sheepman!" he cried. "I'll tell them our side. Of the need for haste. And provide horses for our trip."

"And I'll go too!" called a musical voice from the back of the crowd. The crowd parted, to let the pretty, curvy horseman's bride through.

"Too dangerous, Lilly!" a witch wailed. "The horsemen will seize you back again."

"But don't you see, it's perfect," Lilly answered, passionately, looking around at everyone. "Who better than me to crack the horsemen's minds open, show them how wrong they were about the witches, and help make the union?"

"It's risky," said Vild. "It could backfire. But I salute your courage, Lilly. Are you really sure you're prepared to undertake this? It cost you so much to get here."

"Yes, and I've learned so much here, I've *grown* so much here!" cried Lilly, gripping her hands together. "Anything I can do to protect Witch Crag – to keep it safe – I'll do it. Anything."

Kita looked at Lilly, stunned. Then she looked at Vild, who was looking straight back at her. "What fine, courageous young women we have among us," she said, smiling. "Thank you, Lilly. Thank you indeed. I'll contact our two witchmen at the horsemen fort. Tonight they'll dream that the change they're working for is about to lurch violently towards them. They'll be waiting, ready, for something to happen. And if Arc succeeds in convincing his people, and a council of war is called, they'll make sure they're among the horsemen who come to it. To help make the union, alongside Lilly."

"One of the witches must go too," said Wekka.

"Not you, dearling," said Nada. "They're not quite ready for you yet."

"No," agreed Wekka, grinning. "A young male warrior. To shake their prejudices about us hags. To show that witches have children too."

"I volunteer!" cried a voice. A tall, elegant boy with brown hair to his shoulders strode forward.

"Accepted," said Wekka. "Thank you, Flay." Then she looked around at everyone and said, "So! A desperate, bold plan. But are the witches agreed? Do we support this venture?"

There was a rustle of excited discussion, of fearful consideration, then one by one the witches called out, "Agreed! *Agreed!*"

Then Arc spoke up again. "A fifth member." He turned, and pointed steadily at Kita. "*She* must come."

Kita took in a huge breath. Then she exhaled, and looked steadily back at him. "Agreed," she said.

"You don't have to go," whispered Quainy, some time later, as they all huddled round the great oval fire pit, waiting for dinner. "I don't know why he's trying to make you go. Well, I do – but it won't do. Putting you in danger just so he can get his hands on you. Don't trust him, Kita. *Please.*"

It had been arranged that the five would descend the steep north face of the crag at first light, then ride to the sheepman hill fort. If all went well, they would be there by the second day. Pitch's three men had already left, to arrange mounts and provisions to be ready at the foot of the crag.

"Quainy, dearling – you don't understand," said Kita, softly. "Which isn't surprising, because I'm not sure I do. But it's got nothing to do with trusting Arc – it's gone far beyond that. If the tribes don't unite against the invasion of the old city, one after the other we'll be enslaved, destroyed. And like Lilly, I think I can be of use, I think I can help bring the union about."

"I wish Lilly wouldn't go, either. I'm scared for her."

"Oh, Quainy," Kita sighed.

She couldn't explain that when Arc had pointed at her, she'd recognized the "what was to come" that Vild had spoken of. She'd seen that her purpose was to come to Witch Crag – then leave it again.

And now Quainy was frowning, wailing, "Kita, we've only just *got* here! And it was such a terrible journey – and now you want to put yourself in danger again—"

"We're *all* in danger!"

"I know, I know," persisted Quainy. "But why d'you always have to be in the front line?"

Kita smiled, and took hold of her old friend's hand. The jealousy she'd felt, the anger – it had evaporated. But Vild was right. They could never go back to their old closeness, to how it used to be. She'd moved beyond it, somehow.

On the opposite side of the fire, Arc was hunkered down next to Wekka. The warrior witch kept her eyes trained on him; she was still coiled, untrusting, ready to strike. But she was also speaking to him.

Pitch was with another group of witches, talking too much, waving his hands nervously. Lilly and Flay sat beside each other some way away, conversing in low voices.

"I don't know what they're all talking about," muttered Kita. "There's nothing we can plan for. None of us has any idea what to expect."

*

The next morning, just as dawn was breaking, Vild woke Kita and led her across the compound to the snail-shell bathhouse. "Part of the preparation," she whispered. "For your quest."

Lilly had just had her bath when they arrived; she was sitting, white faced, in the outer ring. She tried and failed to smile at Kita as she came in; a young witch was plaiting her mane of glorious chestnut hair, and trying to encourage her to eat one of the mushroom pasties that were laid out on a tray.

"New garments for all of you," murmured Vild, indicating the line of clothes hanging on pegs on the curved wall. They were the kind the warrior witches wore – elemental colours, the cut streamlined and strong. "Except for Arc. He insisted he'd stick to his footsoldier gear. He's probably right. The sheepmen need to recognize him. Ah well – we tried to clean it up for him."

Soon, Kita was submerging herself in the hot silky water of the bath, her hair floating out behind her. A tangy, invigorating smell flooded her senses; it reminded her of pine forests and sharp, frosty mornings. Vild had told her special herbs and essences had been added to the water. She washed carefully, surrendering herself to the ritual of cleansing, allowing her mind to empty. Then she heard Arc's voice, from outside. "All right, if you insist we have this *bath*, Pitch and I can sluice off together. We need to hurry. It's almost light."

Immediately, she clambered out from the pool, dried herself, and pulled on the dark red tunic and trousers that Vild had chosen for her. Soft and pliable, they fitted snugly. Then she combed back her hair with her fingers, and went out into the outer ring.

Arc looked straight at her, and she met his look. "Ready," she said.

He responded by pulling his shirt off, still staring at her. She laughed, refusing to let her eyes drop below his.

Pitch grinned, then swaggered into the bathhouse, yanking off his worn clothes as he went. Arc followed.

"*Whoooo*," breathed the young witch, tying a green thread round the bottom of Lilly's plait. "I wouldn't mind spying on those two as they get in the water."

Kita laughed again, and picked up a pasty from the tray. She was hungry.

Chapter Thirty-Four

It had been agreed that only Wekka and two other warriors would escort the five down to the base of the crag, where their horses would be waiting, but a murmuring crowd of witches was gathered at the graceful willow gates, waiting to see them off. Raff and Quainy were there, too, holding hands. As soon as they saw Kita they came over to her, and Quainy threw her arms round her. "It's not too late to say no, Kita," she whispered.

"Quainy – *please* don't."

"Sorry. Sorry. Just – it's been so weird between us! I feel like I found Raff – but lost you! And I hoped that now we're here, and that awful journey's over – I hoped we might be able to spend some time together. The three of us. Didn't we, Raff?"

"Yes," said Raff, simply. "We miss you, mad one."

Kita took in a breath. "I miss you too. I really do. But things have changed – everything's changed. And I have to do this."

"I know," said Raff. "I'm beginning to see that."

"You seemed. . ." croaked Quainy, "you seemed so angry with us."

"I was," said Kita. "I'm sorry."

"No, *we're* sorry—" Quainy broke off. Arc had suddenly appeared beside them.

"The other two runaways," he said. "I thought I saw you in the distance."

"Hello, Arc," said Raff. "We both made it to Witch Crag, then."

"Yes. Funny, eh? Was it you who stole Drell's knife? Before you scarpered?"

"Yes," said Raff, squaring up to him.

"Make good use of it, did you?"

"No. You and your footsoldiers didn't get close enough."

"*Hah*," snorted Arc.

"And, apart from that, I just used it to skin a few rabbits. Waste of time nicking it, really."

"So give it to Kita now. She might make better use of it."

"I would do, but Geegaw – the seer from the old city the witches keep dreaming of? – he relieved me of it."

Arc said nothing, just stared witheringly at Raff, as though losing the knife was the ultimate proof of his uselessness. Raff stared unblinkingly back.

Then Vild pushed between them. "Kita," she said, "I have something for you. The boys have their own weapons. This is for you." She held out a wide leather belt, with a holster holding a dagger attached to it. The belt had the shapes of oak leaves burnt into it. Vild buckled it solemnly round Kita's hips; Nada was doing the same to Lilly, nearby. Then they kissed and hugged them. Flay too was kissed and hugged, but Arc and Pitch hung back, Arc scowling, Pitch smiling nervously, neither wanting to be touched.

"Five of you," said Vild, softly. "Five is a good number – from the ancient symbol of the pentangle."

"Time to go," said Arc.

Three little girls darted from the crowd and threw up fistfuls of tiny leaves that swirled in a magical green and yellow cloud, then settled on the hair of the travellers. As they walked through the gates, the witches started a low ululation, mournful and respectful.

"Is that a spell?" muttered Pitch.

"Yes," said Vild. "They're sending you off with their love and support. And great hope."

Wekka led the way down the sheer north face of the crag, leaping from rock to rock, the five working hard to keep up with her and put their feet where hers had been. The two other warrior witches brought up the rear, eyes sharp, scanning for danger. There was no breath for conversation. Lilly found the steep descent frightening and hard going, but Flay kept beside her, helping and encouraging her. Halfway down, Pitch stumbled badly, but Arc threw out a hand and caught him before he fell. Kita, deft and athletic, focused hard. She was determined not to need help.

As they reached the base of the crag, they heard a low whistle. Then a shock-headed boy appeared from behind a group of low trees, leading a large black horse.

The three witches bowed to everyone, and melted back in to the crag mist.

"Well done, Skipper!" said Pitch.

"We only just got here," said Skipper, as two boys and four more horses appeared behind him. "Didn't want to be late for you – but didn't want to give any wandering thugs the chance to take a pop at us neither. Here's yours," he added, holding out the reins.

Pitch took them and the horse neighed happily, then nuzzled the side of his head. "Hello, boy," murmured Pitch, patting him. "You may not look so happy when you know what I've got planned for you."

"These are for the men," Skipper said, indicating two more mounts, "and these for the girls." The third boy walked forward two piebald horses with charming fringes of hair round their hooves.

"Oh, what beauties!" cried Lilly, her fear evaporating. "Can I ride this one?" She took hold of the reins of the larger horse. Then – as though it was all part of the same movement – she sprang up on to its back. "Bliss!" she cried.

Kita had never ridden before. But something in her responded to the fluid way Lilly had mounted. She took hold of her horse's reins, and looked up at it. It was the nearest she'd ever been to a horse. She suddenly remembered Raff's beautiful sculpture in the old city, and what he and Quainy had said to her before she'd set off down the crag, and she felt a wrench of loss and grief. *All that's over*, she told herself, fiercely. *What's to come is all that matters now.* Then she jumped, and landed, inelegantly and too hard, on the beast's back. It lurched, and bucked, but she stayed on, grinning in triumph and determination.

"Oh, well done, sheep girl!" said Lilly. "You're a natural! Ride beside me, and I'll give you some tips as we go."

Flay had his arm round his horse's neck, pulling its head down to his, whispering into its ear, pulling tenderly on its mane. Arc glared at him, then grabbed the reins of his own horse. Spooked, it reared up, neighing, but Arc yanked it down again.

"*Gently!*" scolded Lilly. "That's no way to treat a horse!" She trotted over to them, and put her hand on the horse's neck. "*Steady*, sweetheart," she soothed. "Steady. Arc, give me the reins and I'll help you get up."

Kita could tell Arc was dying to tell Lilly to clear off, but knew he needed her help. He chucked the reins at her and, while she steadied the horse, he clambered on. Meanwhile, Flay had managed to spring up on his own.

"Right then," said Pitch, mounting effortlessly, "looks like we're all set."

"There's good provisions in these bags," said Skipper, handing a couple of crude sacks tied together by rope up to Pitch. "Water and nutty bread, and as many carrots as those thieving bastards left us."

"Thanks, Skipper," said Pitch, slinging them over his horse's back. "You've done us proud."

There was a chorus of agreement from the others – even Arc gruffly agreed. Then Pitch said, "Right. We'll go slow at first while you three learners get the hang of it. Just focus on staying on – your horses will follow mine."

"Let me ride beside you!" cried Lilly, eagerly. (It was quite astounding, thought Kita, how her earlier terror had given way to joy, just because of the horse.) "I think I know the direction of the hill fort from here."

"Very well," said Pitch.

And the five started to trot forward.

"I've made friends with my horse," said Flay, in his smoky, subtle voice, as he drew alongside Arc. "We trust each other now. I know he'll take care of me."

Arc's mouth twitched; he didn't reply.

They rode for an hour along tracks and across spaces in the forest, Lilly taking the lead more often than Pitch.

"I hope to get most of the way through the forest by nightfall," said Pitch. "We can camp and then make our way on to the wastelands and then the sheep grasslands the next day. We need to arrive in daylight, I think."

"No question," said Arc. "If we want the gates to open for us."

Kita slewed her eyes sideways to look at him. She'd relaxed into the rhythm of the horse, and was now enjoying riding, but Arc still seemed very uncomfortable. He held the reins too short and tight; he gripped too hard with his legs.

"Arc, *relax*," she called out. "Your horse knows what he's doing – you don't have to control him."

"He tried to throw me off a while back," Arc grumbled.

"That's because you keep trying to bully him. He's not a *sheep*!"

There was a silence, then Arc said, "You're very keen to look after me, tree rat. Saving me from the witches' arrows. And now this."

Kita could feel herself colouring up. "That's because I know this work won't succeed without you," she said. "And I want it to succeed." Then she cantered off to join Lilly.

"Isn't this wonderful?" said Lilly. "Riding one of these lovely noble beasties again – it's the only thing I missed on the crag. One of the few privileges horsewomen get – is to *ride*! All very contained and controlled, just to exercise the horses, but I loved it. Then in the last months, my horrible husband-to-be would take me riding. I'd ignore him totally and focus on my horse. *Fabulous!*"

Almost two hours later, Pitch called for everyone to stop. "There's a stream over there," he called.

"You have water in those sacks," said Arc.

"The stream," explained Pitch, slowly, as if to an idiot, "is for the *horses*."

Arc glowered, and reined in his mount.

"Lord, but the sheepman's grim," Lilly murmured to Kita, as they stood watching their thirsty horses drink. "Are all of them that grim?" She imitated Arc's frown, which looked hilarious on her pretty face.

"Most of them," giggled Kita. "Although Arc is particularly skilled at it."

"Don't they ever have *fun*?"

"Yes, but even their idea of fun is grim. Pushing people's faces into the mud, that kind of thing."

"*Adorable*. Ah well. When all this is over you can go back to Witch Crag, can't you? And maybe, if the revolution succeeds, give the horsemen's fort a try, too."

"You really see it as a revolution?"

"Yes, I do. Most of the young people and nearly all of the women – they're ready to rise up. If we get through this war with the city, the horsemen won't be allowed to go back to their old ways."

"I wish I could say the same about the sheepmen," mourned Kita. "Change must come to them, it *must*. I just wish I could see – how it could happen."

"How *what* could happen?" demanded Arc, walking over to them – then he broke off, and thrust a warning finger at his mouth.

Some distance away from them, a twig had cracked. They listened, barely breathing. A rustling noise – then a branch snapping.

Pitch and Flay had become aware of the danger, and were creeping noiselessly over to join them.

"Get ready!" muttered Arc.

Chapter Thirty-Five

Two thickset men burst through the undergrowth, and stood facing the five. They each had an ugly, jagged knife in their right hands – they crouched like beasts about to pounce. "We want your horses," one of them growled. "That's all. Hand 'em over and you can live."

"No," said Arc.

The smaller of the two laughed nastily. "Call the rest," he snarled.

"You going soft, mucker?" demanded the other. "They're kids. And *girls*. We can deal with them. Get the horses."

The smaller man spat on the ground. Then he advanced towards the horses, now looking up from the stream, spooked by the appearance of strangers.

Arc drew his knife. "Don't be silly, boy," said the man.

"Take one step closer to those horses, and it'll be your last," said Arc.

"*Oh*. Fighting talk. Come *on*, then!"

Arc and the robber faced each other, eyes locked. Then the robber started to smile. "Bravo, laddie. Now give in."

And Arc suddenly sprang forward, slashing the man's right arm. A great spray of blood spurted over the leaves and branches, the jagged knife fell to the ground, the man screamed and collapsed on top of it. The other robber, roaring, launched himself at Arc but buckled at the knees before he reached him with Pitch's knife in his neck.

Arc stooped, and slit both robbers' throats, fast and efficient.

Like sheep, thought Kita watching, frozen in horror.

The horses were neighing, panicking, getting ready to bolt. Lilly raced to them, seizing their reins, calling out words to calm them.

Pitch retrieved his knife. "More coming!" breathed Arc. "Get *ready*!"

Kita just had time to draw her dagger and stand next to Pitch when three more men burst through the trees. On the edge of her vision she saw Flay race to a tree and scramble up it.

Then five more men were upon them. She had no idea how to fight. She'd never fought before. But Arc threw himself forward and killed two men in swift succession, Pitch fighting beside him, slaughtering two more, and then there was only one robber left standing, and Arc had him in his sights.

But yet more men were crashing through the trees. A huge man launched himself at Pitch, grappling with him, overcoming him. Kita sprang, landing on the robber's back, and slashed at an artery in his neck. Pitch dodged away before the robber collapsed like a giant tree being felled.

More men, more men. The ground seemed to be covered with bodies, more than they'd killed. Something kept whistling past her head. A man ran at her – she thrust her dagger upwards into his guts, and as he fell sideways, she saw that Arc had stabbed him from behind, and their eyes locked as his body slumped.

Then there was an unearthly vacuum of silence. Kita, heart thundering, looked around, dazed, disbelieving. Bodies everywhere – and four right in front of Lilly and the horses, with black arrows sticking out of them.

Arc nodded to Pitch, and they began gathering up the knives of the fallen, piling them into the sacks hanging each side of Pitch's horse. Then they heard shouting, at a distance. Angry, bellowed shouting.

"There's more of them!" barked Arc. "Get your horses. *Ride!*"

Pitch led the way on his horse, crashing through the undergrowth, swerving round tree trunks. Arc was the last. They rode on for what seemed like an age at breakneck speed, then Pitch slowed down, and after a while steered his horse between close-growing trees, to where the forest was denser and the canopy provided good shelter. "Stop here?" he called over his shoulder.

"Please!" sobbed Lilly.

They all dismounted. Pitch pulled open the two sacks and drew out water, lumpy bread and great fistfuls of carrots, most of which he threw to the ground so the horses could snaffle them.

Then they all sank down in a tight ring, knees almost touching, and drank. Lilly couldn't stop shivering; Flay put his arm round her, and rocked her gently.

And Kita heard herself saying, "Arc, you were *amazing*."

"He was," said Pitch. "A proper leader."

"A death machine," added Lilly, through chattering teeth.

"You led us," said Flay, "with such courage and resolve. None of the witches could have done as much."

Arc stared at them all as though he couldn't quite believe what he was hearing. "Thanks," he said gruffly. "You were at one with me – all I could hope. Although –" he laughed – "when I saw Flay shinning up that tree, I thought he was getting himself out of harm's way!"

"And then his arrows started flying," said Lilly. "Four men came at me. I watched them all die." She nestled into Flay's neck.

"Yes," said Kita. "Flay, you must show me how to use a witch's blackbow. I want to learn."

"Of course," said Flay. "My pleasure."

"If we can fight a big battle like we fought back then," said Pitch, "Arc taking the lead, everyone backing him up—"

"I didn't do anything," said Lilly, mournfully.

"You kept hold of the horses!" said Arc, warmly. "No point fighting to the death over them if they'd bolted!"

"I did think . . . I did wonder if we shouldn't just have handed the horses over," Flay murmured.

"No," said Lilly, firmly. "My tribe was always up against thieves. They kill you whether you hand your horses over or not. You just make it easier for them if you think you've made a bargain to stay alive."

There was a collective sigh around the group, as if everyone was finally letting go of the adrenaline and fear, and understanding that they were safe now. They munched on the bread, which was filled with seeds and nuts and was very satisfying, and crunched the carrots.

"It's getting darker," said Pitch. "Shall we camp for the night?"

"Yes, let's," said Lilly. "I'm shattered."

Soon, the horses were tethered and settled, and everyone was curling up on the ground. It was warm, and companionable, and they could rest while they waited for sleep to come.

Kita found herself lying between Lilly and Arc. *There's a bond between the five of us now*, she thought, *a chain connecting us. And Pitch is right, if all the tribes can act together like that, each using their own strengths. . .* She had a sudden, violent flashback of her first kill, slashing the robber's neck, and shuddered violently. A hand gripped her arm; she turned towards Arc.

"It's OK," he murmured, "it's OK. It's the shock."

"I can't stop seeing blood."

"I know. It will fade. We had to do it, or they'd have killed us. You were great, Kita. You saved Pitch's life, jumping on that giant's back."

"And you saved mine."

"No. I think you'd stuck him already."

Their faces were very close. She could smell sweet bread on his breath, and the sharp, iron smell of drying blood. They were all of them covered in blood. She looked at his mouth; remembered kissing it that night before she'd escaped from the hill fort.

Lifetimes ago.

Or maybe seconds ago, it was so vivid still. She whispered "goodnight" and rolled over towards Lilly.

Arc was awake before any of them the next day, standing some distance away, looking into the forest. "All right, mate?" called Pitch. "Want some breakfast?"

Arc didn't answer.

"Leave him," murmured Flay. "He's going to have to make the speech of his life today. On his words depend our lives — and the future of our tribes."

"Kita, you know the headman," whispered Lilly. "Will he listen to Arc, d'you think?"

"I don't know," said Kita. "I honestly don't know."

Flay took hold of her arm, led her apart a little. "When we reach the fort, use your powers, Kita. The ones I heard you used to stop wild dogs attacking. And I'll use mine, though they're frail in comparison. We must both focus on the headman while Arc speaks, and make him open his mind to Arc's words."

"I will," promised Kita, although she was full of doubt that the headman could be influenced by her or by anyone.

Except perhaps Arc. All her hopes were on him.

Soon, they were mounting their horses and riding through the forest. After an hour of painstakingly making their way round tree trunks and under branches, the forest started to thin. Then they were cantering out on to the bleak wasteland, with its scrubby bushes and giant hogweed. Pitch quickened his pace; the others followed, and before long they were crossing through more trees and wading the defensive ditch on to the sheepmen's vast, upward-sloping grasslands. It was still too early in the spring for the sheep to be out grazing, and the plains were deserted. In the distance, the hill fort loured, the great gates gleamed in the morning sun.

They drew to a halt.

"All right, this is it," said Arc, his eyes fixed on the gates, his hands on the reins rigid with tension. "We'll ride straight for it. The headman will parley with us over the walls. Whatever I say, trust me. I need to get us all inside the fort and then I need to get the headman on his own. So he can make the great leap he's going to have to make – without the need to keep face in front of his people."

"Good luck, friend," said Pitch. "We're with you."

"And when it's your time to speak," Arc went on, "just tell it straight. Say who you are, what you are, what brought you here. There's to be no trickery in all this, except maybe in the beginning, to get inside the fort. We show our union, show it in its essence – it's the only chance we have to convince the headman."

Kita turned to look at Arc, moved by the words he'd used. The great leap he was talking about the headman making – he'd made it himself.

Then Lilly broke the silence. "We can do it!" she cried. "We're the pentangle!" And she kicked her horse forward, and the five of them spaced out and galloped up the grasslands towards the great hill-fort gates.

CHAPTER THIRTY-SIX

The hill fort grew closer and closer, and soon the five were reining their horses up outside. Arc threw his head back. "Open the gates!" he roared. "It's Arc – I'm back. *Open the gates!*"

Kita heard shouting from behind the walls; orders, and exclamations. Then the parley ladder was thrown against the gate, and after a few moments, the headman appeared at the top of it. Just as he had done, she thought anxiously, when Arc had hauled poor Finchy out of the forest, and the headman had ordered her slit.

The headman gazed down long and hard at Arc. "We thought you were dead, boy!" he shouted. "Boiled and eaten by the hags!"

"No, as you see," Arc replied.

"Who have you got with you?"

"One missing horseman bride, and Kita, brought back again," Arc said. "And two from the farmers' tribe, who have grave news. News you must hear, sir! *Open the gates!*"

Flay's horse shifted in place; Kita remembered what

Flay had said to her, and focused her gaze up at the headman's heavy-jawed face. *Trust us*, she chanted, silently, willing him to hear her. *Open the gates.*

"The last your men see of you is being dragged off by witches," retorted the headman. "What's to stop me believing you're part of some new necromancy?"

"The evidence of your eyes, sir," Arc replied. "And of your good sense. I'm the same. Please – *hear me*."

The headman glared down at them, silently. Then he disappeared; then the ladder disappeared. The great gates swung slowly open, and eight footsoldiers jogged out, knives drawn. They surrounded the five, ordered them to dismount, relieved them of their weapons, and seized the horses' reins. And for a few stark seconds, Kita was face to face with Drell, and her blood seemed to freeze. *He'd slit me, too*, she thought, *if he was ordered to*. Then the footsoldiers ushered them inside the gates, which rumbled shut again.

"So," said the headman, walking towards them. "The horsemen will be glad to get their bride back again. What of the other bride though? And Quainy? She was good trade for us – a bad loss."

He suddenly rounded on Kita, raising his fist. "A worse loss than you, you treacherous bitch!" Before Kita had time even to duck, Arc threw himself in between them and caught the blow on his shoulder.

"She's no traitor!" he cried. "It's because of her that we stand a chance of avoiding mass slaughter. Headman,

271

you trusted me before. *Trust me now.* Talk to me alone. Or with guards to hold knives at my throat if you must. But you need to hear me. Calmly and wisely, as a headman should."

There was a heart-stopping pause, everything hanging in the balance. Then the headman, still scowling, growled, "Very well. Follow me, and we'll speak. No – no guards. I can deal with that *boy* if I need to. But guard those four close."

Then he turned on his heel and stalked off to the headman's hut, Arc following behind.

Kita followed Arc with her eyes, willing him strength and success. As soon as he was out of sight, she subsided on to the ground, Lilly next to her.

"Stand up!" barked one of the footsoldiers.

"Oh, shut up, Bray," she said, tiredly. "We want to rest. And we could do with some water, please."

Bray looked for a moment as if he might grab her and stand her upright, then he jerked his head at one of the youngest footsoldiers, and ordered, "Water!"

This wasn't like Witch Crag, where by now a small, curious crowd would have gathered round the newcomers, staring and asking questions. A few sheep people hurried by on various errands and glanced over, burning with curiosity, but no one dared approach.

"So," said Bray, in an attempt to regain control. "Farmers, ay?"

"S'right," said Pitch, cheerfully.

Bray peered suspiciously at Flay. "You don't look like a farmer. Your hands are too soft."

"I'm a farmer of soft fruit," said Flay, as the others laughed.

"They won't send me straight back, will they?" whispered Lilly. "I nearly died when I heard Arc introduce me as the runaway bride."

"No, of course they won't," said Kita. "Arc – he meant what he said about us standing together." But she couldn't know this for sure, of course. She couldn't know anything. All she could do was wait, and trust, and hope. She stared unseeingly at the ground, twisting the thin chain bracelet that the witchman had given her, remembering the way Arc had protected her from the headman's blow.

Water was brought to the four of them; then some cold mutton, which Pitch and the girls devoured with relish but Flay was suspicious of. The time dragged by slowly, everyone focused on the headman's meeting with Arc.

Kita looked up and saw Drell striding towards them. He spoke briefly to Bray, and then he ordered Pitch and Flay on their feet and escorted them over to the headman's hut.

"Great," said Lilly. "Just the men."

"Yes, but the headman knows us," said Kita. "Knows who we are. Maybe he needs to satisfy himself with who those two are."

"Will Arc tell him Flay's a witchman?"

"If he sticks to the plan, he will. Flay's supposed to be the acceptable face of the witches, remember."

Lilly laughed, nervously. "Imagine if Wekka had come instead!"

"She'd've been good," joked Kita. "She'd've terrified everyone into unifying."

A few minutes later, Drell marched back again, unaccompanied. Kita took in a breath and called out, "Drell, did you hear anything? D'you know what's being said?"

Drell ignored her, jaw clenched.

"Drell, it's still me. It's Kita. You can talk to me, you know."

More silence.

"It must've been horrible when the witches seized Arc," Kita said, softly. "You must've felt really bad, just abandoning him."

"Is it good to have him back?'" asked Lilly.

Drell clenched his jaw harder, and stared into the distance.

A long time passed as the girls sat on the ground, waiting. The raw spring sun climbed in the sky. Then suddenly there was a commotion from the direction of the headman's hut, and the harsh clanging of iron against iron, which meant only two things – danger, or rain.

But the skies were dry.

Everyone began to surge towards the sound of the alarm.

"On your feet!" ordered Drell, then the footsoldiers ushered Kita and Lilly over, too.

The headman was standing on a rough bale of straw, elevated above the crowd gathering quickly all about him. Arc, Pitch and Flay were grouped behind him. Kita scanned their faces for news, but they looked impassive. Exhausted. The footsoldiers close to them had their knives sheathed now, but could still, she thought, be guarding them. She waited, heart drumming, for the headman to speak.

"Sheep people, we're entering dark, dangerous times," he said at last, loudly and grimly. "What I have heard today has convinced me that war will soon be upon us. From the direction we most feared – the old city."

Kita looked at Arc, and against the murmur of horror rising from the crowd, he looked straight back at her. Intent, unsmiling. *He's succeeded*, she thought. *Or at least, he's got halfway.*

"Reports from the footsoldiers a while back told us of the weapons those creatures are forging. And now Arc and Pitch, the farmer there, have described further signs of their intent to invade and plunder. But there's not enough of us to defeat the city alone."

"The horsemen!" came a swelling cry from the crowd. "Yes, the horsemen – call them to us, they'll join with us!"

"They will," answered the headman. "They must,

for their own survival. And the farmers. And one more tribe will join. The witches from the crag."

There was a kind of universal groan of terror then, of disgust and disbelief. As if they'd been told that crows and wild dogs would fight by their side.

"*Silence!*" roared the headman. "They are not as we thought. Their vile acts of desecration upon our dead were for their own protection. To keep us away from them. This man here −" he threw out an arm at Flay − "he is one of them."

The groaning rumbled louder, became threatening, and for a moment Kita thought they'd rush at Flay to tear him limb from limb, but the headman roared for silence a second time.

"*What of her?*" shrieked a woman, daringly, pointing at Kita. "Did she get to the hags? Is she bewitched?"

"No more than you are!" Kita retorted loudly. "I left this fort because I wanted to live freely. The witches are different, alien even, but they are not our enemies. Our enemies are *right now* making metal weapons and wagons to come at us, pick off the tribes one by one. We have no chance against them unless we all join together."

"In quieter times, I'd have killed her myself as a runaway," said the headman, nodding at Kita. "But these are not quiet times, and I say she is right. Now − these are my orders. At first light, three swift footsoldiers will run to the horseman's fort to give notice of a council of war to be held on our plains the morning after next. The farmer will return to his lands, with the same message; the witchman will take the news back to the crag. There are three horses spare. I need volunteers to go with the farmer and the witch as guards."

"I'll go with the farmer," cried a young footsoldier, stepping forward. "I've ridden with the horsemen – I can do it."

"Very well," said the headman.

"And me, sir," said another. "With the farmer."

The headman nodded, adding, "That leaves one horse to go to Witch Crag."

Silence. No one volunteered. Kita knew that no one would volunteer. "I'll go," she called out. "I'll keep Flay company, and watch his back."

"*I'll* go," countered Lilly, loudly. "I'm the better horsewoman."

"No," said the headman, grimly. "No females. Your place is here."

CHAPTER THIRTY-SEVEN

The rest of the day passed uneasily. Arc, Pitch, the headman and the leading footsoldiers were in constant military conference. The sheep people kept to their demanding routines; chores were carried out, food was cooked and served. Kita felt as though suspicious eyes raked her everywhere she went, and she kept to Flay and Lilly's company. No one asked them to work, so they huddled by the lifeless fire pit, and talked.

Lilly told them all about her flight from the horsemen fort – how the two witchmen, the infiltrators, had helped the brides believe that they could do more than just yearn to escape. "They'd find chances to talk with us," she murmured, "*listen* to us. I felt they were drawing out my courage, my resourcefulness, making me believe in myself. And then they revealed who they were, where they were from. We were terrified! But we still liked them, enormously – witchmen are made of very precious metal, Kita! So we just kind of *leapt*, and agreed to go. And after that it was all surprisingly easy. I stole the horse, one that knew me, and the witchmen unbarred the gates and barred them again once we'd gone. . ."

"It didn't cross the horsemen's minds that anyone would help you escape," said Kita. "They thought you were spirited away by sorcery."

"No, no spells, no hexes. But the witches knew to come and meet us. Remember, Flay?"

"I do," Flay said softly. "You looked like a centaur riding up to us, graceful, and strong."

"And *you* — we were so frightened when you all materialized out of the mist! Then we were blissed out!"

"I remember you laughing. As though you hadn't laughed for months."

"I hadn't!" giggled Lilly, and she turned to Kita. "We left our horse to make his way back. Witch Crag is no place for horses. It's the one fault I find with it. But Flay knows that the horseman fort accommodates *witches* very well. . ."

There was a pause. Kita looked from Lilly to Flay, at the way they smiled at each other, and thought: *They're going to be together. Maybe he'll move to the fort with her, and help free the horse people.* And she felt a stab of envy, and grief for her own loneliness.

"Kita," said Flay, kindly, as though he'd sensed her thoughts, "Lilly has to see to the horses now, she promised Pitch. And I promised to teach you the art of the blackbow. Do you know somewhere we can go?"

Kita nodded gratefully, and they made their way

to the back of the compound, behind the sheep pens, where he gave her an archery lesson.

She was a quick pupil, and shot the mark accurately three times out of five. No one came near them; the sheep people regarded the witch's blackbow as a thing of necromancy. But Kita loved its flexibility and strength. Flay explained that the arrows were lethal only at short range; they were tipped with poison for longer shots. He promised to bring another blackbow to the council, so that she could have one of her own.

Very early the next morning, the messengers set out. Three footsoldiers jogging to the horsemen's fort; three riders to the farmers' lands; and Flay cantering out on his own. Lilly was distraught about this but Flay assured her he'd be fine – he had a bond with his horse now, and was sure the swift beast would keep him from danger. And he was confident the warrior witches would come out to meet him halfway. "They'll know," he said. "They'll have sensed what is happening. And they'll be ready for this council. Expecting it."

The impending war hung over the hill fort like a lowering thundercloud. The headman ordered all weapons to be honed and sharpened – the haul of robbers' knives was a good addition to the arsenal. Kita and Lilly requested the return of their witch's daggers and belts and, with Arc's support, the headman granted this.

Arc began to put the footsoldiers through relentless training. The cooks baked hard bread and stockpiled it against a time when there would be no time to cook. The sheep were penned more securely. The footsoldiers' clothes were mended, with extra layers sewn in for protection. The hill fort was getting ready.

Kita kept expecting the headman to call her in for questioning, but the summons didn't come. She spent the two days before the council of war solely in the company of Lilly, and both of them were ostracized. They went into the food hut to eat, but no one came near them. They slept at one end of the girls' sleeping hut, avoided by all. Lilly didn't let it bother her. She spent time grooming the horse that had been left behind; she preened rather than cowered when the sheep people stared at her long chestnut hair and pretty face; she kept her head high and moved freely. But Kita was more subdued. She was on edge, waiting – knowing she had to be at the war council, but not sure what her role was to be. Anxious that the headman would try to stop her, and dreading what was to come. She saw Arc only from a distance, always surrounded and in the thick of things.

The night before the council, Arc came to find her. "The headman sent me," he said, simply. "You're to come with us tomorrow. We leave at first light."

Kita took in a long, shaky breath. "Good," she said. "I need to be there. Is Lilly coming too?"

"Yes. Stick by each other, Kita – protect each other. I'm afraid of what will happen when the horsemen see her."

"Me too. Arc, why didn't the headman call me? Talk to me himself?"

"He should have done. It's hard for him to let go of the old ways, I guess. He kept insisting women had nothing to do with war."

"Even though he's accepted the witches as allies?"

"Not deep down he hasn't. I persuaded him that you were the vital link between us and them, and in the end he gave in."

"You're not going to let *Drell* come to the council, are you?" Kita blurted out.

Arc looked at her steadily; the memory of the young witch dying was vividly between them. "No," he said. "But he's still one of the best footsoldiers we have, Kita. When he slit Finchy, he was following orders. It was me who was out of line."

There was a silence, the two of them looking at each other in the dusk. Then she said, "Well, I'm glad you were out of line."

He sighed, looked down, muttered, "I'm dreading tomorrow. The headman, he—"

"What?"

"I don't know. He took the decision to act on what we'd said, he took control, but now he's . . . withering. Flailing. It's like the ground's collapsing beneath him."

"Well, in a sense it is. *Reality's* giving way beneath him. And getting the sheep people to accept the witches as allies – that's more daunting than a battle!"

"And I think there's more to it. He ordered witches to be slit, killed them himself. How can he let himself admit now that they're just women, good women?"

"I don't know," muttered Kita.

A sudden wind wailed over the top of the wooden barricades, and Arc murmured, "Well, tree rat, we'd better get some sleep." That childish nickname seemed almost affectionate now. The wind wailed; the darkness gathered all about them. He drew a little closer to her; she could hear him breathing. For one wild moment, she thought he was going to reach out and touch her.

"Sleep well," she said, stepping back.

"You too, Kita," he said, and disappeared into the night.

Seventeen people left by the great gates of the hill fort at dawn the next day. The headman and five of the older fighters led the way; then came Arc and six of his elite footsoldiers; then Kita, Lilly, the matron of the infants' pens and the head cook.

It was a great surprise to everyone that the headman had ordered the two older women to attend. They were powerful and capable and full of good sense, but they were still women, and therefore usually left within the hill-fort walls.

It was clear they'd more than risen to the challenge, however. They strode forward, keeping pace, as the seventeen walked down the steep slope of the grasslands to set up the council space. An eerie, early-morning mist hovered over the grass, waiting to be dispersed by the rising sun. The headman walked forward into it, half disappearing, then he suddenly halted and held up his hand.

"Shapes!" he hissed. "Lots of them! Moving towards us!"

His words froze his followers. Everyone drew together, peering forward into the spectral whiteness. The shapes looked like an army of ghosts in the mist, coming slowly, steadily, towards them.

The sheep people began to retreat, stumbling backwards in panic. "*Hold!*" ordered the headman. Then he cried, "Arc – advance! Reconnoitre!"

Kita looked anxiously at Arc's face as he began to walk slowly forward. She could see fear there, mastered by determination.

Then she heard him cry, "*Pitch!* What, man? What's *happened*?"

Pitch staggered into view out of the clinging mist, leading his horse with three small hunched figures on it, followed by more of the farmers. Freed from the whiteness, they still looked like ghosts – bloodied, frail and exhausted. There were about fifty of them, men, women and children. The two footsoldiers who'd gone with Pitch came behind, leading their horses burdened with children.

Arc ran forward and seized Pitch's arm, supporting him. "I'm not hurt," Pitch croaked. "Look to the others."

The farmers were subsiding on to the grass all around, sobbing and groaning. "We got back too late," Pitch muttered. "We rode on to the outskirts of our farmlands and were met by this heartbreaking sight – what's left of my people, fleeing. The city had invaded again. Sooner than we feared – and worse than before." He heaved a shattered sigh. "Many more killed, many taken captive. To work the land as slaves, growing our produce for the city dwellers. They've left creatures with metal whips in charge. I led those who escaped here, to you – I didn't know what else to do."

"You did right!" said Arc, still gripping his arm. "And we'll get your farmlands back – we'll unite, and invade them!"

"You may not have time to invade," said Pitch, looking for the first time directly at Arc. "As we fled, we saw something new. They're clearing the great road, the one that leads from the old city, and passes not far from the wasteland beyond. Clearing it of broken wagons and scrub and fallen trees."

"To make easy passage for their infernal cars," breathed Arc.

"Yes. I fear it."

"So it's happening already. They're coming for us, now." Arc turned back to see the headman's reaction, but the headman was staring at the ground, as if overwhelmed by all that he'd heard.

Seven huge crows materialized out of the mist, circling hungrily. A dog howled in the distance; another answered it.

"It's the blood," said the matron. "They can smell it from here."

Startled, the headman looked up at her. "The blood," he echoed.

"We need to get the wounded back to the hill fort," she said, firmly, scooping up a young child and sitting him on her hip. "Get these little ones to safety before the crows come."

"Yes," said the headman. "Of course. Footsoldiers – move! Help as many as you can, then return as swiftly as you can. The horsemen will be here soon for the council of war."

"Which is now of even greater urgency," said Arc, grimly.

"Yes," said the headman. "Arc, you wait with me. The horsemen must be greeted by their hosts or they may turn back."

"And I'll wait too," said Pitch, shakily. "I represent the farmers."

The matron took complete control. Calmly, efficiently, she divided the wounded among the footsoldiers, gave two sobbing babies each to Kita, Lilly and the head cook, and led the whole cavalcade back up the grassy slope to the great gates, yelling for them to be opened as she went.

The sheep people gathered around the incomers. They were anxious, muttering, demanding to know why so many needy strangers had been brought into the fort.

The matron drew herself up tall. "These people are our allies now," she announced. "Look at them – they're the same as you and me. Decent people trying to scratch a living in the soil, and they've been reduced to this by the scum from the city. *Now.* We all have work to do. See to the wounded. There's some young men who just need a patch and a stitch, and they'll be fit to attend the council. Food and drink for all. Then I want two of the sleeping huts converted to hospitals. We're going to need them."

The well-drilled sheep people immediately began to carry out her orders. The footsoldiers who'd helped bring the wounded up to the fort ran back to the council place; Kita, Lilly and the cook gave the babies they'd carried honey-smeared crusts to suck on, and stowed them safely in the infants' pens. Then they too hurried back to the gates.

"We must go!" Kita called out to the matron. "The headman wants us at the council."

She was half expecting to be ignored, as she had been

ever since her return to the hill fort. But the matron hurried over, took hold of her hand, and said earnestly, "Thank you for your help, Kita. Not just in this – in everything."

"Of . . . of course," stammered Kita, taken aback.

"Say your piece in the council. Make sure you do. And when the witches come, send some of their best healers up to us, h'n?"

Kita's mouth dropped open. "You *trust* them?" she breathed.

"I have to trust them," said the matron. "We all do, now." Then she headed over quickly to a young boy who'd started wailing in pain.

CHAPTER THIRTY–EIGHT

Kita, Lilly and the cook got back to the council place just as eight horsemen thundered towards them across the plains.

"The witchmen!" breathed Lilly, pointing to two riders on the left flank of the group. "They've come! Oh, this is good for us. This means change!"

Kita wouldn't have known they were witchmen. They were a little slenderer than the other horsemen, perhaps, more elegant in the saddle, but essentially the same.

Now Lilly was pointing to the lead horseman, who had a great scar across his cheek and grey hair flying out behind him. "He was my intended," she said, grimacing. "Well, he'd just better not start, that's all."

"Welcome!" shouted the headman, as the horsemen wheeled in and dismounted.

"Well met," said the lead horseman. His eyes scanned over everyone gathered there – and settled on Lilly.

"Hello, Gath," she said, coolly.

He glared at her, then spat on the ground.

Here we go, thought Kita, nervously.

*

The preliminary discussions lasted without a break while the sun climbed high in the sky. Flay had been asked to delay the witches' arrival until midday, when they hoped to have reached a basic agreement; Kita, seated between Lilly and the head cook, thought sundown might have been more realistic.

First, the headman gave a dour description of the threat of invasion from the city. Then Arc spoke of it passionately; then Pitch, desperately. But Gath the lead horseman dominated the proceedings, endlessly challenging and questioning and growling his dissent, unconvinced by what he called "hearsay" and "panic mongering".

By late morning, he and his supporters not only flatly refused to accept the witches as allies, they refused to accept that there would be a war – or one that would involve the horsemen, anyway.

Then one of the witchmen stood up to be heard. "Horsemen," he said, "we're trying to tell ourselves that this war won't come to our homelands. But all the evidence suggests that it will. The farmers were invaded and enslaved. Now the road is being cleared. Do we wait until the hordes from the city have eaten our allies the sheepmen, and are on their way to eat us, before we fight back?"

There was a faint rumble of agreement from the younger horsemen. Gath got slowly to his feet. "Causing trouble again, Onga?" he demanded. "You like to do that, don't you? Getting the young bloods on your side, stirring them up with your sneaky talk of change, of *freedom* – and now of war. A war to protect the sheepmen. I say it's always been an unequal alliance with the sheepmen. Far better for them than for us. We horsemen can stand alone in the world."

"They're our allies, sir!" cried Onga.

"We can break that alliance! And refuse to join their sickening union with the hags! I'll never be convinced of the rightness of that." He glared round at everyone, and roared, "You've been bewitched, all of you – sheepmen, farmers – all of you! Infected by the hags!"

"There's no bewitchment!" Arc roared back.

"Oh, I say there is!" Gath yelled. Then he jerked his chin up, and cried, "Horsemen, we're going! I've heard enough!"

"You haven't heard me yet," said a cool, fluting voice. Lilly stood up. She took three slow, steady steps towards Gath, and stopped, just out of arm's reach, while the men of the council watched her, amazed.

"Look at me, Gath," she said. "Look at me and know me. How do I seem?"

He glared at her. "Don't talk to me, you treacherous bitch."

"Treacherous? So I wasn't bewitched? I went of my own free will?"

"Don't twist my words, *bitch*."

"Gath – *how do I seem?*"

Gath turned away from her, face thunderous. She followed him, saying, "I seem happy, don't I? More alive. If I'm infected, it's a good infection. Even with this war hanging over us, since I went to the witches I *seem* to have richer blood in my veins than the sour, thin stuff that barely pulsed when I was going to marry you."

Gath spun back to her, violently, fist raised. A young horseman sprang to his feet and got between them. "Gath, *sir* – this must come to a vote!" he gasped. "We eight were chosen to represent our tribe. You lead us, but you're not the only voice here. I've heard enough to know I – *I support the sheepmen!* We can't live in isolation in this world. Or break our word when we've sworn to support them, sir!"

"You *puppy*," snarled Gath. "We let you youngsters attend this fear-birthed council and this is how you repay us." He lowered his fist, but looked as though he might erupt into rage at any minute. "Very well," he gritted out finally, through clenched teeth. "All who agree with Jayke – stand beside him."

Onga and the other witchman went over to Jayke. Then another young horseman scrambled bravely up, and joined them.

"Four against four. That's the trouble with voting," sneered Gath. "It often decides nothing."

There was a tense pause, then a thickset man heaved himself to his feet, trudged over to Gath, and clapped his hand on his shoulder. "Gath, man," he said, "I've fought alongside you for years, I've stood up for you,

you know that."

"I do. I rely on your support," said Gath. "And reward you for it."

"I know you do. But I have to say what I think. And for a while now, I've been thinking you're wrong."

Gath shrugged the man's hand off violently. "You think I'm *wrong*?"

"Yes. Onga speaks a lot of sense – why don't you ever listen to him? Change is inevitable. Change must come if the young will it. We need to open out a bit."

"Well, you're a fool," snapped Gath. "And what's that got to do with this council of supposed war?"

"Because I stand with the young 'uns on that, too. This war is coming. We need allies. So it's five to three. And decided, all right?"

There was an electric silence, everyone staring at Gath, waiting for his anger to blast them. Kita felt the skin on the back of her neck prickle; she put her hand on her witch dagger, nervously. Then she turned and stared out towards the woodland that flanked the open plain.

"Yes, it's decided," Gath grated out, at last. "I can't go against the vote."

There was a muted rumble of relief, but no one dared make eye contact with Gath. He crackled with hostility. "So where are the hags, our *allies*?" he spat. "The sun's as high as it can go. Looks like they've let you down, headman."

"They won't do that," said the headman. "They're as

much at risk as the rest of us. As much in need of allies."

"Unless they've made new allies," said Gath. "With the city."

The headman didn't answer.

Kita was still staring at the woodland. "No," she said. "They're here."

Among the shadows in the trees was a strange, dark shifting. It was as though the shadows were growing blacker, denser, and beginning to move into the light of the plain.

"It's dogs!" said Gath, drawing his long knife. "A pack of 'em – get ready!"

Three great hounds erupted from the woods and loped out into the open. Then seven women and two men, all cloaked in dark red and green, materialized on the plain's edge, and began to walk slowly forward with the dogs.

Anyone who had still been sitting now got to his feet and faced the witches. It was a powerful, eerie sight, the great dogs keeping pace with the walkers, dark cloaks billowing around them.

"Sheathe your knife, Gath!" Arc rapped out.

"*No*," snarled Gath. "I don't trust 'em."

"They've got bows, and arrows," one of the young footsoldiers yelped. "They can shoot us."

"If the dogs don't get us first!" cried another. Panic was spreading among the men, and anger fed by the panic – they bunched together, muttering, threatening, and more of them drew their knives.

And all the time the dogs and the witches continued to walk towards the council, steadily, silently. They were close enough now for Kita to recognize Flay, and Wekka. She darted over to Arc. "This is going up in flames!" she hissed.

"He needs to *take control!*" Arc said, flinging a desperate glance at the headman. "Look at him, mouth open, hands slack—"

"He's scared. He thought he knew his world, and now – Arc, we need to *bridge* this somehow. *Come with me!*" And she started walking purposefully forward. Immediately, Arc was at her side, walking in step with her, then Lilly ran over to join them, then the two witchmen, all of them advancing steadily to welcome the witches.

The great dogs circled the two groups as they conjoined. "Well done, tree rat," breathed Arc. "Let's hope this will sheathe the knives."

Everyone swiftly exchanged greetings, Flay seizing Lilly's hand briefly, then Wekka asked, "Are the horsemen with us?"

"The young ones," said Onga, "but not Gath and his cronies. He's suspicious, very hostile. And he has strong support back at the fort."

"And the sheepmen have a problem too," said Arc. "Since our headman agreed to this council, it's as if he's – dazed. Broken."

"Then you must take over, Arc," said Wekka, gravely. "You must lead. And now – we must join the council."

CHAPTER THIRTY-NINE

Nobody at the council sat down again; everyone fanned out to form a large ring. The witches were flanked by the sheepmen and the farmers, and faced the horsemen, who had sheathed their knives, but still kept their hands on the hilts. The dogs, on the insistence of the horsemen, had been sent back to the woods.

Everyone waited for the headman to speak, but he stared at the witches as if struck dumb. Wekka turned to Arc and nodded, then she stepped into the centre space. Arc, scowling with determination, followed and stood beside her.

Kita, watching him, knew the risk he was taking, aligning with Wekka, and taking charge like this – the courage it cost him. She focused on his face, sending him energy, and saw that the witches were doing the same.

Arc bowed to the headman, then to Gath, and said, "Sirs, this is Wekka, the lady who captured me. Who, with her sisters, opened my eyes to the truth of the witches. And who then let me go so we could form this alliance to defeat our common enemy."

Wekka bowed solemnly to the headman and to Gath; neither gave a response. Then she turned to Pitch, bowed, and said, "It is a great grief to the witches that the farmers were attacked again."

"And enslaved," said Pitch, bitterly. "This council has come too late for us."

"No," said Arc. "Not too late. We will rout the city and win your lands and people back."

Gath folded his arms across his chest and snorted, loudly.

"Tell me," said Wekka, "who was there when the city invaded? Who saw them arrive?"

There was a silence, a scuffle, Pitch muttering to the lad standing next to him, pushing him forward into the ring. Kita recognized the shock-headed boy who'd brought the horses to the base of Witch Crag for the five of them to ride. He'd had his head shaved as a warrior now, though, and the three dark slashes cut into his scalp.

"This is Skipper," said Pitch. "He was leading the farmers from the carnage when I met up with them. He's a sound lad."

Skipper had a gash on his cheek, and his arm in a rough woollen sling. "I didn't want to leave," he muttered. "Abandon our people, and our lands. But the fight was lost."

Wekka took a step towards him. "You did the right thing, Skipper," she said, gently. Kita noticed that the witches were all now focused on him; she gazed at him too, trying to send him strength and warmth. "If you'd stayed, you'd be dead – all of you. Now, please tell us what you saw."

Skipper took in a long shaky breath, and began. "At the front, murderous warriors. Running in time, ranks of them, two hundred maybe. Great metal weapons with jagged ends. Then behind – the wagons. Lines and lines of them. Each drawn by four slaves. A sight to chill your soul."

A shiver went round the ring, as though everyone's worst fears had been realized.

"Did you see what occupied the wagons?" asked Wekka.

"No. Whatever was in there had no need to get out to fight. Their warriors outnumbered our riders almost four to one. They slaughtered us with their pikes, and grabbed the horses. While they were harnessing the poor beasts to the wagons, the rest of us ran for it. They sent a posse after us – some of us were cut down as we ran. Some turned to face them and died in the attempt." He paused, hung his head. "Sacrificing their lives to let the rest of us escape."

"Lift your head, Skipper," said Wekka, passionately. "You were as brave as the rest of them. You led your people to safety, and now you contribute to this council of war. You've given us a picture of our enemy."

"Yes, a pretty one," said Garth. "How many wagons, boy?"

"Fifty, maybe."

"So there's another two hundred men, drawing the wagons. Who can also fight. And perhaps four more men in each wagon? The numbers stack up. They're stacked against us."

"Numbers aren't everything," said Arc.

"No, but they certainly help. Especially if you fight as a unit. We don't even do that."

"No, but that could be our strength," said Arc, fervently. "In our differences – lie our *strengths*."

Gath turned to the headman. "This boy speaks for you, does he, sheepman?"

The headman shook his head, eyes lowered, and didn't answer.

"Our strengths," jeered Gath. "Let's look at that. What can you witches do? Apart from shoot arrows and heal with herbs? You brought dogs with you – can you call up huge packs of 'em to rout your enemies?"

"Those dogs you saw were trained," retorted Wekka, "domesticated. The wild dogs in these woods are just that – wild. We could scare them off, perhaps, but not call them to do our work."

Gath turned from her, rejecting her, and confronted Arc. "So," he said. "Together, we have fewer than half the fighting men the city has. And we can't know for sure that they sent everyone against the farmers. Tell me, laddie, where *are* our strengths exactly?"

But Arc was silent, staring fixedly at the ground. Kita

glared at Gath, loathing him, loathing his arrogance and undermining comments. As if he felt her look, he glanced up at her, and bared his teeth.

"You said you wanted to trap the city hordes," said Pitch, despairingly. "Wait until they made their second attack on our farmlands – then surround them, meet them in open battle, cut off their retreat to the city. It's too late for that now."

"No," said Arc. At last, he lifted his head, and looked round at everyone, intently. "No, the plan's still good. It's just changed its place. Headman – can I lay it out?" The headman nodded, bleakly, and Arc continued. "For years now, we've hacked down the growth at the edge of the wasteland and the forest, where it encroaches on these plains. We did it again a few weeks back. There's a ditch full of brush and dead wood all around the edge. Wekka – can you witches ignite it? All at once?"

"Nothing easier," said Wekka. "Fellfurze is a plant that explodes into fire when it's lit. We'd strew it all along the ditch, in among the waste wood. Then, when the time comes, shoot flaming arrows simultaneously. You'd have an almost instant ring of fire."

"Excellent," said Arc, keenly. "The trees are more sparse on the wasteland at the far end of the plain. We hack down more of them, clear a route through them. Then we construct a wide, lightweight wooden bridge at the end of it, across the ditch. We cover it with earth and fellfurze and flattened brush, to hide it."

"Oh, brilliant," sneered Gath. "A secret bridge. If that's all you've got—"

"Oh, *LISTEN!*" broke in Kita, so loudly and fiercely that everyone looked at her, at the hot haze of witch rage surrounding her. "You don't *know* what he's got, you won't hear him!"

Arc stared at Kita, eyes wide, and she looked back at him, unblinking.

"We horsemen *are* listening," said Jayke, bravely. "Arc, please go on."

"We know the city creatures are clearing the old road to here," Arc continued, "preparing to invade us. We watch the road. When the hordes set out on it, we make our move. Thirty or forty sheepmen and farmers advance to meet them. Challenge them, confront them – then take flight. The hordes think they've routed us, and they follow. Swilling the taste of victory in their mouths. We race on, leading them off the road, across the wastelands, along the route we've cleared and over the makeshift bridge. On to these grasslands. They see our hill fort ahead of them – see us, running to it – they surge on, triumphant. But the witches and the rest of the footsoldiers are hidden in these trees."

"*Yes!*" breathed Jayke. "Go on!"

"When the city warriors are all across the bridge, the witches shoot their flaming arrows. And suddenly they're cut off from half their army and all their wagons – surrounded by a gigantic ring of fire. They're trapped, terrified, disoriented. That's when the advance guard stop running. We turn back to face them. The witches rain down arrows on them and the rest of the fighters run out from the trees. *And we bury them.*"

There was a rumble of assent from the footsoldiers – men turned to each other, excitedly discussing the plan. "And we horsemen ride in on the wagons," said Gath, drawn in despite himself.

"Yes," said Arc, earnestly. "You deal with the army on the other side of the fire. You ride in and slay the creatures who pull the wagons. Then you despatch whatever lurks inside."

"Yes," said Jayke. "We bury them."

The plan was set. No one could better it. Even Gath stonily agreed to it.

The witches offered to be the ones to watch the road. "We won't be seen," Wekka said. "We can melt into a landscape." Then she drew an arrow and shot it into the sky; a flare of vivid red streaked upwards, trailing bright silver. "That will be the sign that the city is on the move," she said. "We'll shoot three. They can be seen for miles, even at night, even from the horseman's fort. Keep careful watch for them."

"Well, if there's no more to discuss," said Gath, gruffly, "the horsemen must return. Prepare our weapons, ready our army. We have close on eighty horses, and other fighters can be carried pillion."

"Good," said Arc. "We need all the fighters we can get."

"And we'll go back to Witch Crag," said Wekka, "to do the same. We'll travel all night and be back by dawn. We'll start watch on the road immediately; we'll gather fellfurze and spread it along your ditch. And with your permission, headman, we'll bring healing herbs and ointments to your hill fort, to help the wounded."

The headman wouldn't look up from the ground.

"The matron will welcome you," said Kita, loudly. "She's converting two of the sleeping huts into hospitals. She asked for your help."

"We'll give it gladly," said Wekka.

"My task is to hack back the wasteland scrub. Then get all our fighters licked into shape," Arc said. He looked exhausted, thought Kita – but triumphant. As though he'd run a long hard race, and won.

"How many fighters do you have?" demanded Gath.

"Seventy – more maybe," said Arc. "We can match you."

The headman cleared his throat and said, flatly, "I declare this council over. We've reached a good decision. Now we must prepare, and wait. No one knows when this invasion will happen. But I sense it may be soon."

Onga, Flay and Lilly had been talking quietly to each other. Now Lilly sidled over to Kita, and murmured, "I'm going to go back with my people, Kita. Even if there's only a few days till we're called to war, I can do a lot of good in that time. Getting ready for the revolution. Talking to the women, telling them the truth about the witches. Showing them I dance when I choose to now, not because I'm told to by men."

Kita smiled. "Just the sight of you will convince them. You look so happy and rich and free. But will you be safe? What if Gath—"

"I don't think he'd want me now even if I crawled back naked with a flower between my teeth."

"*Lilly!*"

"And if he wants revenge I know the witchmen and Jayke and the others will protect me. I'll be fine, Kita. We're going to win this war. Whatever it costs us. And then we must be ready to fight for real change. And I want to play my part in that." She pulled Kita's face down to hers, and kissed her. "Till we see each other again," she whispered.

She walked, head high, over to Gath, with the infiltrator witchmen beside her, and Kita watched as Gath cursed when he heard what Lilly proposed. But like before, he was outvoted; he mounted his horse, and rode off. Lilly and Flay held each other silently for a few moments, then Onga pulled Lilly up behind him on his horse, and he and the other horsemen followed Gath back to their hill fort.

"Well," said Wekka. "A troubled exit, h'n? But I sense even Gath is convinced, now. They'll answer the flares when they go up. They'll come back."

"They'd bloody better," grunted Arc. "Come on. We should get back. And the farmers, obviously, will come with us. We'll make room."

"What about you, Kita?" asked Wekka. Her berry-red cloak swirled round her as she spoke. "Will you come home with us, to Witch Crag?"

Kita sighed, thinking of the colour and the herb scents, the laughter and the songs.

"Here," said Flay. "I bought you the blackbow I promised you." Kita took hold of it gratefully, feeling its smooth, whippy strength in her hands.

"Look at her," said Wekka. "She holds it like one of us."

"You can fight alongside us, Kita," said Flay.

"Are you coming?" urged Wekka, softly. "See – our escorts are here." The three huge hounds had crept out of the forest again, and were waiting for the witches. Kita looked at them with longing. Looked at the dark, mysterious shades of the forest with yearning.

At her side, she sensed Arc waiting for her answer, as if everything hung on it, and she was filled once more with a strange, strong sense of purpose.

"No," she said. "I'll go back to the hill fort. There's work to do there."

CHAPTER FORTY

On their return that afternoon, the headman summoned everyone together and told them that the union of the four tribes had been agreed at the council. Then he announced that Arc was now captain of the sheepman army, responsible for readying it. "Obey him as you would me," he said. Then he went off to his hut, alone.

If the sheep people were alarmed by this, they were too disciplined to show it. The same went for Arc. He stepped forward and shouted, "The enemy is larger than we feared. We have a fighting elite of some thirty footsoldiers – I need more than double that. All men who've retired from fighting because of age, but are still able bodied – step forward. Those lads who hoped to be fighting in a year or two, your time has come right now. Men and boys never chosen, who shared the women's work, this is your chance to prove yourselves. And those farmers not too injured to fight, all of you, come forward now."

As the men surged forward, Kita melted away with the women.

"I suppose our role is to keep things going without

the men," said the head cook.

"I suppose it is," said Kita.

"I've lost three of my best helpers to that army. And now there's more mouths to feed with those farming folk here."

"A lot more."

"Well," said the cook, "now you're back, *you* can give me a hand. Come with me and get chopping."

Kita worked hard for several hours in the kitchens, then she was sent over with soup to the hospital huts. Arc had set out with his little army to hack down a route through the scrub of the wasteland, then he'd taken over the whole of the central yard, in front of the great gates, for drilling purposes. She crossed behind the ranks of men.

At the huts, the matron immediately put her to work sweeping the bloodstained straw from the ground, and laying down fresh. "You could've been in charge of the infants' pens," she said. "But young Erin came up as my successor when you did your bunk. So she's in charge now."

Kita, busy with her straw, didn't answer. She felt as if the old suffocating ways were claiming her again, making her dull and obedient.

"So?" said the matron, after a while. "Did you say your piece at the council?"

"Oh, I don't know. A bit. It was mainly Arc. He led it."

"He'll be named the new headman when this is over. He's stepped up to the line, that lad. Do you know, I thought you and he would get together this spring. But I don't suppose there'll be any time for all that pairing up and sneaking off now. . ."

"No," said Kita. She felt suddenly weird. She stopped spreading straw and turned to face the matron. "The witches are coming back soon," she said, loudly. "They promised to bring you healing salves and potions."

"Good," said the matron, complacently. "They're needed."

"Have you no curiosity," Kita demanded, louder still, "at *all* about why I did *my bunk*, as you call it? And what happened to me after I did?"

"Yes," said the matron, looking straight back at her. "Of course I have. Enormous curiosity. But it's not the time to go into it all now. Maybe after the war, if we survive it. Now off you go. There's the summons for the end-of-day meal."

A night and a day went by, filled with endless mundane chores. It was both the same – routined, regimented, fuelled by sheep-bone broth – and utterly different, because of the looming war. The farmers they'd taken in quickly became absorbed into the sheep people's routines and ways, so much so that Kita had trouble telling everyone apart.

The end-of-day meal came round again. And like

the evening before, Kita ate alone. The other girls still nervously avoided her. She'd look up sometimes, and catch them looking at her, whispering, then they'd look away.

Arc was seated in the middle of his elite footsoldiers, loudly discussing that day's training. How best to use the old, how best to use the young. What could be expected from each. She looked over, and thought that deep down nothing had changed: she was back here now, mucking out and chopping mutton, and Arc was still top dog. . .

She was wrong about her purpose here. Lilly's purpose was clear, to help with a revolution that was already fermenting. Her purpose was in her imagination. She should have gone back with the witches to the crag. She thought of them disappearing into the woods, the dogs pacing beside them, and was gripped by longing, and regret.

And that turned into witch rage, simmering.

The unjustness of it. The waste of her. Not long ago she'd stopped the witches putting a poison arrow in Arc; then convinced him, through bars, of the need to become the witches' ally. Then she'd fought to the death alongside him when the horse thieves attacked. And led him to welcome the witches and save the council. But now, *now*, just the thought of going over to him, of speaking to him, of running the gauntlet of his entourage – it was unthinkable.

No it wasn't. She'd go over there and *demand* he

recognize her, her part in the union, recognize what she'd done, *what she could do*—

Something struck her, and her heart pounded with horror, which mixed with the rage. Her mind crackled. She jumped to her feet, marched purposefully over to Arc's table, and stood right in front of him. All the footsoldiers looked up at her, but no one said a word.

Arc raised his eyebrows, questioningly.

"The watch for the arrows. Arc, *who's doing the watch?*" she said.

For a moment, he looked stunned. Then he shot to his feet, pushed past his men, jerking his head at her to follow, and together they left the food hut.

Outside, he leant against the wall, and covered his face with his hands, rubbing furiously. "Oh, lord," he groaned. "Oh, lord help me, I clean forgot it. All I could think of was my army, getting the men ready. . ."

"Well you're lucky I only had a load of menial chores to do," she retorted, "so I had space in my brain to remember."

He dropped his hands and stared at her. "I am. I am lucky. Oh, lord save me, the headman put his trust in me, and I've failed."

"Bollocks," she said, robustly. "You've done anything but fail and you know it. You're headman in all but name."

"Could the witches have sent the flares up yet, d'you

310

think? Could we have missed them?"

"No. *No*, Arc. The city was still clearing the road, wasn't it? Pitch saw it. Wekka was being super careful, saying she'd watch the road from dawn today."

"The *flares* – everything depends on them. We need to watch *now*. The hordes could set out under cover of darkness."

"They could, but I doubt it. They're not afraid to be seen."

"All the same, we can't afford to risk it. *The parley ladder!*" he suddenly erupted, pushing himself off from the wall, and heading over to where the ladder was propped. "We can see the whole sky from that!"

"I've got a better idea," said Kita. "Follow me, footsoldier."

Five minutes later, they were sitting side by side on Kita's secret flint ledge, overlooking the dusky grasslands. Arc, still panting from the climb up the rock face, scratched from his crawl through the brambles, looked around in awe. "So this is where you disappeared to," he breathed. "I used to wonder. I thought maybe you were just crouching behind the scrub at the top."

"Course I wasn't," scoffed Kita. "I was looking *out*."

"I kept thinking I'd come after you, but I never did. It seemed . . . I dunno. Cruel. And intrusive."

"It would've been both," she said, as her mind slinked over what he'd just told her. That he'd been watching her. That he'd respected her wish for privacy.

"We escaped from here," she said, boldly. "Dropping down into the brambles below. And it was from here that I saw Nada's funeral – only it wasn't a funeral. And saw you slit the witch."

He flinched. "Not me," he said. "It was Drell."

"I know."

There was a long silence, both of them with their arms wrapped round their knees, looking out over the grasslands as the night came in. "You're still in your witch clothes," Arc said, at last. "Your tunic and trousers."

"Of course I am," she retorted. "They're a lot easier on the skin than hairy sheep's wool. And more free to move in."

"They suit you. You look – I like how you look."

Kita didn't know what to say to this. Her pulse quickened and she hugged her knees harder. Then after a while she said, "Arc?"

"Yes?"

"Have you told anyone that . . . that Nada's still alive?"

Arc blew out a long breath. "One step at a time," he said. "Actually, I played down the witches' powers, a bit. Went on about their archery skills. I didn't mention Vild either. Didn't want to freak the headman too much."

"You *know* about Vild?"

"I remembered the name. The oldies used to mutter it, scaremongering. *Vild, gone to the witches*. I asked Wekka, and she told me her history. After all this is over . . . that'll be the time to tell everyone everything."

Another potent silence, humming between them. "You should get back," Arc murmured, at last. "Get some sleep. I'll watch tonight."

"No. *I'll* watch while you go down to your men, and organize a rota. There's plenty of time before bed and you're too important to be sat up here pinching yourself to keep awake, and you know it."

He grinned. "You should be in charge, tree rat, not me. OK, I will. Thank you. It's good of you to. . ."

"What?"

"Oh, you know. Everything. Come back here. Make your ledge public. Let it be used."

"It seems so long ago, that it was mine, my secret place."

"I know. Everything's changed, hasn't it? Everything's different, right down to the bones. I know what the headman's going through. I feel like it myself."

She turned to look at him. "You're OK, though, aren't you, Arc?" she said. "You'll be OK?"

"Yes. I think so. I just – I hope with all my heart that we can get through this. And *live* – on the other side of it. Kita—"

"Yes?"

"Can I hold you? Just for a moment. *Please*. I won't try anything. I just want to—"

He broke off because Kita had thrown her arms

round him and was hugging him with all her strength. He folded his arms round her too and they stayed locked together as the night grew darker. Then she let him go, and without another word, he crawled through the brambles and climbed back down the rock face, and she sat on, waiting, looking up at the stars crackling above her.

Chapter Forty-One

The next morning, not long after breakfast, the lookout on Kita's ledge yelled out, "Strangers! Strangers on the boundaries!" Then – several octaves higher – "*Witches! Witches on the boundaries! Leading a horse!*"

Kita was just coming away from the infants' pens; she nearly collided with Arc as he ran into the central yard, bellowing for the parley ladder to be thrown up against the great gates. She watched while it was fetched, and Arc launched himself at it and practically ran to the top. Then he scrambled down again. "Yes, it's the witches," he said. "Laying fellfurze in the ditch. Open the gates! We need to go out to greet them, and start building the makeshift bridge. Drell, you lead the drills while I'm gone. And choose five good men to come with me."

Kita darted out in front of Arc, blocking his route to the gates. "I need to come too," she said, loudly.

He stared hard at her for a moment; Drell scoffed, waiting for him to shove her aside. But then he said, "You're right. Our witch interpreter. Yes, you come too."

*

"Witch *interpreter*?" she queried, as she hurried along beside him through the gates, the five footsoldiers following. "Since when have we spoken a different language to the witches?"

"Not in words, maybe," he said. "In all other things. Look, the lads were shaken enough by me allowing a girl to come along, I had to give you an official title."

"Thanks."

"And interpreter sounds less threatening than friend. . ."

"You're right. Although all the sheep people think I'm actually a witch, never mind just a friend to them – they avoid me like poison."

There was a pause, then Arc said, "Do you wish you were?"

"What, a witch?"

"Do you wish you'd gone back with them, to Witch Crag? When you turned down Wekka's offer, and came back to the fort, I saw your *face*, Kita. When they disappeared into the forest without you, it cost you, didn't it? You wanted to be with them."

"Yes. But I'm in the right place right now, Arc. I just feel I am."

He pressed his open hand to her back, so quickly that the footsoldiers behind them might have thought it was a push, and they hurried on.

*

316

Before too long, they'd reached the far boundaries. Seven witches, male and female, were there, stooping under great bundles of spiky, rust-coloured fellfurze. Flay was leading his horse, which was also burdened by fellfurze – Comfrie walked alongside with Wekka, who hailed Arc and Kita eagerly.

"Welcome!" called Arc. "You've worked hard!"

"We gathered these bundles yesterday," Wekka said, "and travelled all night with them on our backs."

"Don't you need to sleep?" Arc asked.

Comfrie smiled. "We have ways to get round the need for sleep for a few days. We'll rest when we return."

"You must," said Kita, hugging her. Then she hugged Wekka.

"Raff and Quainy wanted to come," Wekka murmured, into Kita's hair. "They wanted to see you again. But this skill of travelling without sleep – it takes time to perfect it. Flay would let his horse sleep, and catch us up."

"Send them my love," said Kita.

"Have you set someone to watch on the old road?" asked Arc.

"From yesterday morning," said Wekka. "Nothing. Although the road is now cleared, and there's an ominous emptiness about it. But no sign of any movement from within the city. Yet."

"We're keeping good watch for your flares," said Arc, then he glanced over at Kita, and grinned, and she knew he was thinking of the night before, and all that had happened between them.

"Right then," Wekka said. "Let's crack on. With your help, footsoldiers, we should finish by midday."

"And then I hope you'll come to the hill fort, for a meal, before your journey back," said Arc.

Wekka bowed. "Thank you. We have those healing salves I spoke of."

"I can show your matron how to use them," said Comfrie. "And we've got some delicious mushrooms we gathered on the way."

Everyone set to work. Slender felled trees, long dead, were found for the bridge; lashed together and laid over the ditch they made a sturdy platform. "But one that will burn easily," said Arc, grimly.

Kita laboured hard, helping thrust the spiky strands of fellfurze in among the ditch debris. "This wood's tinder-dry," said Wekka, approvingly. "If the heavy rain holds off till the hordes invade, we can make a ring of fire as tall as the grisly weapons they've been making."

By the time the sun had reached its height in the sky, they'd finished. They headed up to the hill fort, Wekka and Kita walking either side of Arc, with Flay just behind leading his horse, and Comfrie and the other witches behind him. But the footsoldiers, following, gave the witches the widest berth they could without actually separating from the party.

Inside the fort walls, it was the same story. The mushrooms were viewed with deep suspicion, even after Flay had swallowed two raw. Food was brought out to the central yard and left there, the cooks scuttling back to the kitchens as fast as they could. *A bit like we dump bodies outside our gates*, thought Kita, crossly, *and leave them for the dogs and crows*.

Luckily, it was a fine spring noon, and almost warm, and Arc made his footsoldiers sit down with the witches to eat, so it wasn't too inhospitable. He also sent news of their arrival to the headman, who appeared halfway through the meal. The headman didn't sit with the witches, but he bowed to everyone, and when Arc gave him a report of their morning's work, he seemed pleased. Then he trudged back to his hut again, alone.

"We must go," said Wekka, wiping her mouth and springing to her feet. "Flay, Comfrie – bring those little bundles, would you? Kita, take us to the hospital huts?" Kita loved walking across the fort with the witches. The boldness and beauty of them, the freedom and fluidity as they moved – this time, she enjoyed being stared at. The matron welcomed them into her hospital gravely, and showed them the preparations she'd made. Comfrie, whom Wekka introduced as one of the best healers on the crag, gave the matron the ointments, potions and bundles of herbs they'd brought, and explained how best to use them.

"Aaah," breathed the matron, unwrapping a large packet. "Wonderful. Shadewort."

"You know it?" asked Comfrie.

"Oh yes. Nada would risk her neck to gather it. We all relied on it – for childbirth, for pain from injuries. . . She left me a stock of it, but it's running low."

"I can show you where to gather it," said Comfrie. "When—"

"When the war is over. Good. Thank you."

"We must head back now," said Wekka, apologetically. "It's growing late. Flay—?"

Flay grimaced, and unwrapped the oddly-shaped bundle he'd been carrying. "We're not sure if this is a good idea, now," he said, revealing half-a-dozen newly made blackbows. "We thought, Kita, that you might teach some of the girls to use them. But there's still such fear—"

"Oh, I'd love to," said Kita. "If anyone would—"

"Leave them with me," interrupted the matron, firmly. "I'll sort them out."

The witches left, leaving behind the horse, who, Flay explained, had done his job and missed the company of other horses. The second watch on the flint ledge was relieved, and the afternoon wore on, filled with military training and preparations for war. Kita was working in the sheep pens, shovelling dung. Ma Baa the old ewe was still alive, hugely pregnant, and more vindictive than ever. But Kita wasn't unhappy working her long shift, because she had six visitors. One after the other, six girls, all around her own age, all quite well known to her, sidled into the pens and asked her to teach them the blackbow. They told her the matron had singled them out for their courage and strength, and suggested they come and see her. Kita was struck by how eager and excited they all were – as if they were at last being given permission to break through the boundaries, and become more than before. She arranged with them to hold a lesson that evening, in the same place that Flay had taught her to shoot.

The lesson went well, everyone showing a good level of aptitude, and a couple of the girls showing real skill. Then Kita, resetting the target, was suddenly aware of the girls giggling and shuffling and she spun round to see Arc standing there, arms folded, watching them all.

"Well?" she shouted, annoyed.

"Can I talk to you?"

The jaws of the six girls dropped. A footsoldier – *the* footsoldier – making a *request* to a girl, not just barking an order?

Kita smiled. "OK, archers," she called out. "Well done. We'll practise here tomorrow after start-of-day meal, right?"

They trooped off, still giggling, and Arc came over to Kita. "They're good," he said. "Better than I expected."

"The blackbow is an amazing weapon. Were you watching for long?"

"A few rounds. Before they spotted me. Kita, the headman's spoken to me. About this."

"Oh, *typical*. He wants me to stop?"

"At first he did. The oldies – they're just so freaked by the witches. They came to him wailing about the weapons they'd left here. I had to pretend I knew all about it. Stop smirking, you could've told me! Anyway. No one can countenance our girls mixing in with the witches in the woods, when it comes to the war. So I came up with a compromise. You and your six archers stand on your flint ledge. Protect the hill fort."

"Oh, *what*? We'll have nothing to do! I thought the plan was to let the hordes nowhere near the hill fort?"

Arc looked at her steadily. "That was the plan, yes. But plans don't always work out. A flank of the city army could make a break for it, and scale our walls – and if they do, you shoot them. And if we have to retreat – I mean really retreat – you cover us while the gates are opened."

"Oh," said Kita, in a low voice. "I see. What happens to the witches if we retreat?"

"They come in with us."

"If they can get here."

He looked down. "It's a war, Kita. Nothing's sure. Look, please agree to this. Or the headman will order these blackbows destroyed."

"Then I don't have a choice, do I?"

"No," he said, and touched her arm briefly, then walked away.

She stared after him and found herself wondering if part of the reason he'd come up with the compromise was — he didn't want her out there in the woods with the witches either. He wanted her away from them, safe within the fort.

She found herself wondering what she felt about that.

Chapter Forty-Two

There were five horses now to care for on the hill fort. The sheep people were still frightened of them, but the farmers tended them lovingly and rode them on the grasslands every day.

Arc sought out Kita again, and talked through his plan to let five farmers ride out with the footsoldiers when the flares went up. "Horses make a big impact," he said. "They'll swell our ranks impressively. But it's not only that. I want Pitch and the farmers involved from the start, for their pride – there's so few of their fighting men left."

"I understand," said Kita. "It's good you thought of it."

Sometimes Kita felt as though she was drawing closer to Arc than to anyone else on the hill fort. Which was strange, and sweet, and bitter, with the war waiting to happen. She didn't know if it was Arc the headman she was drawn to, Arc the hero whose task was to lead them all to safety and a new way of living. Or grey-eyed Arc who called her tree rat, whom she'd held on to so tightly on her flint ledge in the dark. Maybe the two were inseparable.

*

As well as teaching them archery, Kita took her six girls climbing up the rock face to her flint ledge. None of them were as nimble as her, of course, but none were as fearful as Quainy had been. Soon they'd all mastered it, and could get to the summit in minutes. It had been cleared of its brambles now; there was room for a crowd of them. They'd tease the poor lookout until he went scarlet, and gaze down over the grasslands, shivering as they imagined the hordes of the city swarming towards them, and practise drawing their empty bows. In only two days the seven had become a close-knit band. But they still kept Kita at a little distance and none of them asked her about her escape, or about Witch Crag.

Another day went by, another night. Drilling, preparing, training, and waiting, waiting. And then, right after the start-of-day meal on the sixth day after the council, a wail of terror went up from the young footsoldier on watch.

Everyone knew what it meant. They all rushed out into the open and stared in the direction of the old city, and up at the sky. Three thin streaks of red scored the clouds, with shimmering slicks behind them. Barely noticeable if you weren't expecting them; unmistakable if you were.

Arc ordered the alarm; iron clanged on iron, and everyone seized their knives and staves and clubs, and gathered in front of the great gates, Pitch and his four men leading their horses. The headman lumbered out to the front. "Well, sheep people," he said. "It's upon us at last. The greatest threat to our survival that we've ever faced. I've been your headman for more years than I can count now, and I know all of you. And I know each of you will play your part. . ." He broke off, overcome, and motioned to Arc to speak.

Arc stepped forward hurriedly. "We're all prepared!" he cried. "Each of you knows what your part is. Don't think about what faces us, just think of playing your part, playing it to the utmost. One step at a time, one minute at a time – one death at a time. Just try for it not to be yours!"

An attempt at laughter followed this; then there was the dismal sound of a young footsoldier being sick, and a child crying.

"All right," said Arc grimly. "Those riding or running out with me – come forward." Pitch and his men mounted their horses and rode to the gates. The elite core of some thirty footsoldiers jogged behind them. "Now," said Arc, "those who are going to fight from the woods – line up."

Drell had been put in charge of this group; he marched them up behind the advance guard. They were mostly older men looking grim, and young boys looking terrified.

"Kita!" called Arc. "You and your archers – get in position!"

The six girls ran over to the rock face, and began

nimbly scaling it, their blackbows on their backs. It was an alien, almost shocking sight to the sheep people, and a murmur started up among them, but when the girls reached the top and waved their blackbows, the murmur became a low cheer.

"Yes!" shouted Arc, on the tail of the cheer. "Yes, we're an army! A proper army! And in our differences lie our strengths. We've come together, and we've trained, and – backed by our allies, our true allies – each one of us is going to fight to the death for what we've built here – for what is ours – for our *home*!"

A louder cheer followed. The sheep people had never shared passion before; they looked around at each other, eyes alight, amazed.

"Now – open the gates," ordered Arc. "It's time."

Heart in her mouth, Kita watched as Arc jogged out of the gates with his footsoldiers, all of them running in time, a warlike rhythm. The horses paced beside them, heads tossing, with their shaven-headed riders on their backs. "They look fearsome," muttered the girl to Kita's left. "I hope the city creatures aren't too scared to chase them here."

Drell was watching by the open gates. Once the advance guard had reached the far edge of the grasslands and disappeared from sight over the makeshift bridge, he raised a wildly trembling arm. "Right," he called out, harshly, "it's our turn. We'll spread out through the woods, like we practised. What we couldn't practise is holding our nerve when the witches appear. They'll be swarming into the trees above your heads. *Don't look at them!* Just keep focused on—"

He broke off. The headman had taken hold of his arm, and lowered it, keeping hold of it. "Drell," he said, "I appoint you my second. I'll be relying on you when I lead this band to the woods. I see many of my old comrades before me – I'm proud to lead you into battle once more. And you young uns – you've stepped up, you make me proud too. Watch out for these young lads, men – give them comfort, give them courage. *And don't fear the witches!* Give them a welcome when they come. They're our allies. They're saving our skins. Now, *forward!*"

As he yelled the command, the older men raised their weapons and roared, then they jogged determinedly towards the headman. Kita, looking down on them, felt suddenly intensely moved; this was the same courageous band she'd watched as a tiny child, being led off by the headman to fight off marauders. The young footsoldiers and boys followed, all infected by the sudden confidence, the uplift in spirits, now the headman was back in charge. And then they too all went through the great gates.

The matron strode forward and, with another woman, closed and barred the gates. "Back to your posts!" she cried. "Look to the little ones, keep them calm! We must be ready when they start bringing the wounded in!"

More waiting, waiting, waiting, the six girls seated on the flint ledge, peering into the distance, longing and dreading to see the return of Arc's small army, and whatever horror would be chasing it.

"Shouldn't the witches be here by now?" asked one of the girls. "In the woods?"

"How do you know they're not?" snapped Kita.

"Well, I can't see anything. . ."

"They're good at that. Now keep your thoughts to yourself."

"I'm just *saying*—"

"Well *don't*!"

The truth was, Kita had been peering at the trees for some time now, and she could see the sheepmen all spaced out on the ground, even though they were supposed to be hidden, but in the branches of the trees – nothing. Her mind was full of the horrible vision of Arc turning to face the hordes and then – nothing. No fire. Just utter devastation as his small brave band was annihilated.

The girls waited on.

And then, at the far end of the grasslands, a horse rider erupted on to the makeshift bridge and galloped over it, followed by the other four farmers on horseback, and then Arc and his men came into view, running, running, a long column of them snaking across the bridge and on to the plains.

"Oh, lord," breathed Kita, as her heart seemed to seize with terror, "oh lord help us, the hordes will be next."

As soon as the runners were all across and spacing out across the grasslands, the horse riders doubled back, as though rounding them up, and the band jogged towards the steep slope that led up to the hill fort.

And the bridge seemed to shake with emptiness, with the horror of what was to come. "I can hear them," croaked one of the girls. There was a dull, rhythmic chant, low and menacing and still faint, and in time with the thud of hundreds of feet. And then the first of the city warriors came into view.

They were slow, steady, relentless, as they made their way four after four across the bridge. Jagged metal spikes bristled above their heads; ragged metal plates protected their bodies. They came on, endlessly, fanning out across the grasslands, forming one wide line, then another behind it, fed by the terrible flow across the bridge. When three lines had formed, they began to advance slowly on the hill fort, while the flow across the bridge was as steady as ever, forming line four.

The girl next to Kita began to sob. "When will they *stop*?" she whimpered. "There's hundreds of them!"

Kita didn't trust herself to answer, but she seized the girl's hand and squeezed as she yet again scanned the woodland, desperate to see witches in the trees.

And now a fifth line was being formed, as the fourth

line set off up the plain. There were far more than the two hundred that Skipper had counted at the farmlands. The union was outnumbered by three to one, maybe four. The chant was so much louder now they were closer, and it had quickened; it was violent, hateful, the city men stamping in time as they moved forward.

Arc and his men and the horses were now up against the hill-fort walls. Looking down, Kita saw Arc order everyone to slow, to hover, as though they were waiting for the gates to open. She could sense their fear; she could smell it. And they, like her, were casting frantic glances at the trees.

And now, something different. As the fifth line started to move forward, there was a clanking, rumbling sound, and then a battered black van lumbered its way into view on the bridge, pushed by four squat men, all stripped to the waist.

Witches, witches! Kita's mind screamed. *Where are you? Fire the arrows!*

The first line of the city army quickened its pace further, the lines behind copying. Arc and his men had turned round now, to face the hordes. Army facing army. *"Hold!"* Arc roared. The gap between the armies narrowed, relentlessly. *"Hold!"* Arc yelled. A second vehicle came into view on the bridge. Kita felt like she'd been slammed in the stomach.

The witches hadn't come.

They hadn't come.

Then suddenly, like a glorious explosion of rage, from the woodlands on the left, dozens and dozens and dozens of arrows shot into the sky, a great screaming sheet of them, crackling with fire. As they fell to their mark in the far side ditch, a second flaming sheet of arrows went up, from the right this time, soaring up and swooping, whistling down into the nearside ditch.

Kita felt a great breath fill her. Silently, she cheered the witches, sent her apologies for doubting them.

The dreadful chant had stopped, the hordes had shuddered to a stop. They looked up at the sky, panic stricken – and then the ditches exploded into fire, a fire that grew higher and hotter and wilder with every piece of dry brush and wood it devoured.

The witches had judged their timing perfectly. The two wagons were engulfed by flame, a terrible barrier completely blocking any chance of escape.

The hordes broke from their lines, shoving and pushing each other, stumbling or dropping to the ground, their arms over their heads as the fire mounted higher. A horrible animal wailing filled the air.

Then there was another deadly rain of arrows. Twice as heavy and tipped by poison, this time, not fire, and shot simultaneously from the woods on both sides, over the raging ring of fire, straight into the heart of the city army.

Chapter Forty Three

"*ON 'EM!*" roared Arc. The horses and the footsoldiers raced down the slope and ran at the hordes. If they weren't dead, they were dying; if not dying, they were disoriented, and unequal to the fight. The clash of weapons filled the air, as Arc and his men scythed through their enemy.

The ring of fire had engulfed itself; it was beginning to dwindle.

"*Charge!*" bellowed the headman.

Out from the woods, jumping the dying flames, came the old campaigners, canny and deft, and they laid straight into the enemy. The boys followed them, darting and ducking and learning fast. Then the witches stepped out from the trees and through the heat haze. They aimed at close range, and shot only when sure they'd reach the right target.

Kita stared down at Arc, unable to wrench her gaze away from him. He was in the thick of it, lunging at the city men, stabbing and slashing with his long knife – he looked indomitable. She focused on him, willing him strength and safety, and the battle raged and boiled around him.

"I wish we could *do* something!" exploded one of the girls. "We're stuck here doing *nothing!*"

"Maybe not," said Kita. She walked right to the edge of the rock ledge, and gazed down. Then she raised her blackbow, and slowly, carefully, let fly. A monstrous man with a bloodied, three-pronged pike roared and clutched his eye, Kita's arrow jutting from between his fingers.

The six girls all lined up next to her. "Well done, boss," breathed one.

"OK, take care," said Kita. "Only shoot when you're sure of an enemy hit. That might be when one of *them* has just killed one of *us*. Don't think it's too late – it'll stop the next death."

Steadily, relentlessly, carefully, the girls fired down at the grasslands, and the pile of enemy bodies grew around the steep slopes of the hill fort. The ring of fire had sunk right down now, and nearly died away. Kita, shouting encouragement to her band of archers, told them that the battle was nearly won, but her words felt hollow. True, the first assault had been overwhelmingly successful for Arc and his men. The hordes had been panicked by the fire, shocked by the three-fold attack, and easy to slaughter – but now they'd rallied. Now they were holding their ground. And there were still so many of them. Still far more than Arc's men and the witches.

Arc hadn't buried them.

"*Kita!*" shrieked one of the girls, pointing down.

Several wiry-looking city men were swarming up the rock face towards them, hand over hand, knives in their mouths. "*Fire!*" screamed Kita. "Fire *fast!*"

The arrows found their marks – the climbers screamed, peeled off and fell. One man made it right to the top, but the girl to Kita's left aimed straight at his face and he arced back, wailing.

"Well done," croaked Kita, breathing slowly to stop herself gagging. "Well *done.*"

But it was no time for celebration. At the far end of the field, the burnt-out wrecks of the two vans suddenly lurched forward, as if being heaved from behind by giant hands. Kita groaned. She knew what it meant – what it had to mean. The horsemen had failed to defeat the rearguard of the city army, and now some huge vehicle was shunting the wrecks across the remains of the bridge. Then the city army would roll on to the field, indomitable in its metal boxes. She watched the burnt vans heave, and anguish seized her.

It can't end like this, it can't. We've fought so hard, given our all – overcome huge odds to unify and fight together. We can't just be mown down and destroyed by the spawn of the city.

Wildly she slewed her eyes over the field, searching for Arc. And then she saw him. Three of the horde were on to him, surrounding him, baiting him, jumping back as he tried to knife them. She could tell even from that distance how exhausted he was. Her anguish intensified.

And then, like fire licking up through her veins, the witch rage came in. She felt it, pounding in her heart, behind her eyes, an intense, murderous pressure. She turned on Arc's assailants, felt her rage storming out against them, saw the air around them shaking like a fire haze. Arc was fending off two of them – the third raised his axe to deal a death blow.

Everything in Kita screamed to stop him, her skull scoured by the hate and rage streaming out. There was a shift, a wrenching in the air. Arc's executioner dropped his arm and dropped to his knees, blood trickling from his mouth. The second man dropped beside him – stabbed by Arc, who then turned to deal with the third.

"*What's happening?*" croaked one of the girls, terrified. "Something dreadful's happening."

"Oh, lord, *look*," groaned another, pointing at the sky. It was suddenly black with crows, gathering. "They've smelt the battle. They've come to feast."

"The fighting's stopped!" gasped a third.

It was true. The battle had stopped boiling; both sides were looking about themselves, dazed.

Kita stared down at Arc. He'd slashed the neck of the third assailant, and now he looked straight back at Kita, as if he knew her part in all this. As if he was pulling dark energy straight out of her.

A shattering noise broke the spell, as a huge black

vehicle crashed across the burnt-out bridge, hauled by four slaves. A second was right behind it; a murderous chant started up, keeping the slaves in rhythm.

And then a young footsoldier screamed: "Treacherous *bitches*! Look at them – leaving the *field*!"

The witches were retreating. Moving together, they turned, and melted once more into the forest.

"*Cowards!*" railed Drell, as his neck spurted blood.

"*Victory!*" bellowed a gore-spattered city fighter.

For a moment, absolute despair gripped the sheep people and the farmers, as they watched the second great van roll over the ruined bridge. Then Arc roared, "*Back, men! We're not finished – back!*"

And the fighting started up again, more desperate and bloodier than before. The light on the grasslands had been dimmed by the black cloud of crows. They hovered, eerie and ominous, cawing. Waiting.

Kita's eyes followed Arc, willing him to stay alive. He fought like a man possessed, slashing, stabbing, urging his men on. But the slave-drawn vehicles kept rolling over the broken bridge – a fifth now, then a sixth – and the numbers on the ground were still so weighted against them, especially with the witches gone.

Kita couldn't bear to think about the witches going.

"Why have you stopped shooting, boss?" wailed the girl to her right.

It was true, she'd stopped. She strung another arrow in her blackbow, and gazed down. The battle raged right up to the gates of the hill fort now; shooting clean was impossible. "We should go down," she whispered. "Fight on the ground." Then she remembered what Arc had said about a retreat – how the archers should cover the men as the gates were opened. Was it that time now?

She stood helpless for a moment, hands hanging. Witch rage spent, she felt exhausted. And what had it achieved? Nothing. Nothing that could last.

Suddenly there was another shift in the air. A weird wrenching. The fighting froze – everyone stared up at the sky and the crows who were now descending, coasting menacingly down. The great dark shadow cast by them seemed to surge into the forest, boil around the trees . . . and then it flooded out again, blacker than before. And Kita saw that the shadow was dogs, hundreds of them, wild dogs streaming on to the battlefield, with the witches walking among them.

It all happened with terrifying speed. The dogs hurled themselves into the fray, snarling, growling, ripping and tearing flesh. Kita stared in disbelief as men everywhere were pulled down, raked with claws and teeth. . . Then it hit her that the witches seemed to be herding the dogs, directing them – away from this man, on to that – steering them away from their allies and towards their foes.

Wekka's voice soared above the nightmare noise. "Get back to the hill fort! Our people – *GO!*" The shattered footsoldiers and bloodied farmers began to stumble towards the great gates, and the dogs let them alone as they savaged the men from the city.

"Follow me!" cried Kita, scrambling over the edge of the rock and starting to climb down. The six girls threw their blackbows across their backs, and went after her at speed.

"We have to open the gates," she panted, "then stand guard with our bows and make sure only our people come inside."

She reached the ground, and raced for the great wooden stake that barred the gates; the two quickest girls joined her, and together they lifted it free. Then they seized the gates and pushed them out as far as they could against the piles of dead and dying, right out into the thick of battle. Men fleeing, stumbling, groaning on the ground. Dogs seizing and ripping and gorging. And the footsoldiers and farmers, staggering towards them in a great, weary mass.

The witches were everywhere, steering, protecting, and now they began to form a barrier between the city men and the allies. Arc was there, next to Wekka, dogs skirling around them, urging everyone towards the hill fort. Line after line, the men stumbled through the half-open gates. A thin dog broke free from its pack and raced towards a young boy limping along on his own. Kita sprang in front of it, glaring, and the dog slunk back.

The ragged army trudged on, reeking and bloody. Maybe half the number that had started out that day. Arc and his elite men, those that were left, began to gather up the wounded and help them in, and the witches helped too. The archer girls held their place, arrows ready, but no more dogs and no one from the city tried to get through the gates. Behind her, Kita could hear the matron bellowing orders, and all the women coming to the aid of the survivors.

Then Arc was in front of her, with Wekka behind him. He had a great gash under his left cheekbone, pouring blood, and another on his arm. "Close the gates, tree rat," he said, gravely. "It's done."

For a moment, the three stood looking out as the hordes continued to surge towards the broken bridge at the far end of the grasslands, desperately fleeing the great tide of dogs.

"You witches steered the hounds well," Arc murmured. "Hardly a man of mine hurt by them."

"That wasn't just our skill," said Wekka. "The city scum had never seen dogs before – the dogs smelt their terror. And they worked with us. They can tell the difference between people – and carrion."

And now the crows were coming down, in great, black drifts, to gorge on the dead and the dying. Kita and her archers closed the gates.

CHAPTER FORTY-FOUR

Just as the gates were rumbling shut, a great shout went up from outside. The horsemen, thirty or more of them, were galloping towards the hill fort, with many riderless horses racing alongside, half crazy with fear from the dogs and the crows. Kita nodded to the girls, and they reversed their direction and ran out in an arc again, opening the gates as wide as they could.

The horsemen thundered through, as the exhausted and the wounded scattered to get out of their way. Onga the witchman dismounted first. Arc came forward and grasped his hand, and everyone drew close to hear as the gates ground shut again.

"Terrible losses," Onga croaked.

"Us too," said Arc.

"Gath led us heroically. He paid for it with his life."

"I saw our headman die, but while he fought he was a beacon for us all."

"There were so many of them," grieved Onga. Jayke had dismounted now, and stood beside him, his sleeve dripping blood from a wound on his shoulder. "We wheeled in on them when the fires went up, and at first we had the upper hand, slaughtering the slaves who pulled the wagons. But then the fighters leapt from inside the wagons – savage, all of them. Berserkers. Death wishers. And then more running fighters came from behind – a second flank. They took us on, and some of the berserkers got back in their cars, and started to advance on to your field. And we thought it was all over. And then. . ."

"Yes," said Arc. "*What?*"

"Witch rage like I've never felt before. Reality fractured, torn out of joint. And then the hordes came flooding back across the bridge – and the dogs. The blessed dogs."

"They left you alone?"

"Completely. They avoided the horses. We simply pulled back and watched the killing. They fought in packs, fluid, fast – the weapons missed them, but they got their marks."

"Like here," said Arc. "Five hounds on to one."

"Those who could, started running, of course, back to the city – and the dogs followed. As soon as the bridge was clear, we rode over to you. The dogs saved us. Where did they come from? Wekka, was it you?"

Wekka smiled. "We felt the witch rage too. It charged our power. We'd sensed the dogs gathering behind us, waiting for the battle to be over – and we walked among them, drawing them along with us on to the field. I've never been able to call dogs like that before – none of us has."

"And the crows?"

"The crows came on their own. They felt the rage too." She paused, then raised her hand in a salute to Kita. "It was her," she said. "It was Kita's power that tore things apart. None of us has anything to teach her, now."

For that night, no one went anywhere. For that night, it was just resting, and settling the horses, and recovering, and drinking bone broth from the great cauldrons in the kitchen, and trying to understand what had happened to them all.

Nearly half of the allies had been slaughtered. The horsemen, the farmers, the sheepmen and the witches gathered in their own groups, apart from each other, and talked in low voices, numbering and honouring their dead. The witches and sheep women who were skilled with healing moved among them, stitching and bandaging wounds and applying poultices, while from outside the gates came the dreadful ceaseless sound of the dogs and crows feasting on the dead.

Arc sat with his men as they mumbled out their grief and relived the battle, silently supporting them. Everyone was exhausted; shattered.

They had victory, but no one could celebrate it yet.

As the thin moon rose to her zenith, some of the witches started up a low, keening song, full of sadness and acceptance and gratitude. The other tribes fell silent as they listened; some of the men curled up on the ground, to sleep where they were.

Kita, though, was wide awake. She sat apart from the rest. No one seemed to know what to say to her; and she had nothing to say. She was dazed – burdened. She wondered if she'd ever come to terms with what had happened that day. With the rage that had coursed through her; with what had created the rage.

Anguish that they were losing the battle had fed it – but Arc had sparked it into life. Seeing him about to die had sparked it into life. She looked over at him as he sat with his men, and couldn't imagine speaking with him face to face again.

"All on your own?"

Kita spun round at the sound of the low, soft voice, to see Vild, her white hair streaked with blood and dirt, smiling at her. "Vild! I didn't know you were here! Were you—"

"Fighting? Oh yes. I'm a sure hand with the blackbow. The only ones who stayed behind on the crag were the very young and the very old."

"Nada stayed?"

"Of course. The babies needed her, with all their parents gone. And now she'll be singing them to sleep with a song of victory. . ."

"She'll know. . ."

"Of course she'll know. She'll have sensed it hours

ago." There was a pause, and Kita became aware of two shapes, standing so close they were really one shape, drawing nearer to her in the dusk. "Everyone of an age came and fought, Kita," Vild murmured.

With a long, low wail of emotion, Kita was on her feet and rushing at the shape, throwing herself on them, crying out "Quainy! *Quainy!* Raff!"

"They fought well," said Vild. "True citizens of the crag."

The three were hugging and sobbing and kissing each other, and Vild drew them down to sit on the ground together. Quainy had her arm around Kita's shoulders; Kita nestled into her neck, comforted and warm. "I didn't *see* you," Kita said, for about the third time. "I can't believe I didn't see you on the field."

"Oh come on, were you looking for us?" said Raff. "You had enough else to do."

"We saw you, dearling," said Quainy, warmly. "Brave and bold, up on your ledge with your archers. . ."

"You're not hurt, are you, either of you?" said Kita. "It's so good you're not hurt."

"Archers don't tend to get hurt," Vild said, softly. "Especially if they know when to melt back into the trees. That's why we chose it, way back, as our method of fighting. Kita, only two of the witches were killed. Two. I do hope this doesn't cause trouble with our allies."

"It won't," said Kita fervently. "You were the reason we won that war."

"No," said Vild, firmly. "You were."

Another silence, Kita subsiding lower on the ground. She couldn't look at her friends. She thought: *They'll be more wary of me now than ever before.* But they were being so kind, and it was so good to be with them again. . .

"Is Lilly OK?" asked Quainy, anxiously. "I didn't see her – did she fight?"

"No. She's safe," said Kita. "She went back to the horseman fort. To tell the women the truth about the witches."

"Ah, I thought she would," mused Vild. "Little of the witch about her, but enough human warmth to make up for it. She's where she can do most good."

"So many have been killed," mourned Quainy.

"Arc was an absolute hero," Raff said, abruptly. "He fought like a wolf with a lion's heart. I will never, ever take the piss out of him again. Well, not for a while, anyway."

"He *was* a hero," Kita agreed, solemnly. "The way he came forward to lead when the headman was overwhelmed. . ."

"Yes," said Quainy. "Those qualities that made him so obnoxious in the old days – they found their place, didn't they? And they mellowed, and matured. I suppose he'll be headman now."

"He is already," murmured Kita. "Oh, Vild, there's so much ahead of us. What's going to happen? How will all this be resolved? How will it move on?"

"What's going to happen is we all sleep, tonight," said

Vild, firmly. "Sleep and let our bodies start on their road to recovery. In the morning, Arc will call a council. This work isn't finished yet. But it will be soon."

"And then we can go home," said Quainy, hugging Kita, carefully settling her down so she could sleep.

Gratefully, Kita let herself be settled, while she thought, *where's home?*

CHAPTER FORTY-FIVE

It was hard for Kita to wake on the hard ground with the sun barely warm and a sprinkling of spring frost on her body. But it told her she was alive. She stood up, and stretched, and looked around at everyone else getting to their feet, too. Groaning and stamping and shuffling, but like her, smiling. Glad to be alive.

It seemed completely natural to Kita, then, to run over with Quainy and Raff to the kitchens, and offer her help with theirs. Her old friends acted like a shield against the stares she was getting; they were warm and relaxed with her, whatever wariness they felt inside.

The cooks had been up for an hour or more, preparing vast cauldrons of nourishing mutton porridge. Vild had charmed her way in among them, and persuaded them to add the mushrooms and some of the healing herbs that the witches had brought to the hill fort. "We all need healing, this morning!" she cried, gaily. Then she winked at the three friends, muttering, "And it will help *immeasurably* with the taste."

The three helped carry the cauldrons outside, along with every wooden trough and bowl that the kitchen possessed, and began distributing the steaming porridge, and ladles of water from the great stone well. Everyone came together, the four tribes merging again, and hunched on the ground, eating hungrily.

When the troughs and bowls were empty and being gathered in again, Arc stood up. One of the witches had stitched up the gash under his cheekbone; it showed red against his pale, exhausted face.

"People!" he cried. "We had a victory yesterday."

A half-hearted cheer went up; someone called out, "You mean the dogs did!"

He smiled. "Yes. Maybe we'll call it the Battle of the Dogs. But it's not the time yet to celebrate, or rest. We've still got work to do. We must go with the farmers to reclaim their lands, although I imagine they've already been deserted by the hordes. Then we must invade what's left of the city – gather up the children and anyone who is prepared to change their ways and move on into the future. Then we must burn the place to the ground so that this never happens again."

Pitch stood up. He was limping, wounded, but determined. "I'm ready to go when you are, footsoldier," he said. "And our horses are too. I checked on them at first light."

Jayke got to his feet, but with only Onga beside him – the other witchman had died in the fight. "The horsemen must decline this new task," Jayke said. "We lost over half our men in the battle. We must return to our fort, and break the news, and shore up our defences. Our fear is that roving robbers will hear of this devastation and seize their chance to break in on us."

There was a rumbling among the older horsemen, who began to help each other up. They stood together in a pugnacious group. "Have we voted you to speak for us, Jayke?" one demanded.

"I understand your need to return," broke in Arc, hastily. "And we can manage without you. But the horsemen must be represented in this alliance. Perhaps—" he raised his voice a little — "perhaps some of the senior men might come with us. To add weight — to share their wisdom."

"Indeed!" cried a grizzled, stocky horseman, with a bandage about his neck. "Now Gath is slain, I am the most *senior* warrior here. I'll come — and some of my brothers-in-arms, too, yes?"

"We will!" cried the older men, one adding, "I've slaughtered more boar than you, you old pretender!"

Arc bowed modestly — almost submissively — and said, "Thank you, all of you. You honour us with your presence."

Kita, watching intently, saw him glance at Jayke and Onga, and nod. *Oh, clever, clever, clever,* she thought. When did this communication happen? When did Arc start . . . *flowing* like this, like the witches flowed? It was clear to her that revolution would happen at the horseman fort over the next few days. Jayke, Onga and the other young men would return and, with Lilly leading the women, they would institute change that would be all in place and irreversible by the time the old warriors got back. . .

Change, change for the horsemen. But who would help the sheep people change?

Wekka stood up. "All we witches will come with you," she said. "We can help with the children. We can help smoke out the ruins of the city."

"And you can help with the final fire, too," said Arc. "Thank you. But don't some of you need to return to the crag, to assure your people that it's over?"

Wekka bowed. "They know," she said.

It was all bustle and hurry, as packs of food and water were prepared, weapons cleaned and sharpened, and the horses got ready. Pitch and Skipper and the other farmers, yearning to see their homelands again, were standing ready at the gates with their mounts. Everyone who had fought in the war and was still fit to fight was expected to come; Kita organized her archers two to a horse. Even with all the deaths and the young horsemen dropping out, there were nearly a hundred of them. They were wounded, exhausted, but still a potent army.

The matron was to be in charge again once they had all gone. Kita found herself wondering about this formidable woman's status when they returned. Surely Arc couldn't expect to be a headman as all-powerful as his predecessor had been? Surely he couldn't want that?

These musings kept her from thinking about her own future. The witch rage that had possessed her — that had caused reality to be wrenched out of joint — it haunted and burdened her. She felt even the witches saw her as a freak, and were afraid of her.

"We're ready to go!" Arc shouted, as he mounted his horse. "It will be grim work, riding across the grasslands, with the half-eaten corpses of our people, but we must keep our minds on the living! *Open the gates!*"

Soon, they were picking their way across the grisly plain, some riding, some jogging alongside, and on to the wastelands beyond.

They arrived at the outskirts of the farmlands well before dusk set in. The whole area had a dismal, abandoned air. It seemed that the city men had gone, swept back with their defeated army. Arc sent Pitch and the others to ride on ahead, their faces set and anxious.

"Anybody there?" yelled Pitch. "The battle's over. You're safe now. Come out, show yourselves!"

There was a long, bleak pause, then stooped, ragged figures began to emerge silently from their hiding places and gather wearily round the newcomers. Too much had been lost, too many of them killed, for them to feel much joy at Pitch's return. But they raised their faces when Pitch greeted them; and they answered his careful questions.

It didn't take long for the story to be told. They'd been

working in the hell that their fields had become, planting, digging, starved and thirsty, while the metal whips screamed around their heads. Then, suddenly, there'd been a shift. A great noise, growing louder – screaming, howling, snarling – terrifying. Their tormentors had gathered together, arguing loudly about its cause. One man, wailing that the city army had been set upon by demons, was knocked to the ground by the gang master, who then sent a group out to reconnoitre. When the group didn't return, panic spread – and soon all the slavers were dropping their whips and sidling out one by one.

"To head back to the city," said Pitch. "Let's hope the dogs intercepted them."

"But before you tell our tale of the battle," said Vild, firmly, "let's start a cheering fire and cook some food, and let us witches do our healing work."

"You're right, Vild," said Arc. "We'll camp here tonight. This place needs our energy and support, I think. We can make an early start on the city tomorrow."

An hour later, Kita was helping shred cabbage for a great pot that was bubbling on a large log fire. Several of the witches had gone hunting for rabbits; since the time of the Great Havoc, large rabbits overran any land with fresh green shoots on it, and they especially loved the farmlands where they were trapped, but inefficiently. Some of the farmers, impressed by the witches' haul, asked about the blackbow and were promised as many as they wanted. So the future – even if it meant just a plentiful supply of rabbit stew – was already looking more promising.

Newly orphaned children were grouped together with the children who'd been snatched from the city in earlier times – and those "slave" children would get kinder care in the future because of this. The farmlands had been devastated, most of their produce stolen, but the earth was still fertile, it would be replanted, and there was enough around the edges to keep everyone going until the new produce grew. The horror of the past days would be acknowledged, then put to rest. The dead would be grieved over, but the living came first.

As the night came in, a night of no moon, everyone gathered about the fire, and ate.

Chapter Forty-Six

Kita found herself riding next to Arc the next morning as they headed towards the ruined city. She wasn't sure how this had come about, but she was glad to be there. She was drawn to him, she kept looking at him, to find him looking back at her. Then she'd look away. But somehow he was the only one she didn't feel like a freak with. Vild was as calm and kind as she'd ever been, but what had happened to end the battle seemed to stand between them like a wall. And even Wekka treated her with – what? Diffidence. *Distance.*

Arc rode easily now, moving with his horse rather than trying to control it. He and Kita kept each other's pace. Behind them came the sheepmen, with the flamboyant old horsemen determined to outpace them. The witches all ran or rode together, two to a horse; Quainy and Raff were among them. They all had bundles of plants that they'd gathered the night before; Comfrie was pleased with their haul, she said it would make excellent smoking through the decrepit alleys and tunnels of the city.

Pitch and a few other farmers had insisted on staying with the army, despite the urgent need for them on their homelands. He said they were representatives of their tribe in the new union, and everyone respected this. Many fighters might be needed, after all.

Soon, they'd veered off the scrubby grasslands and were riding along the great road from the south, the road that the city hordes had cleared for the invasion. The emptiness of it, a sterile gash in the wilderness, and the echoing sound of their hooves, seemed eerie, ominous.

"How you doing, tree rat?" asked Arc, pulling his horse a little nearer to hers.

"All right," she said. "Considering."

"Considering you've just become the most powerful witch on the crag?"

She flinched at that, as though he'd hit her. Then she laughed, relieved. He had the courage to be honest, to tell it straight, and she welcomed it. "Yes," she said. "Considering that. You're not afraid of me then?"

"Terrified. *Witch rage*. I heard Vild talking about it. I'm bloody terrified."

Kita laughed again. "It's — supposed to be the birth of a witch's skills. They come in in a pretty crude way."

"Crude or not, I was glad it happened! So . . . when it's all mellowed down . . . you can see into the future, sense what people are up to, all that stuff?"

"I suppose so. What did Vild say about it?"

"Oh, that it had been immense, and you needed time to recover, no one was to hassle you, that kind of thing. But it's clear they see you as a top witch now."

"Oh my lord. That's so frightening."

"Kita, I'm just as afraid of the role I've taken on."

"But you stepped up so well, you never seemed *afraid*. . ."

"I don't know how I got through yesterday. I don't know how I *did* that. Any more than you know how you did . . . what you did."

She considered, comparing the two, seeing the link; her horse slowed a little. Then she said, "It was worse for you. It must have been. You had to keep on and on, screwing your courage down harder. I just got taken over. It wasn't *me*, what happened."

"I could say the same about me fighting, Kita. *Leading*. I wasn't me. I'd let go of *me*."

There was a silence, then he asked, "What did it feel like, Kita? Witch rage? How did it happen?"

She couldn't breathe. She was longing to tell him it was when she'd seen his life threatened. She was longing to tell him everything had leapt into life when she'd seen that – to be absolutely honest too. But up ahead Flay was shouting, "I can see the infernal place!" and the army stirred and quickened, and Arc kicked his horse on to a canter, Kita following.

Ahead of them was the hideous, towering city wall, made of ruined cars and jagged metal. They rode closer, and soon Kita could see the gap she'd run through with Quainy and Raff, when there were horses behind them, all that time ago.

This time, though, there were horses ahead of them. Twenty or more, wandering nervously, cropping on the grass outside the city, reins torn and hanging loose.

"They're ours!" shouted Pitch. "I'd recognize them anywhere."

"They've been abandoned," said Arc. "That may be a good sign. Pitch, can you distribute them among the army?" Then he wheeled his horse round, and faced everyone.

"This is it!" he shouted. "The last haul. Those riding two to a horse, one of you dismount. I want us to go into this sewer spread as wide as we can, I want us to sweep it clean. If we're attacked, then it's all in, and finish it fast. When we've passed right through, we retrace our route, while the witches burn their smoke. We'll call for peaceful survivors – the children and the oppressed – to come out and join us. We'll give clear warning that we mean to burn the place to ashes. Are we agreed?"

There was a low, determined cry of assent from everyone, while the horses shifted in place, sensing their riders' eagerness to move.

"Then let's go," said Arc, and he sucked in a deep breath and added, "We've done work to be proud of these last days. Alone, we'd have been eaten. Standing together – allowing our differences to shine – we survived. I'm proud to have been part of this. Now, *let's finish it!*"

He trotted forward towards the open gateway in the

ugly metal gap, calling to Kita, "Stay beside me, tree rat!" Unhesitating, she kicked her horse forward, and side by side they rode into the rotting city.

It was a slow, gruesome progression. They passed corpse after corpse lying in slicks of congealed blood, whose death wounds could only have been caused by the teeth of dogs. But of the dogs themselves there was no sign.

The sickly-sweet smell of death was overpowering, nauseating. Kita noticed a fresh, astringent tang mingling with it, and saw that several of the witches were holding bunches of burning herbs.

"You all right?" asked Arc.

"Yes," she answered.

They forged on, a great, loose-linked swathe of them, losing sight of each other briefly when they had to navigate alleys and great piles of rubble, but always coming back together again to keep the line.

The silence was uncanny. There was no movement at all apart from the steady forward progression of the army. They went right through the centre of the city with its alleys and hovels, but saw and heard nothing. Kita found herself wondering where the Manager's quarters were – whether they'd pass by them. Whether they'd pass by Raff's beautiful metal horse.

Then they were out in the open at the other side of the city, crossing the great, concrete killing plains, where rival gangs of killers had fought for amusement and Quainy had danced to save their lives. Chilled, Kita reined her horse in. "Arc. . ." she breathed.

"What is it?"

"I feel – something bad."

"This space is bad. I remember it, from when I came here."

"No, it's more, it's – *get ready!*"

"Draw your weapons!" Arc yelled.

That moment's notice saved many of their lives. From behind the crumbling walls sprang almost fifty of the toughest and cruellest that the city spawned. Wounded, bleeding afresh, they came at Arc's army mad with battle lust.

But the witches were ready with their arrows. And those that survived the arrows were hacked down by the sheepmen and the farmers and the old warhorses of the horsemen tribe. It was all over in ten minutes, with only two men lost to the allies and one horse with a gash to its leg that Comfrie set about binding tightly.

More bodies lying bleeding on the ground.

The army paused to pull out their water bottles, and everyone slaked their thirst. Then Arc waved them on. "To the far side!" he called. "We have to be sure, we have to cover every stretch of this poisoned place."

Slowly, grimly, they paced across, past the wall at the far end, through the final winding corridors, until rubble gave way to grass under their feet and they could see forest ahead of them.

"We're done," breathed Arc. "We can turn around."

When they'd crossed back over the concrete field, and ramshackle roofs began to close them in once more, some of the witches pulled bundles of plants from the bags they'd slung over the horses' backs. They handed them out to each other, holding them like torches. Then Wekka ignited them. "Try not to inhale this smoke too deeply!" she cried. "It will do you no harm but it will make you lose focus. Now, witches – come."

They walked in advance of the army, waving the burning bundles. A strange, hazy, purple smoke rose from the burning plants, and started to fill the air, billowing, swirling, engulfing the army as it walked forward.

"City dwellers!" called Arc. "We have no argument with you survivors. We know you were kept down by the few with power. Their thugs have had their lives ended by dogs. It's over! Come out, bring your children out – start a new life on our farms."

Silence. No movement. And all the time the purple smoke was growing, thickening, sliding along the ground and through doorways and into cracks and holes.

"Be warned, when we reach the far side of this place, we'll burn it!" Arc cried. "We'll burn it to the ground. Take your chance to join with us."

Still nothing. No sound, no movement. He turned to Kita. "All right, you try," he said. "Try a witch's voice."

Kita urged her horse forward. Then on an instinct, she slipped from its back, and led it. She knew it wasn't just her voice that Arc wanted her to use. She breathed in, inhaled the rich muskiness of the smoke, felt it fill her mind. She felt calm, hopeful – this must be what the witches intended for the city dwellers.

But she had not lost focus. The other witches were drawing closer to her, and all of them were walking too, leading their mounts if they had them. Focusing with her.

"A new time is beginning," she called out. "Your children have the chance of a new kind of life. Things are changing for all the tribes – the sheepmen, the horsemen, the farmers and the witches. A new union is coming. A transformation. Be part of it. Come out. Bring your children out. I swear you won't be harmed."

She walked on, staring at the ruins and rubble as she walked by, imagining people crouching there, hidden, scared. . . She willed them courage from the hazy smoke, willed them to come out.

In the hovel to her left, a small movement – a thin hand drawing back a ragged curtain. A woman towing three small children came slowly out into the open.

"Don't stare at her," breathed Kita. "Just let her join up." She focused harder, slowing her pace down further. A young girl carrying a baby hurried up beside her; then three skinny boys darted out and fell in behind Arc's horse.

"We're leaving now," she called. "Leaving this stinking place. Come with us!"

362

Stooped, shadowy people, all with children, and some little children on their own, were materializing out of the smoke on all sides of the army. They were calm, smiling, relaxed, because the purple smoke had done its work, and Kita's magic had, too.

The jagged boundary wall was looming up in front of them now, with its gateway on to the great city road. Wekka nodded to the witches and, as everyone surged forward, they drifted backwards into the city, retracing their steps, to throw down their smoking bundles and ignite the ruins.

Chapter Forty-Seven

Once they'd left the burning city a mile or so behind them, Arc steered his horse off the road into a rough clearing in the woods, where a stream fed a marshy lake. He had two children perched in front of him; every horse was carrying someone from the city. "Dismount!" he cried. "Let's refresh ourselves and let the horses drink. Then we must gather round – we've decisions to make."

The children, forty or more of them, ran towards the lake, lay down and lapped thirstily. The adults and the horses followed more sedately behind. Then the army unpacked its small supply bags and handed food out to the city people, who grabbed it gratefully and shared it with the children who came darting over. They devoured it all ravenously. Afterwards everyone grouped around Arc in a great circle. It was a strange echo of the council of war they'd held, all that time ago, only five days ago, in front of the sheepmen hill fort.

Arc beckoned to Wekka, Pitch and the self-promoted leader of the horsemen warriors to step into the centre with him. He turned and bowed his head to Kita, and she joined them too.

"I believe this is the real end now," he said, looking around at everyone, including them all in the council. "And just as well, as we're all half dead with weariness. Welcome to the city dwellers. The carnage for you has been overwhelming: nine-tenths of you, more, wiped out."

"We're glad to see the back of most of 'em!" a young boy yelped.

Arc smiled. "You made a good choice, to leave your old home. The next choice is where you go now. And that's dependent on your wish, and that of the tribe you want to join. We sheepmen can take thirty of you. A few more, maybe."

"I cannot promise here and now to take anyone from the city," interjected the old horseman, pompously. "It must come to the vote. That is the way we horsemen do things."

Kita and Arc exchanged a look. The vote, they knew, would not go the way the old horseman expected. Jayke and Onga and Lilly would have set change in motion already; refugees would be welcomed into the horseman fold.

Pitch cleared his throat. "Well, we'll take as many as want to work on our farmlands. It'll be hard pickings at first while we get things going again, but the more hands we have, the more food we can grow. And you'll be treated equal with the rest of us."

"You have my boy already!" a scrawny woman cried, bitterly.

Pitch bowed. "Then I hope you'll be united with him. Taking children as slaves is something we regret, and behind us now. All will be equal, as I say."

"Madam," said Wekka, "we have city children at the crag, being brought back to health – your boy may be among them. If he's not with the farmers, please send to us to see." A bow was exchanged between the two women, then Wekka continued, "We welcome to the crag any who understand our ways and wish to contribute to our work. Come and speak to us! Two of your young women have already joined us." She waved an arm towards two girls standing with Vild. "And one man – sir, can you uncover your face?"

A skinny, cloaked figure at the edge of the group reluctantly pulled back his hood, to reveal a skull-thin face, a white plait sprouting from one side of his head, and a long, spiky earring on the other.

Several of the witches gasped. "The vision from my dreams!" cried one.

"The powerful presence!" another called out. "He haunted me. . ."

Raff stepped into the ring. He strode across to Geegaw, took hold of his arm, shook him violently, then yanked him forward. "As we told you before, witches," he said, "this is Geegaw. He worked for the Manager, one of the most powerful, devouring men in the city."

"I didn't have a choice!" sobbed Geegaw. "He made me!"

"How did you manage to save your miserable life, at the end?" Raff demanded.

"We hid, the Manager and I. Then the dogs came. He was a much better meal for them than little me. A meal for all of them, *all* at once—"

Raff groaned. "Spare us the details. And give me my knife back."

Reluctantly, Geegaw pulled a knife from out of his cloak and poked it forward for Raff to take.

Raff turned round to the witches, holding it high. "This is a sheepman's knife. I stole it from the man who used it to slit poor Finchy. He's since paid the price, in battle. What shall I do with it?"

There was a muttering pause, then Vild spoke up. "Give it back to the sheepmen," she said. "It's just a knife. There will be more trouble, from marauders and thieves, and it will be of use."

Raff marched across to Arc, and presented the knife to him. Arc bowed, and took it. Then Raff said, "Careful, witches, if you take this city creature back with you. He does have what he calls *vision* – some kind of mind skill, in line with your skills. But up till now, he's only used it for evil."

"Only because no other path was in front of me!" squealed Geegaw. "*And* I saved your life, ungrateful boy!"

Raff shook his head, smiling. "You're right, you did. And you got me a sculptor's job."

"Two things not entirely evil, then," said Vild. "Don't worry, Raff, we're more than a match for Geegaw. If he gets tricksy, he'll find out just how tricksy the witches can be."

"Oh, hoop-*la*!" carolled Geegaw.

"People!" cried Wekka, glaring at Geegaw. "To our purpose again. A new time has begun. There will be movement and visiting, flow and trade, education and discussion between all the four tribes. But right now we must finish deciding who is to go with whom. So we can return to our homes and rest, before the next stage."

"Then let's break off this council," said Arc, "and talk to each other individually, and decide."

Everyone began talking at once. Pitch made a beeline for three strong-looking boys, and began recruiting them; other lads, shy and admiring, headed for the footsoldiers. Kita's archers were surrounded by girls, calling out questions; many of the women with young children were nervously approaching the witches.

And Vild came gliding over the grass to Kita. "How are you, dearling?" she asked.

"Exhausted," Kita muttered.

"I'm not surprised. You were − you were *elemental*, the way you ended the battle. Awe-inspiring. And the way you called to the poor city dwellers to come out of their hiding places − none of us could have won them over the way you did."

Kita didn't answer. She stared at the ground, as two tears forced their way from under her eyelids.

"You need to rest," Vild soothed, putting an arm around her. "We'll be back at the crag soon. And you shall have a deep, hot bath with rosemary and lavender in it, and as many rabbit pasties as you can eat, and fresh clothes . . . then *sleep*, sweetheart. Curled up next to Moss. Sleep for days, if you want to. And only when you feel better, quite recovered, will we talk about what's to be done."

"What's to be done?" muttered Kita. "What's to be done with *me*?"

"Well, yes, my lovely . . . what else? It's all different, now. You've moved it all on. And you're scared, scared of what overtook you, but we can help you, work with you. . ." She stroked Kita's arm, gently. "That power that came through you, Kita — there's been nothing so intense since I was a young girl. I'd just gone to the witches. Three of them, gathering herbs in the woods near the hill fort, were seized and slit by the headman. Do you know the story?"

"Yes," muttered Kita. "The bloodstained clothes that floated down in the night. It terrified me, as a child."

"Aggie did that," said Vild, solemnly. "She's dead now, dear Aggie. But back then she was in her prime. She was in the woods, too — she saw it all. She watched over their bodies, keeping the dogs and crows at bay. She said the rage in her was like a white-hot core, burning and lasting. When night fell, she stripped the corpses of their clothes. There was a wind that night. She let it lift the clothes in her arms; she focused her rage on it. And the clothes flew up and over the hill-fort walls, carried by the wind and the power of her mind. The fear she put in the sheepmen that night saved many more of us from being killed. And what *you* did, dearling. . ."

"I know," mumbled Kita, "I know."

"I've only just started to dream of how your power might be used. We're starting to harness our power to desire, not rage, Kita – you could do that too. Imagine water, wind, fire – harnessed and directed for the good of all. Imagine your power used to bring about change among people, too. We can all move forward together, sweetheart. Bring about this great change we long for – together."

Kita took in a great, shuddering sigh, then she croaked, "I just – I need to be on my own now, Vild, all right? Just for a bit."

Vild withdrew her arm, and turned towards her. She took Kita's face between her hands, and looked for several moments into her eyes. "Nada warned me you had your own path to follow," she said. Then she smiled, beautifully, and walked away.

Kita stood and watched her go, then she turned and hurried into the trees behind the lake. She was longing to be on her own.

But someone was following her.

Chapter Forty-Eight

"Oh, slow *down*, tree rat!" called Arc. "What's your hurry?"

She turned and faced him, heart pounding. He looked beautiful, standing there under the trees, with his grey eyes and dirty hair.

"So you're going back with them, are you?" he asked. "Back to Witch Crag?"

She shrugged, shook her head, shrugged again, and couldn't speak.

"You're one of them now," he went on. "Top witch."

"There's no top witch, Arc. No hierarchy."

"Whatever. They're all agog to find out how you unleashed that power."

"Well, I'm afraid they'll be disappointed," she muttered. "What happened at the end of the battle – it might never happen again. It wasn't like I *decided* to do it."

"Oh, your witch rage was the channel for something massive. They want to investigate it all. You could end up with that freak Geegaw studying you!"

Kita grimaced. "That's a very big reason not to go back to the crag."

There was a pause, then Arc said, "Well, you could always come home. Back to the hill fort."

"After I went through hell and high water to escape it?"

"But everything's different now."

"I know it is."

"Kita – do you support this new union of the tribes?"

"Of course I do. You know I do."

"Do you support it going forward and bringing about deep change?"

"Of course. We need to share our skills. And not be threatened by our differences – let ourselves be enriched by them, instead."

"Well put. But easier said than done. It's a tough task ahead, leading the sheepmen into the future."

Kita smiled, shaking her head slightly. "I know. But you're going to make a brilliant headman. Who would've thought –"

"– that a thug like me could change?"

"Something like that."

"What happened turned everything inside out for me. Cracked my mind open to the witches, and what they have to teach us. And the women at the fort—"

"Oh, they're ready for the future. In fact if you don't get back soon you might find the matron's taken over."

Arc laughed, then he took a step closer to Kita, and stared at her, wide eyed. "Kita, come back to the fort with us. Come back and help me. I want you beside me. You can teach, you can accelerate this change. Who better? You're the bridge between us and the witches. You can still spend time on the crag with them, let them study you, work with you. But *we* need you too. Look how you inspired your archers with their blackbows. And. . ." He trailed off.

Kita looked at him closer. "What, Arc? What is it? Your face has gone all muzzy."

"That's because I'm a liar. Talking about accelerating change."

"*What?*" She stepped back, aghast.

"No – *no* – I don't mean I'm lying about it. I want it, it's the future. And you'd be brilliant, helping bring it about. I don't think I can do it without you. But it's not the real reason I want you to come home. Oh, *Kita*. I just *want* you. Only you. For ever."

There was a huge, momentous silence. Thrumming and potent. She couldn't look at him. She felt as if she'd started floating – as if every cell in her body was floating and expanding with joy.

"There, I've said it," he groaned. "Kita, *I love you*. I can't think of life without you. Please don't go to Witch Crag. *Please* come home and give me a chance with you."

"All right," she whispered.

"*All right?*"

"I'll come back to the fort. It's true, my work is there, not on the crag. That's my purpose. I've known it for a while now. And Vild knows it too, I could see it in her face. . ."

"*And—?*"

She looked at him again. He was in agony. He was beautiful. "I want you too," she whispered, fiercely. "I don't want to live without you. It wouldn't be living. I—"

She broke off then, because Arc had let out a kind of indignant, joyful, shuddering cry, and then he'd seized hold of her, and was hugging her, kissing her face, her neck, lifting her up, overwhelming her, nearly smothering her. "You made me go through all that," he breathed, "that . . . *begging* . . . and all the time. . ."

"I needed to know how you felt!" she cried.

"Oh, Kita. *How I felt?* Ever since you said you'd go to the huts with me, I've wanted you, I've *only* wanted you – no, before that. I used to watch you, I was infatuated. It broke me up when you ran away. I told myself I bloody hated you then, but I didn't, *I adore you*. You amaze me. *Tree rat.* You always have."

They kissed for the second time in their lives, and it was far more powerful now all restraint and suspicion had gone. They stood there in the trees, arms around each other, and kissed and held on to each other.

"Ever since the witches put you in a cage, and then broke you out of it," murmured Kita, "we've been growing closer, haven't we?"

"Yes. So I suppose it was a good thing. And that time

you held me? When you showed me your ledge up on the rock? I'd replay that to myself every night before I went to sleep."

She took in a breath. "My witch rage . . . you caused it. Seeing you about to get killed caused it."

He let out a blissful groan, muttering, "Tell me more later. I want to hear *everything*, later. I can't take any more now, I'll break into pieces. Like I'll probably do when we make love at last. *Witch*."

Kita laughed and they kissed again, standing there in the shushing trees.

It was Arc who, very gently, hugely reluctantly, pulled away first. "I've no idea how long we've been standing here," he murmured. "We ought to get back."

"Oh, lord. What will they all think?"

"I don't care what they think. I'm the new headman. What will the *witches* think? About your decision?"

"They'll understand. They . . . know already. Arc, you *ought* to care what your people think."

"You're right. And I do care. When we get back home we'll move into the old headman's hut. We'll be together, the model of the new way, Kita. No more animal mating. Equality and free choice for all."

"And the children will be free and happy and stay with their parents – no more cages. Not now I know how to keep the crows away."

"Yes, *witch*. And we'll visit the horsemen, and they'll visit us, so we can all progress."

"I'd love to see Lilly again," said Kita. "Flay will be going to her."

"And we'll visit Pitch and the farmers . . ."

". . . trade mutton for vegetables . . ."

". . . and we'll spend time with the witches, too."

"*Lots* of time, Arc. There's so much to learn from them. They'll help me understand that power that came through me. They'll work with us to bring about this great transformation, for everyone. And we'll see Raff and Quainy and dear darling Nada . . . and eat mushrooms, and dance."

"*Yes*. Oh Kita, you terrify me. How much I love you terrifies me."

"I feel the same about you," she said, "but it's going to be fine. It's all one, Arc. What we feel about each other, the great task ahead of us, all the tribes, all the people, it's all one."

Then she took his hand, and led him back to everyone else.